# A Castle Of Sand

*A Shade Of Vampire, Book 3*

Bella Forrest

Formatting by Polgarus Studio

# Also By Bella Forrest:

A Shade Of Vampire (Book 1)

A Shade Of Blood (Book 2)

A Shadow Of Light (Book 4)

A Blaze Of Sun (Book 5)

A Gate Of Night (Book 6)

Beautiful Monster

For an updated list of Bella's books,
please visit: www.bellaforrest.net

# Dedication

To all the Shaddicts out there…you know who you are.

# Contents

# Prologue: Sofia

My blood was pounding within me. A surge of horror rushed through my body as I scoped my surroundings. Gunshots were being fired all over the place. A fiery bullet hit a vampire about seven feet away from me, who screamed in agony as he burst into flames. He was only one among the many vampires present in those tombs—one among many dying excruciating deaths by those fatal gunshots. A few lucky ones were killed with stakes driven through their hearts, but most were shot with the hunters' bullets, uniquely engineered to mete out death on the vampires.

The sight was sickening, but despite my horror over the sheer magnitude of death surrounding me, my prime concern was Derek Novak.

*I can't lose you.*

He was a vampire. He was a prince. He was the man that I loved. The mere thought of losing him made breathing a struggle.

I looked around and gasped at the sight of him ripping the heart out of a vampire from the Maslen clan before moving on to breaking the neck of a hunter poised to attack him with a stake. He was headed straight for Borys Maslen. Fearing for his life, I stumbled forward. As I weaved through the chaos surrounding me toward my beloved, someone grabbed my arm and pulled me back.

"Get her out of here!" My father, Aiden Claremont, was pointing toward the exit. He was speaking to the stranger gripping my arm. The sight of my father still confused me. *What was he doing here?* After all the years he had abandoned me and left me under the care of his best friend, Lyle Hudson, he seemed out of place in this world—*my* world. His attempts to protect me were irritating. He had no business interfering with my life, not after all those years of ignoring me. Still, his presence moved me beyond words. He was still my father and I wanted to run to him and embrace him, feel his strength surround me, hear whispers of assurances in my ear—assurances that would answer my questions about why he had abandoned me. I wanted to know if he loved me, but there was no time for teary-eyed reunions.

War was being waged all around us and the only thing that mattered at that moment—reaching Derek—was being kept from me. I struggled against the hunter's grasp as he dragged me in the opposite direction. He was far stronger than me and I couldn't break away from his grasp until he was tackled to the ground by a familiar vampire. *Claudia.*

Her mass of blonde curls covered her face as she let out a scream before ripping the man's heart out. Her big brown eyes then turned toward me, a manic smile forming on her face.

"Hello, Sofia."

I shivered as I looked into her eyes. A broken creature, she embraced darkness like no other and had become one of the most wicked beings I'd ever come across. She surged forward and pinned me against a wall with her bloody hands.

"This is my gift to you," she hissed before sinking her teeth into my neck. I'd been bitten by vampires before, but I felt right away that what she was doing was different. She wasn't simply feeding on me. She was trying to *turn* me.

"No!" I gasped, trying to push her away. "Claudia, don't... please..."

Before I could fully wrap my mind around what was about to happen to me, I saw my best friend, Benjamin Hudson, hurtling toward us. His blue eyes screamed bloody murder at the sight of what Claudia, the vampire who broke him in many ways, was doing to me. He aimed his gun at her, but she must've sensed him, because she whipped around and tackled him to the ground.

"Did you really think I wouldn't sense you coming to her rescue? Your blood still pumps through my veins, Ben..."

Claudia's hands rose in the air and claws came out of her fingers, poised to wound Ben. I threw my entire weight against her, hoping to push her away from my best friend, but she easily threw me back, and I crashed to the ground. I cast my eyes away in desperation and scanned the hall, only to be met with another bone-chilling sight.

Across the vast hall, Derek stood bleeding and weakened as he faced off with Borys Maslen and three other vampires. And, in another corner of the room, a vampire rushed toward my father, who was fumbling to reload his gun.

Watching with horror as the lives of three of the most important men in my life hung in the balance, I felt an overwhelming sense of loss. Somehow, I already knew that this was going to happen, that the loss of life was inevitable, but finding myself right in the middle of it was something I wasn't prepared for.

A voice echoed in my mind—the voice of a friend who sacrificed her own life to bring me back into Derek's arms. I could almost hear her—Vivienne Novak, Seer of The Shade—speaking to me. Her words not only confirmed my worst fears but painted a future I wasn't sure I wanted to be part of.

The memory of her spoke to me and said, "Blood will be shed."

# Chapter 1: Sofia

*Vivienne held the blood-red rose in her hand and caressed it fondly. Sadness traced her blue-violet eyes as she stood alone in her greenhouse.*

*Liana Hendry stepped into the princess' sanctuary. Worry marred the features of the lovely vampire with amber gold eyes. "Vivienne? Xavier and I have been worried about you lately. Are you alright?"*

*"I didn't think it would be her. I honestly thought Derek would end up killing her."*

*Liana stood still, a patient expression on her face, waiting for Vivienne to offer an explanation.*

*"But she* is *lovely, isn't she?" Vivienne appeared serene, though strangely bothered, as she took a whiff of the rose she was holding.*

*"Who?" Liana took a step forward. The gaze she was giving the young Seer was pensive and kind, almost motherly.*

*"Sofia Claremont."*

*Liana wrinkled her nose, perplexed. "Your brother's slave?"*

*Vivienne shook her head as she placed the rose into a crystal vase.*

*"She's far more than his slave. I could sense it the moment they first kissed. The premonitions that followed… I can't even speak of them…" Vivienne jolted to a start, as if seeing a vision, before she grabbed Liana's hand. "Promise me you'll be loyal to us, no matter what."*

*"Of course. Vivienne, we owe Derek our lives… He* will *bring us true sanctuary just as you prophesied."*

*"Then support him even if you don't understand what he's doing. It's a rough road ahead and he will need the girl. She's the one the witch spoke of all those years ago. The girl who will help him find true sanctuary."*

*"Vivienne, why are you speaking as if you won't be around for what you say is to come?"*

*"Because I might not be. Our island will suffer severe loss before all this is over, Liana. None of us are safe."*

*The deep frown on her face easily revealed how bothered Liana was over these revelations. Vivienne offered no consolation. Her mind was elsewhere—off to the future where she was seeing her beloved twin's fate. "They are strongest together. They are weakest apart."*

I couldn't help but wonder why I woke up to the memory—one that was given to me by Vivienne before the hunters took her. Her memories always seemed to come randomly, triggered by situations I had no control over.

"Why the frown, beautiful?"

Before I could follow the sound of his voice, Derek jumped on the bed, his knees straddling my hips as the cushions bounced beneath us. Kneeling over me, he held my waist with one hand and ran his palm from my forehead down to my mouth.

"What are you doing?" I asked in a voice muffled by his palm playfully rubbing over my mouth.

"I'm trying to erase that scowl on your face." He chuckled as he removed his hand from my lips and made a face at me. His dark hair was still a wet, tousled mess, his pale white skin a breathtaking contrast to his raven locks. His firm lips were curved up in a mischievous smile.

I loved this side of him. Fun, carefree, boyish. He was only this way when he was around me—especially after his father, Gregor, returned to rule as king of The Shade. To the eyes of most of the citizens of The Shade, Derek was prince of the kingdom and I was his favorite slave, his *pet.* Those who knew us well, however, were aware that we were more to each other than just master and slave. We were in love, but I'd grown to accept that what I had with him was temporary. Losing him felt inevitable. After all, how long could a relationship between a vampire and a human last?

Ben once told me—after ruining a sandcastle I'd built—that sandcastles were temporary. It was better to part with them sooner rather than later. What I had with Derek felt like a sandcastle. I was aware that it was temporary, that the waves of life and time would soon ruin it, but it was too beautiful, too precious to me to just let go of. No. This sandcastle was something I planned to protect and be fascinated over for as long as I could.

I didn't realize that I was looking at him pensively until he took a deep breath and feigned exasperation by rolling his eyes. "What must I do to make you smile?" His legs stretched out on the bed, his elbows holding him up so that his weight—at least twice as great as mine—wouldn't fall on me.

I still felt small and fragile compared to him, but I knew he would never intentionally do anything to hurt me. Staring up at him, butterflies fluttered inside my stomach, even more so when his lips caressed my cheekbone and his voice found my ear.

"I know how to make you smile." He raised his head so he could look at the expression on my face.

I played along. "Oh, really now?"

"It's easy." He traced a thumb over my lips and grinned when he felt me shudder beneath his touch. He knew exactly the kind of effect he had on me.

He kissed me full on the mouth, his tongue thrusting in—exploring and tasting. His hands wrapped around my waist as he began to shift us both to an upright position, so that he was kneeling on the bed and I was planted firmly on his lap.

I felt his hands creep beneath the silk night gown I was wearing and I had to break off the kiss before things got a lot more heated. I had plans for that day and he wasn't about to distract me from them by seducing me back into his bed.

"That's what you thought would make me smile?" I managed to ask as I tried to catch my breath.

His breaths were also coming in pants, but the way he looked at me spelled trouble. "No. This is…"

One hand began tickling me on the side while the other caressed my knee caps, one of my most ticklish spots.

"No! Derek!" I shrieked before breaking into laughter. "Don't! You're supposed to make me smile, not laugh."

He relished my failed attempts to pry his hands off me before my back fell on the bed and he finally stopped the playful torment.

"You're supposed to smile when I kiss you," he announced.

Only I was privileged to see this side of Derek Novak. He was mine and I was his. Derek had this way of making me feel like he knew me. I couldn't help it; the thought made me smile.

"There you go…" His blue eyes twinkled upon seeing my face light up. "Lovely."

"Now that you've got what you want, could you get off me now?" I tried to push him away, but as usual, failed to move him an inch.

"Come on, Derek… I have a whole day planned ahead."

"Do you now?"

I nodded. This was our day. Ever since Gregor Novak returned, he'd been keeping Derek busy with building up The Shade's army. Being the commander-in-chief of the island's military force, he had his work cut out. Much to his father's disdain, he still managed to find time for me.

I pouted at him. "You promised. For the next twenty-four hours, you're supposed to be all mine, Prince Derek."

He frowned. He hated it whenever I called him that. "Fine, but you're not to call me that again. Ever."

I grinned. "I'll try."

He rolled his eyes in response. I watched him as he got up from the bed, admiring his chiseled form, covered only by his boxers. He grabbed his guitar and sat over the edge of the bed with his back turned to me. I listened to him expertly pluck a tune on the instrument. He must've felt my gaze on him, because he looked back at me. "Well? Is this what you had planned? Staring at me all day long?"

"Ha!" I threw a pillow at him. He didn't bother to dodge it. "You wish I were *that* into you."

"Oh please…you know you are."

To that, I couldn't think of a worthy comeback, so I just gave him a light shove on the shoulder and walked toward the bathroom to get myself ready for the day ahead. But I stopped just before the door of the bathroom and lowered the spaghetti straps of my night gown down my shoulders and let the silk gown fall to the ground. I knew I'd caught his attention the moment the melody he was strumming went grotesquely out of tune.

"Too bad you already took a shower," I commented before

shutting the door behind me.

A few minutes later, we were both in the tub, my back leaned against his chest.

"Today's going to be a good day," he said as he ran both hands from my shoulders down to my elbows.

I had to smile. "You have no idea."

# Chapter 2: Derek

To say that I was curious over what my lovely vixen had up her sleeve was the king of understatements. The knowing smile on her face and the way she looked at me as if she knew something I didn't was driving me crazy, but not any more than the way she was behaving as we moved around my bedroom dressing ourselves for the day ahead.

I was watching her as she picked out an outfit to wear and I began thumbing through her clothes. I saw a white dress hanging on the rack and recalled the last time I saw her wearing it. "I love the way you look in this dress."

Sofia winked at me, took the dress from the rack and put it on. She then went and stood in front of the mirror. She lifted her locks high over her head and twisted clumps of them around as if wondering whether to tie her hair up.

"I think you'll look lovely just wearing your hair down," I commented.

Thus, stabbing at my curiosity even further, her long auburn locks stayed down, cascading over her waist—just the way I preferred it.

From the very first night I met her, Sofia had a mind of her own and rarely hesitated to speak out whenever she felt the need to. The fact that she never did bend to my will because of fear over the fact that I was a vampire or that I was prince of the kingdom we were residing in was one of the things that drew me to her. Thus, to have her giving in to my slightest suggestions—willingly and without question—was something that I found delightful, intriguing and slightly suspicious.

Still, my wariness over whatever she had in store was easily overpowered by the temptation to test just how far she was willing to go with catering to my "innocent suggestions".

I approached her from behind as she continued to check her appearance on the mirror. I held her waist and pulled her back against me.

"You look incredible," I assured her.

A soft blush highlighted the freckles on her cheeks. She laid both her hands over mine. "I'm glad you think so."

Testing her playfully, I said, "I'd love a kiss."

No hesitation. No objections. She spun around, snuck her arms beneath my own and around my waist, tilted her head up, stood on her tiptoes and kissed me—first, on the jawline, then the corner of my lips, then full on the mouth.

When our lips parted, I couldn't keep myself from asking, "What's going on?"

"What do you mean?"

"Well, if I said that I'd love a drink of your blood, would you cut yourself and hand me a vial of it?"

A knowing smile formed on her lips as she batted her eyelashes at me. "No, of course not. Why go through all that trouble when I could just offer you my neck?"

"You are driving me crazy."

She grinned. "Good, and for the record, I'm severely overdressed for this occasion."

"What occasion?"

"You'll see." She held my hand and began tugging for me to follow her.

"Not even a clue as to what you're up to?"

"Can't you just trust me, Prince Charming?"

"I told you not to call me that."

"No… you told me not to call you Prince Derek." Laughter was in her voice. "Will you just come with me?"

"As if I had any other choice…"

Excitement sparked in her green eyes. Her zest for life was one of the many things I loved about Sofia Claremont. She lit up the darkness surrounding The Shade, and for a kingdom that had no mornings, only eternal night, her light was life.

We exited my penthouse. I sighed as I looked out at three others like mine; interconnected by glass-covered walkways and hanging bridges, and built on top of the towering redwood trees. One penthouse each for the Novak family, although only two were occupied by our clan. After Vivienne was caught by the hunters, her best friend, Liana and her husband, Cameron, moved into her penthouse.

On the other hand, my older brother, Lucas, was still on the run. After he tried to kill Sofia, I began hunting him down and he left the island. The last I heard of him, he'd completely turned his back on his own flesh and blood by joining the coven of our family's greatest vampire rivals, the Maslens.

Sofia led me to an elevator that allowed us to go from the top of the giant redwoods down to the ground below. We strolled through the woods for about an hour before reaching an open field, one of the few still undeveloped on the island.

"Okay…" I said. "Now what?"

Sofia stuck two fingers into her mouth and let out a high-pitched whistle.

I heard the distinct rumbling of a vehicle's motor and, in the distance, saw a car drive toward us. Behind the wheel was Kyle, a vampire guard I deeply trusted. His passengers were my second guard, Sam, and the three girls belonging to my "harem"—Ashley, Paige and Rosa.

Ashley, with her blonde hair tied up in a high ponytail, looked like she was having the time of her life. The mere sight of her made my blood pound. Of all the girls in my harem, hers was the only blood I'd had a taste of and it took a lot of self-control to resist my craving to feed on her.

Having Sofia around made it much easier for me to hold myself back. I felt Sofia's hand squeeze mine when she saw my eyes on Ashley and the craving quickly left me.

"So… what exactly is going on?" I asked as I watched Kyle park the vehicle. I'd never actually been in a car. Four hundred years robbed me of that indulgence and in The Shade, we did most of our traveling by speeding our way from one place to the other, or taking leisurely walks—like I normally preferred to do whenever I was with Sofia. I was introduced to cars through movies and magazines Sofia showed me when she first began schooling me in the ways of the 21st century.

"Since it's your day, I had Kyle and Sam spruce up this old fixer-upper so you could finally learn to drive a car," Sofia said with a sly smile.

"I don't know if I should trust that smile." I eyed her warily. "What do you mean it's *my day*? And why on earth would I need to learn to drive a car?"

"Because it's kind of pathetic that you're five hundred years old and you still have no idea how to drive a car," Ashley quipped as she got out of the car.

"Must you speak, Ashley? The sound of your voice really does grate on my nerves no matter how hard I try to ignore it."

"What acerbic wit you have, your highness."

"What despicable nonsense you have a talent for spouting out, peasant."

Seeming to have run out of wisecracks, Ashley frowned and muttered, "Bite me."

"Didn't I already do that?"

Sofia began snickering beside me, as did the other two girls and the guards. They were all used to Ashley and me bickering. I knew that Ashley still hated and resented me for the things I put her through during the span of time when Sofia left the island with Ben. It was a time when I completely lost myself and did things I regretted. I couldn't blame Ashley if she was forever unwilling to forgive me. I doubted I could ever forgive myself, but my guilt didn't mean I'd just stand there and take it whenever she threw sarcasm and ridicule my way.

"You two love each other so much," Sofia remarked as she pulled me toward the car. "Come on, Derek. Get behind the wheel." She got in the passenger's seat right after the others got out of the car. I stepped forward and ran a hand over the hood of the car. A smirk formed on my lips as I gave Sofia a questioning glance.

"Are you really sure you want to do this, Sofia?" I started loving the idea of learning to drive a car the moment I saw her nervously gulp. “Oh yeah…” I nodded. “This is going to be fun.”

# Chapter 3: Sofia

"Derek!" I screeched. "You're driving the car right into the woods! Derek!"

He waited until the very last minute before turning the car to the right. He seemed to be having the time of his life.

"You're getting a kick out of this, aren't you?" I frowned.

"You know I am!"

He hit the brakes and I found myself thanking the heavens for the invention of the seatbelt, because had it not been created, I would've been thrown right out of that convertible.

The car's motor died down as Derek pulled the keys from the ignition. We were right in the middle of the field, the vehicle's headlights providing more than sufficient lighting. I felt Derek's gaze taking my shaking form in.

"You're right. You are overdressed for this." He chuckled.

Annoyed, I hit him on the shoulder. "At one point during that crazy ride, I swear I saw my entire life flash before my eyes. Whose stupid idea was this?"

"Yours, I'm sure." He leaned back on his seat, a satisfied smile on his face. "How did this car even get onto the island?"

I winced. I knew the answer to his question and it was one that I was certain wouldn't please him, so I shrugged and said, "*That* is something you ought to ask Sam or Kyle." I checked our surroundings and ascertained that the others had left us alone. I smiled. *Perfect.* However, upon seeing the determined, questioning look on Derek's face, I realized that I wasn't yet off the hook.

"Tell me, Sofia. I'd rather hear it from you. How did the car get onto the island?"

"Your father had a couple of cars brought in several years ago. Before you woke up. Sam and Kyle know the details…they just told me about it, so…"

"No. Tell me what you know. How were the cars brought in?"

I heaved a sigh. "They had to use a special freighter ship to get the cars here. Your father and Lucas wanted to try them out. They have a collection stashed somewhere here. Apparently, Vivienne objected to it, but they wouldn't hear of it."

"Another one of their insane luxuries…" He grimaced.

"Now your mood's all ruined." I pressed the play button on the car's stereo and music added a calming, tropical feel to our surroundings. I then got out of the car and headed for the trunk. Just as I'd requested, a picnic basket was inside.

"I'm starving," I confessed as I returned to the passenger's seat beside him, picnic basket in hand.

I began taking out the contents of the basket. Two bottles—one containing champagne, the other containing blood—two glasses, a sandwich, strawberries and a container containing some melted white chocolate.

"So are you going to answer my original question or not?" he asked. I could hear the impatience in his tone.

I smiled at him as I recalled the night that gave me this idea. We were at the lighthouse, the only man-made structure located outside the thick walls surrounding the island. We had been playing a game of chess. I couldn't forget the sadness in his eyes when I asked him about his birthday and he explained, *"We vampires tend to stop measuring our age in years. We progress from measuring it in decades and then later, in centuries."* I wondered why so much hopelessness seemed to cover his countenance whenever his immortality was mentioned.

"I asked you once when your birthday was and you told me you'd forgotten..."

"Sofia..." His voice was choked with emotion, already knowing what I was trying to imply.

I poured blood into one glass and handed it to him before pouring champagne into my own. "You deserve a birthday, Derek." I couldn't keep a grin from my face as I shrugged. "So I decided to just make one up for you."

I was relieved to find a smile form on his face. "A toast to the day you came into my life."

"It's *your* day, Derek, but hey..." I chuckled. "I'll drink to that." The edges of our glasses clinked as we shared a toast. We spent the next couple of hours, seated on the hood of the car, watching the stars and goofing around with the small meal that came with the basket. Of course, he couldn't really partake of anything but the blood, but that didn't stop him from amusing himself by shoving strawberries coated in sticky white chocolate into my mouth.

"So how old are you now?" I asked in an attempt to distract him so I could wipe off the chocolate he'd just smeared on my face.

"Too old."

His blue eyes were burning with intensity and hopefulness as he looked at me. I didn't have to ask what was going through his mind. I knew that the same thing was going through mine. We'd talked about it before. His immortality made it possible for us to have what we had. If he hadn't become a vampire, our timelines never would've crossed.

He pulled me into his arms and began humming a tune as we stared up at the starlit sky.

"I wish we could be like this forever," I whispered.

He nodded.

But I knew the truth. Things weren't always going to be this way, because Ben was right.

*Sandcastles always fall.*

# Chapter 4: Derek

Upon our return to the penthouse, I was surprised to find Cameron and Liana Hendry waiting for us in my living room. The expression on their faces was enough to tell me that something was wrong. Instinct took over and I removed the arm I had over Sofia's shoulder and gently nudged her behind me.

Cameron and Liana rose from their seats upon seeing us. Both their eyes settled on Sofia in a sad gaze.

"What's wrong?" I asked, not quite sure if I was ready to hear the answer to my question.

"We have to talk," Liana responded solemnly. "About Sofia and the girls."

Had it only been Cameron paying me a visit, I wouldn't have been as anxious, but Liana was there, and her presence rarely ever brought good news. I nodded at Liana to talk as we all took a seat. She took a deep breath before obliging.

"A week from now, Sofia and the girls will have been here at The Shade for a year."

My hand quickly found Sofia's knee and I squeezed tight. I remembered what Vivienne told me the night the girls were brought to me. *"The humans who form the harems are kept alive for a year and whomever owns them gets to decide their ultimate fate after that."*

I swallowed hard. "So?" I asked Liana.

"Your father sent me to tell you that he wants to know your decision regarding the girls so that it can be executed at the appointed time."

I grimaced. "He couldn't have just come here to tell me that himself?"

"He told me that he wanted to, but that he would prefer not to see Sofia."

My father's disdain toward her was no secret. Gregor Novak blamed her for Lucas turning against us and for Vivienne getting caught by the hunters. In my father's eyes, Sofia was turning me against him.

"It's for the best. The farther away my father is from Sofia, the better off we all are." I straightened up in my seat and nodded. "Fine. My decision is easy. The girls stay with me."

Cameron and Liana exchanged worried glances.

"That would mean you'd have to turn them all into vampires and make them a part of your clan, Derek," Cameron explained.

"What?!" I spat out. "Who came up with these rules?"

Everyone knew that I thought the concept of a harem was ridiculous. That was one reason I put a stop to human abductions while my father was away.

"Your father," Liana patiently responded.

*With Lucas' influence no doubt.* I scowled. "What are my other choices?"

"Most harems don't really last a year and when they do, the owners usually just turn their slaves into vampires. A year means that they'd grown quite fond of their slaves and..."

I licked my lips impatiently and turned my head toward Sofia. "Do you want to become a vampire, Sofia?"

Her emerald gaze was moist with tears as she shook her head. She was clearly terrified by the idea. The truth was that though I couldn't blame her for not wanting to turn into my kind, the thought that she didn't want to be what I was hurt.

"If the other three girls want to become vampires, then so be it," I announced. "However, Sofia has indicated that she isn't willing to become one, so what are the alternatives?"

Liana's response was blunt and straightforward. "She is either drained of all blood or sent to live at The Catacombs, where she will be assigned work she's skilled at; therefore, making her useful to the island."

The Catacombs were located at the Black Heights, a vast mountain range north of the island. It contained a complex network of interconnected caves. These caves were divided into two areas—The Cells and The Catacombs. The Cells were our prison system. The Catacombs, on the other hand, were home to The Shade's growing human population—the Naturals. The Naturals were humans born and raised at The Shade—they did the bulk of the labor required to keep The Shade in its self-sustaining state. On the other hand, Sofia and the rest of the humans belonging to the harems were known as Migrates. They were taken from outside the island. Just as Liana implied, most Migrates—if not all—died in the island. Only few were turned into vampires or sent to The Catacombs to become Naturals.

I'd only been to The Catacombs once when Sofia asked to visit. The thought of her living there made me sick to my stomach. *She belongs by my side.*

"I guess that really gives you only one option..." Liana broke the tense silence.

"No. It doesn't. I'm going to talk to my father about this. I'm not having it." I growled and shot a glare at two of my dearest friends. "Where is he?"

"He's at his penthouse, but is it really wise to..."

I didn't bother to hear what else Liana had to say. I was up on my feet and speeding toward my father's penthouse—not far from mine. I pushed the doors open and let myself in. A young woman stood shocked in the middle of the large round hall that composed my father's welcoming room. I immediately saw the bite marks on her neck—fresh blood was still trickling from them. I expected to crave her, but all I felt was empathy. She couldn't have been any older than Sofia.

"Where's my father?" I asked, reeling in my anger so I could speak to her in a soft voice. I didn't want to frighten her any more than she already was.

"Your highness..." she croaked, as if unsure whether or not she should be speaking to me. "He's by the pool. I was just..."

"What's your name?"

"Yvonne."

"Take me to him, Yvonne."

She led me through a series of glass-covered walkways before leading to a large, circular room with a round pool in the middle of it. My father leaned against one side of the pool, sucking on the blood of one of the two lovely maidens sitting on either side of him. Being distracted by them, he didn't even notice my presence. My stomach turned upon seeing the bruises on the girls' bodies. The thought of how Sofia would react to the sight before me was enough to make my blood boil.

Yvonne walked over to my father and the moment he was aware of her presence, he grabbed a fistful of her hair and forced a kiss on her. Her body tensed and I knew that, though she didn't resist, she wasn't enjoying the rough manner in which he was treating her.

Throughout the years, my father had already given me many reasons to be ashamed to call myself his son, but he was still my father, and if only to honor Vivienne, I had to attempt to treat him with some respect. I cleared my throat to announce my presence, no longer willing to witness this wanton display of lust.

Gregor snapped to attention. He grabbed Yvonne by the waist and planted her on his lap, using her body to cover his own as he looked over her shoulder at me. He raised a brow at the sight of me. "Derek! To what do I owe the pleasure of this visit?"

"You would have me send the girl I love to The Catacombs? I won't have it."

"Ah… We're at this again. Every time you come to me it is to bitch about that redhead pet of yours. Must everything be about her?"

"I've done everything you told me since you came back. I've taken my place as commander of the army and I've geared them up for battle just as you commanded. I did not interfere with any of the decisions you've made about the island since you took your place as king. Why do you vex me this way?"

"Vex you, Derek?" He once again grabbed a fistful of Yvonne's hair, pulling on her scalp enough to get a yelp from her before pulling her head to an angle that exposed a generous amount of her neck. "Why do you think that everything I do is about you? I'm merely enforcing the laws of this island. Felix has told me about your manic outbursts and about your delusion that you are the law on this island. You're not, my son. We owe you a lot. You made The Shade possible, but we've formed laws in this kingdom that even you aren't exempt from."

All throughout his spiel, all I could really think of was how awful Yvonne must've felt, with her head so painfully positioned and his words breathing chills over her exposed neck.

He must've noticed the way I was staring at his slave, because he tightened his fist over Yvonne's hair and grinned. "If you don't want your beloved living with the rest of her kind in The Catacombs, then realize that this is what happens to humans at The Shade, Derek. You either turn them into one of us..."

I could've sworn that he was going to bite into Yvonne's neck and turn the girl into a vampire, so I was completely taken by surprise when instead, he smiled and said, "...or you kill them." He then snapped her neck like he would a twig. The sound of bone cracking filled the room. The two other girls beside him shrieked at the sight of Yvonne's lifeless form falling into the water.

My entire body tensed, knowing that women just like Yvonne had met the same fate in my hands long ago. Gregor didn't even flinch. He looked irritably at one of the girls and blurted out instructions.

"Go get the guards and have them bring the body to the chilling chambers so we can drain what's left of her blood."

As she scurried away, he grabbed the other young woman, forcing the brunette to take Yvonne's place.

"What happened to you, Father? Since when were you this merciless?"

"Don't be a hypocrite, Derek." He cast me a murderous glare. "Don't ever forget that it's you who made me this way. Besides, you can't judge me. Not while you're doing the exact same things to that lovely redhead of yours."

# Chapter 5: Sofia

The moment Derek returned, the first words that came out of his lips were: "I need to go to the lighthouse."

We often retreated to the lighthouse whenever he felt particularly plagued by his own darkness. I wondered what his father could've told him to once again make him doubt himself. I exchanged glances with Ashley, Paige and Rosa. We had all been seated on the living room couches, talking over the things that Cameron and Liana had said earlier.

"And you should get dressed in something else." He added, "We'll spend the night there."

"We need to have a talk when you get back," Ashley spoke up when I rose from my seat and walked toward him.

I caught the way Derek swallowed hard upon seeing her. A pang of jealousy hit me over the way he looked at her, like he wanted her. I reminded myself that it was only because he'd already had a taste of

Ashley's blood and that it had nothing to do with his affections toward me.

"Since when was it your place to make such demands, Ashley?" Derek snapped at her.

I was surprised by his outburst, but before I could react, Ashley was up on her feet. "My *place*? What exactly is *my* place?"

I wish she would've just kept silent. Derek wasn't in the best of moods and was already poised for a fight.

"You know who and what I am to this island, Ashley, and despite the liberties I allow you, you also know where you stand."

Though I was relieved that Ashley didn't respond, I couldn't help but wince at his statements. He rarely ever pulled rank on us any more—especially when we were in the privacy of his home. When we were in public, we still had to put on a show sometimes: he was the master and we were his slaves and we gave him the deference he deserved as prince of the island, but when we were alone, we were ourselves and he was Derek. For him to question Ashley and put her in "her place" for simply speaking her mind was unlike him.

"Derek..." I gently brushed my hand over his elbow. "Come on... let's go."

To my relief, he cast one final glare at Ashley before storming toward his room. I kept my cool and remained silent as we both got dressed and packed a change of clothes. Whenever we went to the lighthouse, we lost track of time.

I didn't utter a word as I pulled on a light blue dress. I didn't even speak when he nodded his head toward me and told me that it was time to go. He was anxious to get to the lighthouse. While I loved the structure itself, the trip there never failed to take my breath away because it involved jumping free fall over the edge of the Crimson Fortress' hundred-foot wall.

Derek always got a kick out of seeing how terrified I was by the jump, but not this time. He was too wrapped up in his own tension to tease me about it and all I could do was wait for him to let me know what was going through his mind.

Normally, we would've taken a leisurely stroll along the rocky boulders and stone path that led from the wall to the lighthouse, but this time, he held me by the waist, pulled me against him and sped us both right to the top of the lighthouse.

I took a deep breath the moment he set me on my feet. He switched the lights on and the octagonal room, which I embraced as my second home in The Shade, lit up. I drew the red drapes covering the large windows set on every other wall. I had to admire the beauty of the starry night sky within the lines that defined the island. From the vantage point of the lighthouse, it was easy to see where the night stopped and where the day began. A bright lantern hooked to the building shone light over the open seas.

I turned around to find Derek lighting up dozens of candles around the room. He then moved toward the fire place and lit up a fire to ensure I didn't feel cold. I dropped the backpack we had brought with us onto the hardwood floor and made my way toward the velvet couch in the corner of the room.

My eye caught the large leather-bound book set atop the wooden coffee table in front of me. The book contained the chronicles of The Shade. A lot of it was written journal entries—mostly Derek's. It was a peek into his mind, into the internal torment raging within him over the things he saw, and the things he had to do. I could still remember how terrified he was when he first revealed its contents to me.

"Do you remember what's written in there?" Derek finally broke the silence that accompanied us since we left the penthouse and headed for the lighthouse.

"Of course." I nodded before shifting my gaze toward him. I was surprised to find him unbuttoning his navy blue shirt, pulling it away from his body, before tossing it onto the floor. He gave me a sharp narrow-eyed glare.

Embarrassing as it was to admit to myself, it took effort to shift my eyes away from his chiseled torso and up to his face.

"How can you still look at me that way after knowing about everything I did?"

I swallowed hard. "You're not the same person. Not anymore."

"Why are you so sure of that?"

I was getting tired of the interrogation. "Where is this coming from, Derek? What happened?"

He took deliberate strides toward me and pushed me onto my back on the couch. My heart skipped a beat. *What's going on?*

"Derek?"

He climbed on top of me, his hands creeping up beneath my dress and over my thighs.

"Do you have any idea the kind of self-control I need to have to not suck your blood whenever we make love?" His hands were now on my waist, his thumb brushing over my navel.

"Yes… I know… I've seen you struggle not to…"

"No…" he said through gritted teeth. "You don't know. You won't ever understand… not unless you become a vampire like me."

My heartbeat doubled. "Get off me, Derek," I demanded, firmly placing a palm over his bare chest and trying to push him away from me.

Instead of getting off me, he let his entire weight fall on me, making it difficult for me to breathe. He began whispering in my ear, "You shouldn't trust me, Sofia. I can lose my mind and break you any time." His hands were still beneath my dress.

In my mind's eye, I could see my beautiful sandcastle being hit by its first wave and the despair I felt caused a lump to form in my throat. I then felt another emotion take hold of me. Anger. I could play this game right along with him. *If he thinks I'm just going to lie here and tremble, he has another thing coming.* It was a struggle to squeeze my hands between us, but I managed to and began unbuttoning his jeans.

"Well, I *do* trust you, Derek. Deal with it, because really...what can you do about it?"

"Break your trust."

"Then go ahead," I challenged him. "Do it."

I knew I was gaining ground over him when I felt him suck in a breath. His hands tightened over my waist.

"How do you intend to do that, Derek? Break my trust? You're going to force yourself on me?" I unzipped his jeans. "Feed on me? What?"

"Sofia..."

I gasped when he jolted upward, pulling me like a rag doll in the air and setting me on his lap as he sat up and leaned back on the couch. His breaths were coming in pants, his hands still enveloping my waist. He was struggling to look me in the eye. I, on the other hand, kept a firm glare right at him.

"You're driving me crazy. What's wrong with you?" His jaw was tense, his words coming in between deep breaths, his hands moving from my waist down to my thighs.

If it weren't for the intensity of expression on his handsome face, I would've thought he was joking, but he wasn't. He was dead serious.

"You do realize that becoming a vampire is the only way we could ever be together..."

"And what is all this, Derek? Your way of convincing me?" My hands were laid over his broad shoulders. My blood was boiling inside me, anger still the predominant emotion I had toward him as my jaw tightened.

"You would be able to fight back if you were a vampire. You would be stronger."

I scoffed at this notion. "Really? Against you? Please…vampire or not, you can still easily overpower me. Rip my heart out. Break me like a twig."

"That's what my father did to one of his slaves…broke her neck like a twig. Right in front of me. He didn't even blink an eye." The torn expression on his face moved me.

"Do you know what he told me after?" His gaze was still distant, his eyes refusing to meet mine. "He blames me for what he has become. He told me that it was me who made him this way."

"Your father may be many things, Derek, but he certainly doesn't have the right to play the part of a victim." I grabbed both his hands and began pulling them away from my body. "Get your hands off me."

He obliged and laid his palms on the couch. Part of me wanted to get off his lap and position myself on the far end of the couch—away from him, but I needed to see his face and look into his eyes. It frustrated me that he still refused to look at me.

"Let me turn you." His statement was half a command, half a request.

"No."

"If you want to be with me, why won't you agree to this? If you still think that someone like me is capable of good, then why not become like me?"

I leaned my forehead against his as I weighed my words carefully, trying to understand my own trail of thought even as I responded to his question. "Because I'm not as strong as you are, Derek. If I had to go through everything you've had to go through, I don't think I'd be able to take it. It would destroy me."

"You're wrong."

"I can't risk losing myself that way." I gazed at his face, wishing he would just look at me. He didn't. He kept his eyes on a distant area behind my left shoulder. Annoyed, I grabbed his jaw and made him face me. "Look at me," I hissed, my grip over his chin tightening.

When his eyes settled on me, the sorrow behind them rendered me speechless.

"I'm looking," he stated, a muscle in his cheek twitching as he fought to keep his gaze upon me.

I kissed him on the lips. Gentle. Soft. Caressing. "I'm useless to you as a vampire, Derek. This is what we have right now. It may be temporary, but it's beautiful. Can we not just relish it while it's ours?"

"I don't want to lose you."

"You won't. I'll always be yours. *Always.*"

One look in his eyes and I knew that he wasn't convinced. He was still looking at me as if I were about to slip right through his fingers. I wanted to assure him, but I didn't know how to. Perhaps it was time that he too should accept that we would someday have to let go of what we had. The idea made me ache inside, but it was reality. It was how things were meant to be.

Still, I meant it when I said that I was always going to be his, because I knew without a doubt that I could never love another man the way I loved Derek Novak.

# Chapter 6: Derek

"I've decided that I want to become a vampire."

My jaw dropped. None of us saw it coming. After Sofia and I got back from the lighthouse, we gathered the girls around the living room, with Sam and Kyle joining the bunch. I told them what was about to happen and explained the choices they had. I expected all of them to follow after Sofia's decision and live in The Catacombs, so I was completely shocked when the person I least expected announced that she would rather get turned.

I squinted an eye at Ashley. "You? A vampire?"

"Yes. Got a problem with that?"

"You do realize that if I turn you, you become Ashley Novak…"

"I said that I'd rather become a vampire. I never said anything about *you* turning me."

I sighed with relief. "Thank the heavens then. I wouldn't know what I'd do having to take care of a drama queen like you."

Sofia interrupted before Ashley could respond. "Well, who exactly do you want to turn you?"

She shrugged before pointing at Kyle. "Him."

Even he looked surprised. "Me?" Kyle squeaked.

I tried to hold back my laughter over the shocked expression on his face. "May all the powers that be have mercy on you, man."

Ashley stuck her tongue out at me.

"You're not against this, Derek?" Sofia asked.

"No." I shook my head. "Ashley can do whatever she wants."

Her lower lip twitched and she quickly bit on it. She began nodding. "Okay then. I guess we have our decision."

"Wait…" Paige spoke out of nowhere, throwing her hands in the air. Her eyes narrowed. "If I remember correctly, the night we were abducted was the night of Sofia's seventeenth birthday." She eyed Sofia. "Wasn't it?"

My eyes widened in surprise. Realizing that I hadn't even bothered to ask about her birthday was a sock in the gut. There she was going out of her way to give me a birthday, which I enjoyed without the slightest thought of her own special day.

I stared at her as she blushed and nodded—almost as if she was embarrassed that she had a birthday. At that moment, I realized how selfish I'd been with her.

*My father was right. How could I criticize him when I'm here using the woman I love just like I did all the other women that came before her?* The guilt that settled on my chest was making it hard to breathe. I grabbed her hand and the words "I'm sorry" came out of my lips in a husky whisper. Six pairs of inquisitive eyes shot toward me in question. My grip on Sofia's hand tightened.

"You're sorry for what exactly?" Ashley quirked her head to one side, her ponytail swinging like a pendulum. "Do specify, dear prince, because you have a lot of things you ought to be sorry for."

Sofia frowned as my eyes bore into hers. She knew—like she always did when it came to me—that what I was saying wasn't to be taken lightly. Her grip enveloped mine.

"It's like they're communicating through Bluetooth or something..." Ashley muttered under her breath.

"Shut up, Ashley." I turned back to address Sofia. "I had no idea it was going to be your birthday. I guess that makes me an awful boyfriend."

My sensitive ears didn't miss it when Ashley breathed out "True that" as she rolled her eyes.

Sofia smiled. "You couldn't have known."

"I should've at least thought about it... especially after everything you did for me..."

"It's not a big deal, Derek. Really..."

"It is. And I'll make it up to you."

"This ought to be interesting..." This was a remark that should've come from Ashley, but this time it was Sam's voice. He had a goofy smile on his face, one that quickly disappeared when I glared at him and said, "What are you smiling at? You're going to help."

Before anyone could react, Sofia's arms were around my neck and she placed a soft, gentle kiss on my lips. Tears were streaming down her face. I couldn't understand why she was crying, but it made the kiss—innocent as it was—utterly heartbreaking. Sofia was forever going to be an enigma to me—I'd long accepted that fact, but if there was one thing I couldn't stand seeing, it was her tears.

"What's wrong?" I asked her.

She shook her head and smiled amidst the tears. "Nothing. Nothing's wrong. Not as long as you're here."

And that, I realized, was the reason for the tears. I could be *there* for her for as long as she lived, but she couldn't possibly be there for me for as long as my immortality lasted. The realization strengthened my resolve to make every moment I had with her a memory worth keeping.

My life was no longer about myself or the prophecy I had to fulfill. It had just become entirely about Sofia.

# Chapter 7: Ben

The hunter was lunging toward me at full speed, throwing all the strength he had left into a tackle that I knew wasn't going to work. I grinned. *Pathetic.* I twisted my upper torso to the side in order to dodge him and watched him fall to the ground on his hands and knees. I still found time to run a hand through my hair—wet with sweat—before tripping him with one strong kick to his legs as he tried to stand up.

"You're getting smug, Hudson," our trainer, Julian, warned.

"Way to kick a man when he's down, Ben." Zinnia laughed. I found her lighthearted jibes endearing, but I doubted the man I just sent writhing on the ground felt the same way.

We were right in the middle of the glass-enclosed atrium, which served as the main martial arts training center at the hunters' headquarters. I was going through a final test in order to qualify for advanced training at the hunters' academy. Most hunters went through years of training before advancing into that level, but I'd already been promoted. I guessed that Reuben had something to do with it.

Being the best friend of the boss's daughter did have its perks. Of course, not everyone knew my connection to Reuben. It seemed as if only Zinnia and I knew that Reuben was, in fact, Aiden Claremont, Sofia's father.

Determined to prove that I was worthy of the special treatment I was getting, I positioned myself ready to deal one final blow onto my opponent.

"Enough!" Julian bellowed, sparing the wincing hunter more pain.

I stood to my feet, taking in deep, even breaths as I stood over the hunter. I couldn't keep the smirk off my face. *I got this in the bag.*

"So? What do you think?" Zinnia asked Julian. During my stay at the headquarters, she'd become everything to me from a friend to a tour guide to my closest handler. I could tell from the get-go that she was into me, and I'd already returned her flirtatious attempts with several quips of my own, but I wasn't ready to get into anything serious.

In every way, my heart still belonged to Sofia, and I doubted it could belong to anyone else. The slightest thought of Sofia, my best friend, my Rose Red, was enough to distract me from what was going on around me. I wondered where she was and if she was being taken care of. It sickened me to think that Derek Novak, the vampire she was inexplicably head over heels in love with, could be taking advantage of her.

I wished I'd never let her go back in the first place. After everything I'd learned during my stay with the hunters, I knew that I'd made a big mistake letting Sofia go back to The Shade. The vampires were irredeemable monsters. I should've known that then, but I didn't have the heart to keep her away from what she told me she wanted. I'd been too selfish with Sofia all my life and letting her go was perhaps the first selfless act I'd ever done for her.

"Hello? Is anyone at home?" Zinnia was snapping her fingers in front of my face. She was accustomed to me spacing out on her by now, so I figured the annoyed look on her face was more on Julian's behalf than hers. "Did you hear what Julian said?"

"I'm sorry...what?"

"I think you're beyond any training we can give you when it comes to hand-to-hand combat. And I've never seen anyone master the use of a wooden stake as quickly as you did. The only thing I think you'll need more practice on is firing a gun. In that vein, Zinnia is one of the best shooters we have. I think she's more than capable of putting you through the training required in that area."

A smug smile formed on Zinnia's face, her hazelnut brown eyes glimmering with glee. "Hear that, Hudson? *The best...*"

"I believe he said *one* of the best, Wolfe." I then turned my attention toward Julian. "So what does that all mean?"

"I think you're ready for your first mission. I'll discuss this with Reuben and I'll have Zinnia inform you of the boss's decision."

I glanced at Zinnia just in time to see her mouth form into a surprised "whoa."

"When do you think we'll find out?" I asked.

Julian shrugged. "When it comes to Reuben, we never quite know. He's always so busy—especially with the work being done to locate the Maslen and Novak covens, but since it involves you...who knows? His response may come quicker than normal."

I winced at the implication behind what he said. Even *he* was convinced that I was being given some sort of special treatment. I stood still, fists clenched, as I watched Julian walk away.

Zinnia rubbed a hand over my elbow. "Hey. Don't mind him. I'm sure you'll be able to prove that any favors Reuben's giving you are deserved."

"So you think that Reuben's really giving me favors?" I asked.

"Come on, Ben…you're the only recruit staying in a guest suite. You flew right through training—and yeah… even I have to admit that you're better than all the people you passed by—but still, your time here as a hawk-in-training is, let's say, out of the ordinary."

I looked at the tattoo of a hawk on my wrist. It was the sign that I was now a hunter—one of them, part of the international order devoted to ridding the planet of vampires. I wondered to myself what Sofia would think once she saw the tattoo. I steeled myself for when I had to kill Derek Novak—even if I had to do it right in front of her eyes.

*It's necessary, Sofia. He has to die before he totally corrupts you. When the time comes, I hope you'll find it in your heart to forgive me.*

"You're thinking about her, aren't you?" Zinnia asked me, her brown eyes set on my face. "Sofia?"

I was surprised to hear her mention Sofia. I tried to recall the last time I heard my best friend's name spoken out loud. *Was it from Reuben?* I couldn't remember, but an unwelcome memory did haunt me. It was that of Vivienne Novak, Derek's twin sister. As a last ditch attempt to pry information out of her, Reuben sent me into her cell to speak with her. She was bloodied, bruised and tortured, her fangs ripped from her mouth.

Her words haunted me. *You have no idea how much you mean to her. One day, Ben, you're going to look beyond yourself and you're going to see Sofia as she is. Once you see the world through her eyes, you will understand. You could be* great, *Ben.*

Ignoring Zinnia's question, I shook my head and began walking toward the showers. "What happened to Vivienne? Is she dead?"

Zinnia kept pace with me, having to take at least two strides with every one of mine. "I don't know. I never thought to ask. Didn't Reuben say that he had her executed?"

"Yeah… I just…" I sighed and shook my head. "It's nothing." I stopped in front of the locker room and pointed toward the door. "I'll just take a quick shower, okay?"

*I miss you so much, Sofia.* As I took a shower, I went through for the umpteenth time everything that happened between us. She was into me for so long. I took advantage of that knowledge and in so doing, I lost her. *She deserves better than me, but 'better than me' definitely isn't Derek Novak.* My gut clenched to think that she felt more valued being with the vampire prince than with me. *I really screwed it up with her.*

It felt hopeless, like I could never get her back, but I refused to entertain that particular emotion. She was too important to me to just give up on. I was going to get her back.

I twisted the shower's brass knobs and the steady stream of water rushing down onto my body stopped. My resolution was clear. *I'm going to get Sofia back. Right after I help destroy The Shade and every single vampire within it.*

# Chapter 8: Derek

The Catacombs were composed of several levels of intricately networked caves, located within the base of a giant mountain range known to the island as the Black Heights. The human population not housed within the vampire residences was given quarters within The Catacombs, and it was to be my beloved's home.

I couldn't help but wince whenever I visited The Catacombs. It was no place for a vampire—this was made clear by the stares that came my way; some curious, and some tainted with blatant animosity. I couldn't blame them. The Catacombs was their haven—their place away from our kind, and my presence there only served to remind me that they were a generation of captives—they and their ancestors before them.

Still, I steeled myself against their glares, because I had work to do. If Sofia was going to live there, she wasn't about to live the same way the others did.

Corrine, witch of The Shade, served as the humans' champion. Though one could never underestimate my own position and power within The Shade, she was one of the few people in that island whom I was severely wary of.

"You can't be serious!" she exclaimed when I broached the topic of clearing out half of the entire top level so I could have it turned into Sofia's quarters.

"I want it done," I responded firmly.

"Derek…this is insanity. You do realize that, don't you?" she asked as she paced the floor of the Sanctuary, her home.

"My father made laws that I cannot defy, but if Sofia is to stay here, I will not have her live like a pauper. Not while I'm prince of the island and commander of its army."

"I understand that, Derek." The brunette nodded as she planted her hands on her hips and took several deep breaths. "There's really nothing any of us can do if you demand that this be done, but do you realize that this will only earn Sofia the other human citizens' ire? She's a Migrate, for crying out loud. To give her such lavish treatment is a slap in the face to those who've been loyal Naturals for generations!"

"They know who she is to me. I will have the head of anyone who dares lay a hand on her."

"Does she know about this?"

I shook my head. "I want it to be a surprise. A birthday gift."

"Derek, are you still so naive when it comes to what kind of person Sofia is?"

My ears stung at her words, but I was unrelenting. I ran my hand through my hair in frustration as I responded to the witch. "What would you have me do, Corrine? Would you have me just send her there, living in the same dire conditions as the rest of them?"

"If you help improve the living conditions of *all* the humans there, then she wouldn't have to!"

"That action could turn *all* the vampires against me. Everything I do for Sofia puts me *and her* in danger against the other vampires. If I start siding with the humans..." my voice trailed off, refusing to think of the implications. "Are you going to get this done or not, Corrine?"

Her shoulders sagged in resignation as she looked at me from head to foot, not bothering to hide her disdain. "It's not like I have a choice in the matter."

And thus, it was done. It took barely a week until everything was set up exactly the way I had specified. Her quarters were composed of a master bedroom, two guest rooms, a living area, a kitchen and a dining area.

It wasn't until everything was in order that I brought the girls—after having Corrine and the guards effectively distract Sofia—to the refurbished quarters. While Paige and Rosa were busy exploring the rooms, I stood beside Ashley, knowing that she would never withhold the truth from me.

"What do you think?" I asked.

Ashley crossed her arms over her chest and sighed. "It's gorgeous. I'm sure she'll love it," she replied flatly.

"That's *really* what you think?"

"I mean it when I say that the place looks incredible. I'm astounded at how quickly it was finished, but how many people were kicked out of this space in order to make room for Sofia? Have you even looked around The Catacombs, Derek? Half of the levels barely have electricity and you wiped out families from half of the one level that has stable electricity."

I gave Ashley the same reason I gave Corrine. Sofia chose to live in

The Catacombs. She chose this fate. I wasn't about to stand by and just watch her live an impoverished life while I enjoyed the comforts of my extravagant treetop villa.

"I can't just let Sofia live the way they do. If any of the people here have a problem with this, then they can take it up with me."

"You really do love her, don't you?"

I was surprised to hear softness in Ashley's voice. It was the first time I could remember her talking to me in a tone that was free from spite.

"I feel like I'm losing her," I admitted, surprised that I would divulge something as private as that to Ashley. I realized at that moment that without Sofia, Ashley never could've been safe around me. She couldn't stand in that living room with me without danger of me completely destroying her. I found myself wondering why, in spite of the constant thirst for her, the temptation to feed on her wasn't as all-consuming as it was before. *Love is a powerful force,* I told myself.

"She left *everything* for you. How on earth could you lose her?"

"Time is our enemy."

I took a good look at the young woman standing before me. I wasn't blind to her beauty. Some could even say that the former cheerleader was fairer to the eye than Sofia, but she wasn't the girl I loved. Still, I knew she deserved happiness—something that The Shade had stolen from her.

"I'm sorry for everything I put you through, Ashley. I truly am."

"Water under the bridge…" Ashley shrugged and shook her head.

My eyes narrowed at her. "You're a hunter," I reminded her, the memory of the hawk tattoo on her lower back coming to mind. "Why on earth would you want to turn into one of us, the very thing you wanted to completely eradicate?"

"You used to be a hunter too, right? I saw the tattoo on your back. Yet here you are..."

"That's different. I wasn't given a choice when I was turned. You're *choosing* to be one of us. Why?"

She was silent but a moment as she shifted her weight from one foot to the other. "Because I don't ever want to feel powerless again... I don't want to feel like I don't have a choice." She paused, her gaze distant. "More than that, I envy what you and Sofia have. I want to have that too...with Sam."

I almost choked at her statement. "*Sam*?"

She looked at me with panic-stricken eyes. "You're not going to tell anyone, are you? Only Kyle and Eli know how I feel for Sam...not even the girls know...not even Sofia!"

I was having trouble wrapping my mind around the whole thing. I knew of her closeness to both Kyle and Sam, but I had no idea that she'd also developed a bond with the island's resident scholar, Eli Lazaroff, who along with his brother Yuri, were part of the island's Elite. I'd been sending Ashley to Eli for a while so she would divulge everything she knew about the hunters' operations.

"What do you think you're doing, Ashley? Are you on some sort of quest to divulge your deepest secret to every male vampire on this island?"

She hit me lightly on the shoulder and pouted in that strange way teenage girls have a habit of doing. "Shut up."

"You're one of the craziest people I've ever met," I teased. "That's saying a lot, considering how long I've been alive."

"Come on...the four hundred years you spent snoring doesn't count." She scowled at me.

"I don't snore."

"M-hm...can you get Sofia to vouch for that?"

I paused before changing the subject. "Look, Ashley, if you want to be with Sam, why do you want Kyle to turn you?"

"Well, Kyle's like a protective older brother to me. I'm not sure about the rules on the island, and you made it sound like whoever turns me becomes my family."

"What?! I never said anything like that."

"You told me that if you turned me, I was going to be Ashley Novak!"

Hard as I tried, I couldn't hold back the laughter. The look in her eyes was too precious, the secret she'd just divulged too sacred. Her face deadpanned as she watched me try to hold back the snickers.

"I'm so screwed."

"Seriously…I'm just surprised that you would entrust me with information on this schoolgirl crush of yours." Sam was in his mid-twenties when he got turned. I honestly doubted that he saw Ashley as anything other than a sister.

Before Ashley could react to my statement, Paige and Rosa stepped in.

"Could we please go now?" Ashley stomped a foot. "His highness has once again proven to be the most irritating creature on earth." She began to walk toward the doorway.

Paige and Rosa exchanged knowing glances, smiles forming on their faces. As they followed their friend out, brushing past me, I could hear both girls mutter, "What's new?"

# Chapter 9: Sofia

The moment Derek stepped into the penthouse, I began tapping my foot on the hardwood floor, showing him my impatience. I crossed my arms over my chest, before demanding, "What's going on, Derek? You've been acting *really* strangely lately."

Since Ashley announced that she was going to be a vampire and the subject of my eighteenth birthday was broached, it was almost as if Derek had been avoiding me.

He was barely ever home. I was asleep by the time he arrived and he was gone when I woke up. He kept me busy with either the girls or the guards and when I began questioning him about it, he gave me a string of words that barely constituted a decipherable answer before sending me to Corrine.

I wondered if it had something to do with my birthday, if he was concocting some sort of elaborate surprise. For a few days, that appeased me. Still, as far as I was concerned, it didn't excuse how aloof he was being toward me. At a certain point, I just about gave up trying to figure him out. I wasn't much of a fan of surprises when I was the one being surprised—even more so when I was left out of the preparations for the surprise. I told him that, but it didn't seem to make a difference to him.

Derek took a quick look at me, before diverting his eyes elsewhere. "I'm tired," was all he said, his voice cold and calculated.

"*This* is your way of making it up to me?" I took a couple of quick steps forward in order to block him from walking off toward his bedroom. That was another thing that had changed since that day. He'd moved me out of his bedroom. It left me utterly confused, but I obliged. A succinct "it's better this way" was the only explanation I received from him.

He tried to side-step me, but I blocked his way once more, staring him down. "I don't care if you're tired. You're immortal. *I'm* tired of you avoiding me."

"I'm *not* avoiding..."

"Yes. You are. You can't just walk away from me. Not again."

His shoulders sagged and he looked at me with longing. I couldn't help but feel butterflies inside my stomach at the sight of those blue eyes on me. It seemed I could never really get used to the powerful effect his mere presence had on me.

We remained silent for a few more moments, just staring. I couldn't comprehend what was going through his mind, but this was the longest time I'd been able to spend with him for the past couple of days and truth be told, despite the silence, I was satisfied just to be there with him.

Suddenly Derek squared his shoulders and stood to his full height. He grabbed me by the wrist and nodded. "Fine. Come with me."

"Where are we going?" I asked as he began pulling me outside.

"To take a walk," he responded. "If we're going to have this talk, it won't be here."

I creased my brows, trailing after him, wondering why on earth we couldn't just have the conversation in his penthouse. I stared at the back of his head as I tried to keep up with his long, fast strides. *What is going on inside that brain of yours, Novak?*

We were already at the Vale, nearing the town square when I stopped in my tracks and pulled against him, trying to catch my breath. I looked around us and felt annoyed that he had dragged me to such a public place. People were beginning to look at us, but out of reverence for him, kept to themselves.

"What is going on, Derek?!" I managed to exclaim in between gasps. Frustrated, I placed both hands over my head, grabbing clumps of my hair to emphasize my point. "I can't wrap my mind around what you've been up to lately." I was desperately trying to fight back the tears as I leaned against the stone wall of one of the buildings bordering the town square.

His eyes softened and he heaved one deep sigh before finally addressing my concerns. "You're moving out on your birthday, Sofia. We have to get accustomed to being apart from each other."

That wasn't what I wanted to hear from him. I shook my head and swallowed hard as I stood straight, digging my heels into the ground in irritation. "So it's like that? Is that why you were saying sorry to me? Because you're just going to abandon me? Is this some sort of punishment over my choice to live in The Catacombs and not get turned into a vampire?"

"It's not like that…"

"Then what is it?!" I couldn't understand what was going through his mind. He'd barely looked at me, much less touched me in the past week. My voice softened as I begged him to tell me, "What's going on, Derek? Why are you avoiding me?"

"My father's got me busy. You know what he's like..."

I gently placed a hand on his arm and he flinched away from my touch. That sudden motion of his was painful to experience.

He must've noticed how my eyes were beginning to moisten, because he softened at the sight.

"Sofia..."

*My sandcastle feels like it's about to fall apart.* "I always knew that I would lose you eventually. I just didn't expect that it would happen so soon."

"You know what, Sofia!" he snapped. "That's just it!"

I gasped when he pushed me against the wall. Eyes blazing, he rested one hand against the stone so that he could have his face closer to mine, his breath cold against my skin.

"You keep talking about how we're going to lose each other as if it's something inevitable, as if it's something we just have to accept. I *dread* the day I could lose you, Sofia. It would be like losing my reason to live, and for the past few days all I've been able to think about when I look at you is how you're slipping away from me every second of every day."

The urgency by which the words came out of his lips drew my breath away. Desperation oozed out of every syllable. I stared up at him, not knowing what to say.

He stepped forward and leaned closer so that he was looking right into my eyes. "Why can't what we have last forever?"

A tear ran down my cheek as I spoke the sad truth, "Because we both know that it can't."

His jaw tightened and he began shaking his head furiously as he spat out through gritted teeth, "How could you say that?! How could you just give up like *that*?" Both his hands gripped the sides of my head and his lips crushed against mine. The kiss was passionate and forceful—as if he were punishing me for daring to resign myself to the eventual doom of our relationship.

I found myself frozen beneath his touch, a hundred thoughts warring in the battleground of my mind. I couldn't respond to his advances, but neither could I resist. I missed this, missed his touch so much that the only thing I found myself feeling at that moment was relief. He still wanted me. He wasn't giving up on us.

When our lips parted, I was trembling and I could barely form words through my quivering lips. I stared up at him. "I thought you didn't want me anymore," I admitted.

Fire sparked in his eyes as they narrowed in question. "How could you ever think that?" His hands wrapped around my waist and he pulled me close. "I will always want you." He once again pressed his mouth against mine—tender this time, before kissing my forehead.

Suddenly, we were interrupted by a loud clap. We both looked toward the direction of the noise and found Gregor Novak approaching with several members of the Elite council—members I wasn't quite familiar with—trailing behind him. He had a young woman holding on to his right arm. He shrugged her hand off him and she stumbled backwards.

My gut clenched when I saw the bite marks on her neck. I grabbed Derek by the arm for support. I couldn't keep my eyes off the girl even as I bowed my head in reverence toward the king of The Shade.

"Father." Derek's entire demeanor tensed.

Gregor's eyes were on me. Cold. Cruel. Condescending. When he touched me, brushing his fingers over my cheek, I couldn't help but flinch.

"Jumpy, isn't she?" He chuckled.

Derek glared at his father, his sovereign. "Don't touch her."

"What is it with you and this consuming urge to protect this little firebrand?" Gregor kept his steely eyes on me, amusement and mockery dripping from his every word. "What's so special about her? What makes her so different from all the other women you've brought to your bed?"

My eyes shot toward Derek. I knew that I wasn't the first woman he'd had in his bed, but to hear someone call him out on it felt different. I could practically sense how torn apart Derek was at being reminded of his past. He just hung his head, staring into space as Gregor drawled on, this time addressing me.

"Do you have any idea how many lovely ladies have graced the presence of your prince here? Do you know the kind of women whose pleasures he's willingly partaken of? Do you really believe an immortal could stay faithful to a mortal like you?"

I hated the way he was talking. I knew it was meant to cause doubt in me, but more than that, it was meant to inflict pain on Derek. I gave Gregor the sweetest smile I could manage before turning my eyes toward the man I loved. I hated how dejected he seemed when all his past weaknesses were slapped right into his face. I brushed a hand over his cheek and tilted his chin so that he would look at me and see me smiling.

"I don't have a single doubt in my mind that he can and he *will* be faithful to me," I spoke the words with conviction emanating from every fiber of my being. I knew then that the words were true and from the spark in Derek's blue eyes, I could tell that he too knew that I meant every word.

Gregor laughed wryly. "Sure. You must be really good in bed if you think you can keep him interested for…"

"Enough," Derek spoke up. "You don't talk about Sofia that way.

Ever."

"What? You deny that she isn't the first whore you've taken to bed? That she's just one among many who…"

"I said *enough.*" Derek's glare was so menacing, even I stepped back. "She's not one among many, father. She's the *only one*, the only woman I have ever been in love with."

"*In love?!*" Gregor exclaimed. "Do you even know what that means, son? Is that what you think you feel whenever you have this nubile body of hers writhing beneath yours?"

"It's got nothing to do with sex." Derek looked around at the crowd now beginning to form around us—made curious by the argument going on between king and prince—and raised his voice, "In fact, I vow that I will no longer take her to my bed and make love to her until she's become my wife…until the world knows that Sofia Claremont alone owns my heart."

My eyes widened with surprise. His eyes met mine and if he didn't know it already then he was a fool, but I was his. I was forever his.

Still, he wasn't done astounding me. He looked deep into my eyes and I found my mind reeling at the next words he spoke, "I'm going to marry you someday, Sofia Claremont. I don't know how it will happen, but it *will* happen. We belong together and you know it."

I tried to say something, but I had no idea what to say, so my jaw just hung loosely as I gaped up at him.

"Until that day, Sofia, I can't treat you the same way I treated all the other women who came before you. You're too precious for that, but be sure of one thing…I will pursue you. Relentlessly. I will pursue you until death pulls us apart. I will find a way, Sofia. I'll find a way to make what we have last forever."

I shuddered at what he was trying to tell me. He knew that I could never become a vampire, an immortal like he was, so how he thought that the words he was speaking could possibly become true was beyond me. Still, the determination in his eyes told me that he meant everything he had said.

Moved, I caressed the side of his face with my hand, enjoying the feel of his skin beneath mine. "No matter what happens, Derek," I tried to assure him. "Remember that my heart belongs to you, and it could never belong to any other."

A smile formed on his lips. "That's all I need to hear."

Given that statement, every single person present that night was made aware that Derek's pursuit of me had just begun.

# Chapter 10: Lucas

I didn't know what to expect after the Maslens—our clan's archenemy—offered me sanctuary. It felt like such a gamble, but having been informed that my father would rather send me back to The Shade and face death at Derek's hands instead of taking me under his wing, I really had no other choice. The Oasis, home of the Maslen clan, became my sanctuary.

Thus, I travelled to Cairo where Borys Maslen—lord of the Maslen clan—sent an escort to take me to The Oasis. In a couple of days' time, traveling by night and seeking shade by day, I arrived. At first, I thought that it was some sort of joke. It was exactly as it name implied—a small oasis hidden within the Egyptian boundaries of the Sahara Desert.

A slew of curses escaped my lips as I approached the small lake surrounded by three palm trees that appeared to form a triangle around the lake.

“What is this?” I hissed at my escort.

“Wait and see,” he responded smugly.

I’d already heard a lot of stories about The Oasis. It was said to be a marvel, but nothing prepared me for what I saw.

My escort took out a small velvet pouch and retrieved a brass hexagonal object studded with emeralds. He walked toward one of the palm trees and knelt on the ground, brushing sand away from an area beneath the tree to reveal what looked like a metal plate. He then gently placed the emerald-studded hexagon on top of it. He stood up and took out another brass hexagon, this time studded with sapphires. He walked to another one of the two palm trees and did the same thing. For the third palm tree, he repeated the process with a brass hexagon studded with rubies.

“Earth, water, fire…” he muttered as he placed the third hexagon in place. The moment the ruby-studded plate was put in its place, I felt the ground rumble beneath my feet. The small lake transformed into a whirlpool and suddenly an opening began to form in the center of it. That’s when I spotted a black staircase leading downward. This real-life oasis was actually just a gateway allowing entry to the Maslens’ infamous Oasis.

“Follow me.” My escort motioned to descend the stairs. I stood frozen for a couple of seconds before finally gathering my wits about me and following him to wherever the staircase led.

We descended the stairs surrounded by gushing water, but amazingly I was kept dry. We finally reached the top level of The Oasis’ seven underground levels.

The levels were once Egyptian tombs concealing hidden treasure. After the Maslens found the keys to The Oasis over a hundred years ago, they modernized and renovated all of the tombs’ interconnected halls and chambers. At the center of it all was a huge, round, glass-encased elevator that allowed quick access from one level to the next.

I didn't get a chance to look around much, because I was immediately brought to level four: "The Palace". I was ushered through several well-lit corridors, lavishly decorated with golden-framed paintings and beautiful antiques. Finally, we reached the chamber which was our destination.

Borys Maslen was slumped on a large black throne made of skulls—looking the same way he did centuries ago—muddy brown hair; dark eyes; a stocky, well-built physique; wide and muscular.

Our first conversation was tense to say the least—even more so when I mentioned that the girl prophesied to establish my brother's rule was already at The Shade. When he discovered the girl was actually Sofia, he lost all control of himself—something that I couldn't fully understand until I saw Borys' right-hand woman, Ingrid.

Ingrid used to be Camilla Claremont before she became a vampire. She was Sofia's mother.

It was daunting to me, but from that day onwards, everything about my stay at The Oasis became about finding Sofia. I didn't understand what all the fuss was about. She was just one human girl and yet no matter where I went—whether it be in the middle of the ocean at The Shade or the middle of the desert at The Oasis—everything seemed to revolve around Sofia Claremont.

"I want Sofia," Borys told me.

"As I told you, I haven't figured out how to get her to you yet." I replied.

We were inside my quarters; a one-bedroom suite located at level four, where all the royals and favored citizens of The Oasis resided. To them, I'd been given a privilege to stay there. To me, it was just a comfortable prison, because they forbade me to leave level four.

"What is it with my daughter and getting vampires so caught up in her wiles?" Ingrid said in a slurred tone as she slinked from one side of the room to the other. She lay down on one of the Egyptian couches.

"I have no idea," I lied, wondering how Sofia ended up with such a demented mother.

Having already tasted Sofia's blood, I knew her appeal. I knew how sweet she was. *Sofia has this thing about her—almost as if her blood is a siren call. I don't know how my brother can stand being around her and not suck the blood out of that pretty white neck of hers. She's the tastiest little morsel I've ever had the pleasure of having.* Still, considering Borys' obsession with Sofia, I couldn't reveal that little secret to them. I was sure that the moment Borys found out that I was most likely the first vampire to ever taste Sofia's blood and live, I would be a dead vampire.

"What's so special about her anyway?" I asked.

Borys and Ingrid gave me wary glances.

"I didn't expect that Derek would have such a heavy ace against me. First, Vivienne. Now, Sofia."

I stared at him. *Does he actually think that Derek is keeping Sofia as some sort of hostage to cause umbrage against him?* "I doubt that Derek is keeping Sofia to spite you, Borys," I said carefully, surprised that I was defending my younger brother.

"Then what good would the teenager do him?" Borys frowned.

"I told you...I'm pretty sure Derek is *in love* with her. If you get Sofia in your hands then it's *you* who would have an ace against my brother."

Borys sat up straight on the couch he was slouched on. "How do you propose we get Sofia in our hands?"

I fought the urge to roll my eyes. I wasn't one to boast about my average intelligence, but Borys—cruel brute that he was—really wasn't the sharpest tool in the box. I looked at Ingrid. *Perhaps that's why she's proven to be invaluable to him. She's his brain.*

Ingrid stretched and purred on her recliner before breathing out a sigh. "This conversation isn't going anywhere. It's a waste of my time."

"I'd just like to know why you want Sofia," I pried.

Ingrid gave me a calculating look before finally nodding as if deciding for herself that she could trust me with the information she was about to give. "When I asked Borys to turn me into a vampire, he agreed to do it on one condition. I was to give him my daughter. I agreed. Thus, Borys turned me. When we set off to retrieve Sofia from the States, my husband, Aiden, already realized what we were after. He took my daughter away from me and hid her somewhere. I have no idea how, but he managed to obscure her from all our attempts to sense her and track her down."

I shifted my weight over the edge of my bed as I digested the information she just told me, wondering how I could use it to my advantage. *Too late.* Ingrid stood from her seat and looked at me with sheer agitation.

"Are you not weary of this pointless conversation we're having with your enemy's brother, Borys?"

"I am." Borys nodded, the expression on his face stoic. "And I'm not sure we can fully trust him. Not yet."

I swallowed hard. The conversation had suddenly taken a dangerous turn. "Look…I wouldn't be here if I weren't desperate. Desperation calls for loyalty as a necessity."

"If you really are pledging allegiance to us, you will help us get Sofia." Ingrid tilted her head to the side, not a trace of maternal affection in her expression. She talked about Sofia as if she were talking about a piece of property we were all haggling over.

"I told you… I don't know how to help you… Derek is going to kill me the moment I step back into The Shade. I don't have any allies there." *Except maybe Claudia, but she's more an ally to herself than to anyone else.*

"All I hear are excuses, Novak." Borys now also rose from his seat and walked toward Ingrid. He brushed a hand through Ingrid's red hair, and I had no doubt in my mind that with each fond caress, he had Sofia on his mind. "Make a way. If you don't bring us Sofia soon, you will die. I expect a report on your progress within the week."

I watched, completely stunned, as the odd duo walked out of the room, with Ingrid looking like a redheaded goddess, graceful and stunning, while Borys stomped out with as much grace as an ox. I frowned, wondering how I'd gotten myself into this nightmare.

Still, there was a ray of sunshine—the possibility of having Sofia within The Oasis' tombs. The idea of once again laying my hands on the girl I craved so deeply was enough to make me smile.

I mused over the things I could possibly do in order to get Sofia to The Oasis. The first step suddenly became clear in my mind. *I need to contact Natalie Borgia.*

# Chapter 11: Derek

The look in Sofia's eyes the last time we spoke haunted me. I told her that I would pursue her, that I would find a way for what we had to last forever, but I hadn't the slightest clue how to do that. She was an ache in my heart that I knew would never go away until I was certain that she would be mine to keep for eternity.

When her birthday came, it felt like losing a precious year. The night before it, I was moping around like a dismal sap over the feeling of her slipping away from my grasp. I was being pathetic and I knew it, but I couldn't help myself.

Still, the day came and I was determined to set myself aside in order to make her happy. That was her day. I wasn't going to ruin it with my selfishness.

I sneaked into her room in the wee hours of what could be considered as morning at The Shade. I was disturbed to see that her beautiful face was marred with agitation as she whispered in her sleep. She was clutching her blanket so tightly, her knuckles had become white. She began tossing and turning on the bed and a cold sweat was forming on her brow.

No other person in the world could make me as anxious and worried as she could. I hurried forward and sat near her on the bed, unsure of what to do.

"Sofia?" I breathed out as I tentatively ran a hand over her bare arm.

"No!!" she screamed the moment my hand came in contact with her. She slapped it away. "Don't touch me! No!" Tears began streaming down her face, her eyes still shut.

Panic surged within me, desperate to get her out of the nightmare she was in. All caution toward gentleness left me as I began shaking her awake. "Wake up, Sofia."

"No!" She screamed once again before jolting up on the bed in a sitting position, her whole body trembling. The last time I saw her this terrified was when she woke up to find Gwen murdered in her bedroom.

When her eyes finally settled on me, I was almost sure she'd scream from fright, so I was relieved when she gasped "Derek!" before throwing her arms around me. "Don't let them take me!" she whispered into my ear, her embrace tightening around my neck.

Her words gripped at my chest. "Shh…it was just a dream, Sofia…no one's going to take you away…not while I'm around." My heart began to pound just at the idea of anyone attempting to take her from me. "Everything's going to be alright," I assured her. The way her body was shaking did little to ease my fears, even though I was desperately trying to ease hers.

It took a couple of minutes before she finally calmed down.

"Don't leave me…" she pleaded, sounding childlike and unsure.

"I'm not going anywhere." I pulled away from her embrace in order to take a look at her, but she clung on to me. "I'll be right here with you for as long as you need me." I put my arms around her, my palms running the length of her back in order to reassure her. It was the closest we'd touched for the past week.

I leaned back against the bed's headboard before tapping the space in between us, coaxing her to snuggle against me. She obliged without hesitation. I was once again so keenly aware of her vulnerability, of how fragile she was. Yet at the same time, I was fully aware of her strength and her determination as a person.

"Care to tell me what the dream was about?" I asked after a comfortable period of time, just as she leaned her head against my shoulder. I had my arm around her and was softly brushing her kneecaps with my fingers.

"I'm not sure how to explain it. I was being pulled away by so many shadows. Away from you. Away from here. Waking up, all I can think about is Vivienne's memories of Borys Maslen. What he did to her when he took her…"

My gut clenched at the thought. A lifetime ago, we owned a farm in a small village lorded over by the Maslens. When Borys first saw my twin, he took an immediate liking to her. She couldn't stand him. Neither could I. When our mother died and I, convinced that vampires took our mother's life, left to join the hunters, my father agreed to have my sister betrothed to Borys in exchange for a generous dowry—a dowry that was quickly spent on gambling, women and ale.

Vivienne never talked about what she went through in Borys' hands—enough indication in itself that she must've gone through hell. I never asked. I didn't want to know.

I, however, wondered why Vivienne felt the need to share those memories with Sofia. *Why does Sofia have to know?* I didn't know what to make of the whole thing. The fact that Sofia would connect her nightmare to my twin's darkest memories left me unsettled, but I tried to keep a brave face. "Don't worry, Sofia. I would never allow you to suffer the same fate Vivienne did. I'd rather die."

"I know." She nodded. "But I don't want you to ever die, Derek...especially not on my behalf."

To that, I remained quiet. I knew that if I could trade my immortality to keep her alive, I would do it and I wasn't about to promise her that I wouldn't risk my life for hers, because should the need arise, I knew I would. Without hesitation.

"So today's the day..." she spoke up after a short silence.

I pulled her closer to me, realizing how much I missed her. "Happy birthday," I said and pressed my lips against her temple.

What she said next echoed my heart's desire. "I wish I could stop time."

She was aging and I wasn't. Her every birthday would be a reminder that time was slowly, but steadily, pulling us apart. I wanted to beg her to become one of us—a vampire—but I knew she wouldn't.

*Perhaps she's right. What we have is a sandcastle. Temporary, but beautiful and we can only treasure and enjoy it for as long as nature allows us.*

"Our time together is too precious to waste like this," I eventually said, unable to conceal the tone of resignation that came with it. I grabbed her hand and squeezed. "Come with me."

Thus, though her nightmares still haunted me, I pulled her up, determined to make her birthday a complete dream.

# Chapter 12: Sofia

I was used to people forgetting my birthday. The only time I could remember actually celebrating my birthday was when I turned thirteen. Ben treated me to burgers, fries and milkshakes before taking me to a party I wasn't exactly invited to. To my relief, he stuck with me the whole time. He made me feel special that night—but even while we were dating last year and he was actively trying to pursue me, Ben was never able to make me feel as special as Derek did on my eighteenth birthday.

Our first stop, of course, was the lighthouse. Our secret place. Our private hideout. All the candles were replaced with new scented ones. Rose petals were scattered all over the floor. In the middle of the room was a mannequin. Hanging on it was one of the most stunning dresses I'd ever laid eyes on. The upper part was a tubed pink satin with intricate beading and beautifully embroidered sleeves. The lower part was made of light pink chiffon, its hem reaching just below my knees. A pair of silver, strappy heels were set on a wooden pedestal beside it.

I approached the dress tentatively, tracing my fingers over its beautiful fabric.

"You like it?" Derek asked from behind me.

I nodded. "It's gorgeous."

"Well, put it on. I'll wait outside."

I grinned, wondering what he was talking about. *It's not like you haven't seen me undressed before.* Then I remembered his promise to treat me differently than "all those other women." I searched myself for what this made me feel. After we first slept together, I never told anyone, but I struggled deep inside. As I sketched his image the morning after I lost my virginity to him, I couldn't help but feel a sense of insecurity and fear. I had just given him all of me. Just like that—in the span of a night. He was my first kiss, my first love…my first everything. On the other hand, I was only one among many women that came before me. Doubts of him losing interest in me and finding me unable to equal the more experienced women he'd been with plagued me.

Then he did this. He set me apart from everyone else. That night, as I watched him step out of the room in order to give me privacy, I couldn't help but feel a sense of gratefulness toward him.

I got dressed as quickly as I could, not wanting him to wait too long. When I was done, I headed for the door and opened it. I drew a breath when I saw him wearing a black coat over his outfit. He looked stunning and refined.

"Hey, handsome." I smiled.

He grinned, seeming to genuinely appreciate the compliment, before giving me a good look. "You look incredible."

"Thanks to you." I blushed.

He took hold of my hand, his every motion gentle and much like a sweet caress. He then led me to the middle of the room and gently placed his hands on my waist. He began leading me to a slow dance. He told me once that music was always playing in his head. This wasn't the first time he made me dance to music that only he could hear.

I smiled, enjoying the feel of his hands on me. It was a balm to the yearning ache I'd been feeling for him over the past few days. Being in his arms was bliss in and of itself, so it was even more of a treat when he began humming a tune, allowing me to hear the music playing in his mind.

Just like every moment I spent with him, I wanted it to last for an eternity, but the song came to a close. He then uttered words that sent my brain into a tailspin.

"Marry me, Sofia."

I froze. I guess I should've seen it coming. He was pursuing me. He wanted me. *Why is this request taking me by surprise?* Every fiber of my being was begging me to nod my head and say yes. There was nothing more I wanted than to be his wife, but what kind of life would he have with me? It didn't make any sense for an immortal to commit his entire lifetime to a mortal such as me. I looked up at him, seeing the longing there, mirroring exactly what I felt.

"Derek..." My voice was choked and slightly broken. "I want to...you know that, right?"

"But you can't..." he muttered sadly, his head slowly nodding to show his attempt to understand. His eyes betrayed the pain inside, however, and I wanted nothing other than to ease his pain. But I had no idea how to do that.

My grip tightened over his arms. "I'm so sorry..."

"Don't be. I knew you'd say no, but I wanted to try anyway. I know that someday, I'll hear you say yes to that request, Sofia." He nodded resolutely. "Someday, you're going to be my wife."

*You have no idea how much I want to say yes right now.* A soft gasp escaped my lips when he pulled away from me. He kept on talking about marriage as if only he wanted it, as if I didn't want it just as much as he did, but how could we take such a step? I didn't even want to think about tomorrow, because the hopelessness I felt whenever I thought about the future always ate me up. I didn't want to think of a future without Derek. I wanted to just live today. Marriage was a commitment that forced me to look ahead and wonder what would happen.

Confused, I stepped away from him and looked into his eyes, wondering what was going through his mind. I was relieved to see his melancholy fade away with one bright smile. He lifted his forefinger in the air in a gesture for me to wait.

He walked toward a small chest placed on top of a wooden desk in one corner of the room. He took out a square blue velvet box just about the same length and width as my hand. He brought it to me and opened it. Inside was a golden chain with a small heart-shaped pendant. I brushed my fingers over the pendant, marveling over its beauty. I really had no idea how to tell if a piece of jewelry had any worth, but my gut told me that the necklace he was offering to me was more expensive than I would care to know.

He verified this when he announced, "It's a diamond. It was my mother's. It was the most valuable thing she owned. She had to pawn it off before she passed away, because of some difficulties we were having at the farm. It took me years to find it."

"Derek, I can't possibly take this. It's too valuable..."

"No. I want you to have it. I know that *she* would've wanted you to have it." He took the necklace from the box. "Lift your hair up," he instructed.

"Derek..." I said breathlessly, wanting to object, knowing how precious the item he was offering to me was.

"Sofia...please..." His voice was husky. "I want you to have it. Wear it always. It will remind you of me. Take it as a promise from me—a promise that I will find a way to be with you."

I lifted my hair up with my hand. My skin tingled as he put the necklace over my neck. I was fighting back tears. I couldn't remember anyone ever giving me something so precious. When he faced me, I could barely look at him.

"Thank you..." I brushed a hand over the pendant. "I love it."

"I have another surprise..." He smiled, his hand squeezing mine.

I adored him for what he showed me next, but a part of me wished he hadn't done what he did, because the moment I saw the lavish quarters he'd prepared for me, Paige and Rosa in The Catacombs, I knew without a doubt that life there wasn't going to be easy.

# Chapter 13: Ben

BANG! BANG! BANG!

A smirk formed on my lips as each bullet hit the target right on the mark, smoke billowing out of the place the bullets struck.

"Watch it, Zinnia. I think it's possible I could take your spot among the order's best shooters."

Zinnia scoffed as she traced a finger over the small scar on her left cheek, a scar I never actually thought to ask about before. "You wish, Hudson." She aimed her gun and fired five rounds—all hitting the red circle on the target.

She looked at me with a wide grin on her face. "You may be one of the best fighters the academy has, Hudson, but you're still not as good with a gun as I am."

I rolled my eyes, hating to admit defeat. "Still, you have to admit…I'm ready for this mission."

"Well, you certainly look like you're ready to murder just about every vampire you lay eyes on."

My eyes narrowed at the thought. It was true. I wanted to make my first vampire kill. Desperately. *Soon, Ben...very soon...*

We were off to New York. We'd been tipped off that a group of vampires—whose coven had recently been destroyed by a team of hunters—would be passing through the city that night on their way to seek refuge at a new coven. The plan was to attack at the break of dawn—thus giving us the advantage of sunlight.

"Have you ever seen a vampire die by one of these bullets?" I asked, holding my gun up, pointing it at the mock vampire target a considerable distance away from us. We were using ultraviolet-ray bullets.

Zinnia licked her lips and nodded. "It's an interesting sight, though it's not as lethal as a stake through the heart."

"Why's that?"

"We're not sure why, but the bullets have different effects on different vampires. Some immediately combust...others...well, they die a slow, painful death. We're not really sure yet why the effects aren't the same for everyone."

I imagined what it would feel like to shoot one of those bullets right through a vampire's heart. I wondered what it would feel like if the vampire was Claudia. Seeing her scream in pain, her lithe body writhing on the ground...after everything she did to me, I couldn't keep the wicked smile from forming on my lips as I pulled the trigger once again.

"It's a different kind of feeling. You really don't expect it to be like that," Zinnia said pensively, as if reading my mind. "Killing vampires...especially your first kill..."

I frowned at her, surprised by the careful tone her voice took on. I straightened to my full height, slightly bending my neck in order to look her in the eye. "What do you mean? What's it like?"

"It's hard to describe. After what you lost at the hands of vampires, after all that time training to kill..." She shrugged, her eyes glazing over with tormented memories. For a moment, I thought that she felt sorry, but I realized that the glaze in her eyes was not out of regret, but glee. "There's just this sense of pure satisfaction, knowing that in a small way, you've avenged those you've lost."

I stared at her, never before having been introduced to this cold, dark side of her. The look in her eyes sent chills down my spine. I never thought I'd be so disturbed by a girl as petite as Zinnia Wolfe.

"The horrified look in that girl's eyes as I saw life fade away from her...I'll never forget it. It's true what they say...your first kill will always stay with you. I still see her in my dreams..."

"And you didn't feel any regret or compassion toward her?" My breath slightly hitched at the thought. "Ever?"

She shrugged. "There's a reason I say 'in my dreams' and not 'in my nightmares'."

I studied Zinnia carefully, wondering if she was serious. She was always so fun and lighthearted. She was definitely one of the toughest girls I'd ever come across in my life. Still, she was a teenager like me. *What could've caused her to harbor this much apathy and hatred?* It was strange seeing her act and speak in such a serious, pensive manner. It was so unlike the Zinnia I'd gotten used to.

"Once you go on this mission, Ben, understand that things will never be the same for you again. You really should know exactly what you're getting yourself into, because once you do this, there's no going back."

I gave it a moment's thought, but I couldn't relate to what she was saying—not at that moment, not completely. Thus, I just nodded and said, "Thanks, Zinnia. Don't worry about me. I know exactly what I'm getting into."

I didn't realize what a lie that was until the morning of the mission.

Everything started out as planned. We flew by helicopter to New York. Since I'd been paired with Zinnia, I was supposed to stick with her at all times. After landing on the rooftop of a building right across the street from our mark, the rest of the team quickly ran toward their assigned positions. I was about to do the same thing, but Zinnia quickly grabbed a hold of my arm.

"Wait..." she whispered.

"What?" I asked impatiently. "We're supposed to get into position, Zinnia..."

Cat-like, her eyes darted from one side of the roof to the other. Her gaze stopped on a specific spot on the rooftop.

"Zinnia! Ben!" our squad leader, Quinn, spat out in a muffled hiss. "What are you two doing?"

My eyes widened when I saw a red dot on Zinnia's forehead. I was about to push her to the ground, but she had already done so, screaming, "Duck!" before tackling me to the ground.

Gunshots were fired and from my peripheral vision, I could see one of the hunters fall to the ground. I was looking for a trace of panic among the hunters in my squad, but there was none.

Quinn had a faint smirk on his face as he ran for cover. "They knew we were coming," he said through our communication system. "Just take cover. The sun is about to rise. They won't have an advantage for long. The other squads are already in position. All we have to do is stay alive until sunrise. Keep cover."

The words had barely registered in my brain when I saw Zinnia roll toward one of the concrete banisters lining the rooftop. A small grin was on her face, her eyes still focused on the same spot in the rooftop she'd laid eyes on right after we got there.

I crawled my way closer to her, my stomach still flat on the ground. I followed the direction of her eyes as she began to aim her gun. All I could see were old wooden crates and piles of black netting.

"What exactly are we looking at, Wolfe?"

"Shut up." She fired a shot right through one of the crates.

Within seconds, a piercing scream came from the other side of the crate and a female vampire emerged from behind it, walking around as if she was burning. It was the strangest sight, because the area where the bullet hit her began to glow from the inside—channeling through several parts of her body. She seemed just about ready to implode, and then she just fell to the ground, burned to a crisp before finally turning to ashes.

My jaw was wide open with shock. "That's insane."

After that first kill, chaos ensued. I couldn't quite keep track of everything that went on around me, but what I knew for sure was that the vampires seemed to be winning. We didn't expect them to know that we were coming. They were prepared for us—stronger, more agile. Keeping cover, like Quinn suggested, was difficult to do considering that the vampires were attacking us from all sides.

One of them lunged at Zinnia. I crouched to the ground and swung my leg and tripped him. I was surprised by how easily the big lug fell to the ground. Of all the times I'd tried to fight against Claudia, I never once succeeded in harming her in any way. *Maybe this is a baby vampire.* I was about to stick the wooden stake right through his heart, but a girl screamed behind me.

"No!" her cry was piercing. She obviously held affection for the monster I was about to kill. She pushed me away just in time for Zinnia to shoot another UV ray bullet at the guy.

"No..." the girl who had attacked me whimpered as she watched the man struggle and implode. Tears began to stream down her pale face. "He's my brother..." she whispered, her voice hoarse and broken.

Taking advantage of her distracted state, I tackled the blonde vampire to the ground. I took a quick look at her. I tried to ignore how much her appearance reminded me of Claudia. I knew I couldn't afford to lose time waiting for her to snap back to attention. Thus, without hesitation, I drove the wooden stake right through her heart. As I looked into her bright blue eyes, I wanted to feel the elation and satisfaction that came with my revenge against all the vampires that she represented. There was none.

*Where's that 'pure satisfaction' Zinnia was talking about?*

All I felt was the life of another living creature draining away—a life force that coursed through my entire being before fading off into oblivion.

I'd just made my first vampire kill and all I could think about was the tortured look on Vivienne's eyes when she firmly, but pleadingly told me that she was not the vampire that destroyed my life.

She wasn't Claudia, and neither was this girl I'd just killed.

# Chapter 14: Sofia

"Do you like it?" Derek asked me with such a hopeful tone, it broke my heart to even think of telling him the truth.

"I love it, but don't you think it's too much, Derek?" My tone was tentative and unsure. "I really don't need to have something as lavish as this. I could've easily lived here just like everyone else. Surely someone is more deserving than..."

"Nonsense," he interrupted, shaking his head firmly. "You're the woman I love. In my eyes, you're practically princess of The Shade. You're not like everyone else, Sofia. No one here is more deserving than you are. Accept that."

I forced a smile, knowing how stubborn he could get when he set his mind to something. I looked at my surroundings and felt my gut clench when friends I just recently made at The Catacombs showed up. The widow, Lily, and her children, Gavin, Rob and Madeline—seventeen, seven and five years old respectively—appeared at my doorstep. Lily's eyes widened upon seeing the quarters' modernly designed interior. The two younger children went inside without hesitation, eager to explore the home, their eyes bright with delight and curiosity.

"They said The Palace was stunning, but I didn't expect it to be like this…" Lily muttered under her breath.

I remembered what their home looked like. It felt garish to live in such a place when the family of four was squashed together in one room.

"The Palace?" Derek asked.

Lily's eyes once again betrayed her terror when it came to Derek. She never really did get used to his presence and she always looked as if she were frightened that she would say or do something that would displease him.

"That's what the Naturals call this place…" Gavin was a lot more confident around Derek. Sometimes, he even bordered on defiant—something I admired, but still found myself fearing for him, because not all vampires would tolerate his insolence the way Derek did.

"What do you think?" I asked Gavin. I'd long realized since I first met him how much I valued his opinion. I found it refreshing that he always spoke his mind without hesitation, telling me things as they were and not as I wanted to hear them.

Gavin looked Derek straight in the eye as he crossed his arms over his chest and leaned back on a bare wall. "It's over-indulgent, but I think you already know that."

Derek visibly tensed, most likely surprised that Gavin would have the gall to speak to him in that manner.

"Sofia deserves the best," said Derek.

Gavin's eyes went from Derek to me and to my relief, he nodded. "I'm not going to argue with that. I have to admit that Sofia really is quite special." He then took out a white rose that had been tucked in his back pocket. "I heard it's your birthday." He approached and handed me the rose. "Happy Birthday, Sofia. Now, you can't say I never gave you anything."

From behind me, I could hear Paige and Rosa trying to stifle their giggles. I wondered what they found so funny until I noticed the look on Derek's face after Gavin gave me the rose. He looked just about ready to rip Gavin's heart out.

Derek cocked his head to the side. "Do you have a death wish, boy?" he asked Gavin.

Lily was trembling. I wouldn't have been surprised if she suffered a heart attack then and there. Her face had drained of all color.

Gavin, on the other hand, still had a cocky smile on his face. He stayed calm as he gave Derek a look over from head to foot. "Don't worry, your majesty. I'm not interested in your princess. Not in that way."

"In *what way* are you interested in her then?"

"Not in any way that would be a threat to either her or you, your highness. She's a friend—a sister even. Nothing more."

Gavin said the words in a matter-of-fact way, as if he expected all of us to already know what he'd just explained. He sounded almost bored. Even I was intimidated by Derek's disposition at that point, but Gavin didn't even flinch.

I recalled the first time I had spent time with Gavin. It was right after Claudia took him from the farm and I helped stopped her from making a slave out of him. Claudia attacked him and left some pretty nasty gashes on his upper torso with her claws. I pleaded for Derek to give me a vial of his blood, so we could use it to heal Gavin's wounds.

*"You want me to drink* his *blood?" Gavin spat out, staring at the vial*

*in disdain. "Are you insane?"*

*"It will help you heal..." I said meekly, unsettled by the anger blazing in his eyes. I wondered to myself why I was feeling guilty. It wasn't my fault Claudia caught him and clawed her nails through him. Heck...he should be thankful that I intervened.*

*"Yeah? Well, duh...of course it will help me heal. Doesn't mean I want vampire blood running through my veins..." He stared at me disgustedly. "Have* you *been drinking his blood?"*

*I shuffled my feet uncomfortably. "Several times..."*

*"Migrates..." He rolled his eyes. "No wonder the vampires treat you as pets. What are you doing here, really?"*

*We were in his small cell in The Catacombs and he was lying on one of the four cots belonging to his family. The drab setting and dimly-lit room proved to be rather depressing.*

*"I just wanted to check on you," I responded to his query, wondering why he was throwing so much hostility at me.*

*"You think you're some sort of savior, don't you? Like you're above us just because the prince of The Shade is professing his love to you?" Gavin, despite the bloodied bandages wrapped around his torso, sat up on his cot and glared at me.*

*"No...I just wanted to help."*

*"I've been here all my life, girl. I know the vampires a lot better than you do. Do you think you're the first Migrate these creatures have been infatuated by? You're not. There have been others before you." He snorted as he shot me a condescending look. "It's the same old story. The vampire fell in love. The Migrate got special treatment. Then what? The human gets either turned or killed. If not, they end up with us Naturals—practically useless, because they've been so broken, both mentally and physically, by the vampire who claimed to love them. I could introduce you to one. Anna—stunning beauty, but degraded to nothing but a whimpering child. You're nothing special."*

*A lump formed in my throat as I searched my mind for a response.* You obviously don't know what kind of person Derek Novak is, *was what I wanted to say, but it was clear that Gavin thought himself better schooled in the subject of vampires than I was. Thus, I just hung my head in surrender. It seemed pointless trying to get my point through to him, at least at that moment.*

*The silence seemed to mellow him down, draining the fight out of him. "You have no idea what it's really like to be a human at The Shade, living like every day could be your last. Don't come here holding yourself high above everyone else."*

*"I'm not holding myself above anyone! Is it so wrong to want to help, Gavin?"*

*He studied me carefully, assessing me, perhaps trying to figure out if I was being sincere. His eyes then once again found the vial containing Derek's blood. "I'm not going to drink* that. *I don't think you should either."*

*"Why?"*

*"Because the last thing you want is to owe a vampire anything."*

Standing in the living room of my new quarters in The Catacombs, I couldn't help but form a bitter smile as I realized the extent to which I had neglected to follow Gavin's advice. It felt like I owed Derek *everything.*

Derek continued to study Gavin carefully. He then gave Gavin a nod. "Very well then." He straightened to his full height, once again towering over the rest of us. "I will entrust her to your care. She seems to put a lot of faith in you, so I expect that you will look after her during her stay here in these caves. Do you agree with this?"

Gavin smirked. "How can I refuse? Sure. I'll take her under my wing."

"Gavin…" Lily muttered, her voice hoarse and dry. She still had that terrified look in her eyes. I was about to approach Lily and reassure her, when Corrine stepped into the room. Derek raised a brow upon seeing the witch.

"You told me to inform you once Ashley's turning is about to commence," Corrine said.

I felt myself go pale at what that implied.

"Wait here," Derek instructed.

I shook my head. "I'm going with you."

"Sofia...you don't have to see this."

"No." I stood my ground. "I *want* to see this. I *have* to see this."

Sadness filled his eyes as he nodded. I couldn't place exactly what emotion was coursing through him. To me, for reasons I couldn't entirely understand at that moment, it felt like my sandcastle had just been hit by another wave.

# Chapter 15: Derek

I didn't want her to see anybody—much less Ashley—being turned into one of us. It wasn't the prettiest of sights, neither was it a memory that one could easily purge out of the mind. I was afraid that the sight would haunt Sofia forever. I was afraid that seeing Ashley turn would forever remove from Sofia's mind the option of becoming a vampire.

That's when I realized that I was still hoping that she would agree to be one of our kind. I hated myself for being so selfish.

*How could I wish my curse upon the woman I love?*

We were taking the walk from the Black Heights all the way to The Sanctuary, Corrine's home at The Shade.

The Sanctuary, befitting its name, was located southwest of the island. The white marble structure, with its large round pillars and domed roof, was originally built to honor and house Cora, the witch who made the Shade possible—a dear friend of mine. After her death, the Sanctuary became home to every other witch that succeeded her. One of its chambers also served as my mausoleum during my four-century slumber. Surrounded by lush gardens, complete with a labyrinth, a gazebo and a fountain, it was one of the most lavishly designed structures at The Shade.

Still, I never did quite like going there. This time, in particular, I dreaded reaching the witch's temple. As we walked along the rocky path and past the giant redwoods, I found myself grabbing Sofia's hand.

"You really don't have to see this, you know…" I repeated, a plea for her not to take part in the turning.

"Ashley's my friend. She'd want me there."

"Paige and Rosa are her friends too…you don't see them tagging along."

She squeezed my hand reassuringly. "I'll be alright, Derek."

My gaze focused on what lay ahead. I could already see the Sanctuary coming into view. The sight of the pure white marble façade, seeming to glow under the light of the full moon, should've taken my breath away. It was quite a sight to see. Should I dare look at her, I could almost picture the spark of delight in Sofia's eyes—one that never failed to grace her face whenever we went to the Sanctuary. Corrine, after all, was one of her treasured allies at The Shade. I was never really a fan of the Sanctuary, truth be told. The price paid for such a lavish structure lessened its value in my eyes. I knew what it took for it to get built, but that was only one of the reasons the sight of it made me sick to my stomach. That night, I feared that the sight she was about to witness would lessen my value in Sofia's eyes.

I squeezed her hand tighter. She looked up at me, stood on her tiptoes and pressed her lips against my cheek. "I love you, Derek."

Those words would've been healing balm—hearing them from her always did make all the difference, but not that night. I wondered if she could tell me the same thing after witnessing Ashley get turned.

I kept my silence as we reached the Sanctuary. Corrine, Ashley, Kyle and Sam were already there. Ashley was wearing a skin tight red dress that made her look absolutely stunning. I would've normally been amused at how Kyle and Sam both gulped at the sight of her, but all I could think about was Sofia. Upon seeing each other, Sofia and Ashley embraced.

"Are you sure this is what you want?" Sofia whispered.

Ashley nodded. "Yes. I've never been more sure of anything in my life."

The expression on Sofia's lovely face made me ache inside. She looked like she was about to lose a friend. I didn't know if I was being paranoid, but it was almost as if she was already grieving Ashley.

"Are we ready to begin?" Corrine asked.

Awkward and unsure glances were exchanged across the hall, before Ashley stepped forward and nodded. "I'm ready."

I watched Kyle carefully. I knew for sure that he'd never turned a human before. I wondered what was going through his mind. At that point, however, there was no time to ask. I'd been spending all my free time preparing Sofia's quarters at The Catacombs, I barely gave Ashley's turning much thought.

Corrine nodded for us to follow her and we made our way to the chambers where I'd been kept asleep for four hundred years. The giant round pillars, the stone slab in the middle of the room—each feature triggered unwanted memories from the past.

*"Are you sure this is what you want?" Cora's big brown eyes were moist. It was clear that she'd just hurriedly wiped tears away before I*

*came in.*

*I couldn't look into her eyes. I knew that she loved me. She'd told me many times before. More than that, she'd shown me in more ways than one that I meant more to her than she did to me. I could still remember how she broke into tears when I told her that I wanted to end it all. I wanted to escape The Shade and all the memories that came with it.*

*"You can't leave me here," she sobbed.*

*"I'm sorry" was all I managed to say. She was my best friend and, other than Vivienne, she was the most important woman in my life, but I couldn't stay. Not for her, not for Vivienne. I couldn't bear the guilt anymore—the price I had paid in order to make The Shade what it was, was simply far too high. I couldn't live with myself, yet the thought of dying left me terrified.*

*"You have no idea how hard it is to have someone you love leave you this way."*

*The strongest woman I'd ever known was sobbing right in front of me, a broken, beautiful being I had no idea how to console. She did everything to convince me not to push through with it. She tried to make me see reason, tried desperately to make me realize that there was still something worth living for, but I had made my decision.*

*Thus, we stood there that night, with me entrusting my entire life into her hands. Though she fought tooth and nail against my decision to escape to deep slumber, I knew that she would never do anything to harm me and that she would be true to her word that my sleep would last for eternity, without dreams or nightmares to contend with. Just peace.*

*I never expected her to go back on her promise, because even though no harm did come my way and though the sleep was as peaceful as any slumber could be, I found myself awake four centuries later, madly in love with a girl I feared I would someday lose—the same way Cora lost me.*

Sofia clung to my arm and this motion snapped me out of my

memories. My stomach twisted into a tight knot when I realized that Ashley was already lying on the stone slab. As she usually did, Corrine stood nearby—overseeing the ceremony, making sure that no harm would befall the human being turned. This used to be Cora's role. I found myself missing my best friend, but knew that she was long gone. The thought added another weight to my already heavily burdened chest.

I could sense Sofia's slender form tremble next to mine as Kyle approached Ashley.

"This is going to hurt a bit..." Kyle's croaked.

"It's ok." Ashley gave me a half-amused, sideways glance. "I've been bitten before."

It was obvious from the tone of her voice that she was trying to make light of the situation, but the tremble that came with her words made it clear how nervous she was.

*Who could blame her? This decision of hers will change her life in more ways than she can imagine.* I stared sadly at the annoying little twerp that was Ashley and truly felt sorry for her. Kyle gently brushed strands of her hair away from her neck. Light scars were still present on her skin—my bite marks.

I carefully studied Kyle as he lifted Ashley up into a sitting position. Every move he made was gentle and was meant to keep the young beauty at ease. I could almost see the horrifying memories of the day he was turned flash behind his eyes.

"I can't believe she's really doing this..." Sofia muttered in a low voice that wasn't meant to be heard, but she was close enough for my sensitive ears to hear.

I caught a glimpse of how tightly Ashley was holding onto Kyle's arms, her knuckles turning white as she did. Sam stood in the background, nervously shuffling on his feet, obviously uncomfortable with the situation. We all cared deeply for Ashley. To see her go through what we went through seemed a cruel thing to do—even if it was *she* who made the choice for herself.

*Why am I even allowing this?*

"Wait." I stepped forward just before Kyle was about to position himself to bite her.

I heard a sigh of relief escape Sofia's lips and my heart broke along with it. Still, I had to stop myself from being so selfish. It dawned on me at that moment that the only reason I was allowing Ashley to go through with this was because I was hoping Sofia would see for herself that being a vampire wasn't all that bad. After all, if Ashley could do it, why couldn't she?

*You're the most selfish man in the planet, Novak.*

"I want to have a private word with Ashley."

"Derek, I've told you hundreds of times…I want this."

"I still own you, Ashley. Kyle doesn't get to turn you until I say so. Come with me."

A tense silence followed as Kyle helped Ashley off the slab and she gingerly made her way toward me—not bothering to hide her annoyance. I grabbed Ashley by the elbow and dragged her out of the hall. Sofia motioned to follow.

"Stay there, Sofia."

Ashley was fighting against my grasp. "You don't own me, Derek. *This* is *my* choice. You can't keep me from doing this. You gave us this choice and I've already made my decision."

"You have no idea what you're getting yourself into, Ashley. *No idea,*" I emphasized, unable to hide my exasperation that we had to have this conversation while the others were still around.

"I don't care. I *want* this."

*Stubborn teenager…* "No," I said through gritted teeth. "I don't think you do."

"Maybe you should listen to him, Ash..." Sam offered hesitantly.

I fought the urge to sigh with relief that someone else had seconded me.

"You all do this *now*?" Ashley frowned, unable to hide her irritation. "You guys had all of the past few days to dissuade me from this..."

"Think about what you're about to do, Ashley..." I made a step toward her, towering over her, once again feeling my thirst for her blood after weeks of being able to keep it at bay. "Once you turn, your first instinct will be to kill. Do you really want to live craving every human you come across? Can you really deal with wanting to suck the blood right out of Paige and Rosa?" My gut clenched at the mention of the next name. "Can you bear the burden of wanting to kill Sofia?"

I could hear Sofia's soft gasp as she realized what I was asking Ashley. *Does Ashley really want to turn into a murderer by nature?* I couldn't bear to look at Sofia. I knew then that should Ashley ever try to harm Sofia, I wouldn't hesitate to end Ashley's life.

Based on her silence, I actually thought that I was getting through to Ashley, so I was surprised when she stepped away from me, head bowed and lips pursed.

She nodded her head slowly. "I know what I'm getting myself into."

She then turned her back to me and walked right back to the stone slab. She motioned for Kyle to help her get back on it. Kyle swallowed hard before looking my way to check if I agreed with what he was about to do.

Despite every internal alarm inside me screaming against what was about to happen, I nodded. Ashley was right. I didn't own her. This was her choice.

"Let's do this." Ashley nodded resolutely, coaxing Kyle to do what had to be done.

Kyle stepped forward and placed his hands gently over her waist. I finally forced myself to shift my gaze toward Sofia and found myself wishing that I hadn't.

Her lips were quivering and her eyes were moist with tears. As she stared at Ashley, it was as if she was lost in a daze, her long fingers clenching into firm fists. I wondered then what was going through her mind, because from the look on her face, it almost seemed like she knew exactly what Ashley was about to go through.

# CHAPTER 16: LUCAS

When the gorgeous Italian vampire walked into my chambers, I wanted to jump up and hug her, but this was Natalie Borgia. She was a rogue vampire perfectly capable of ripping my heart out should she decide to. I wasn't about to take my chances, but it was too hard to fight the urge to flirt with her.

It didn't make sense to me how they expected me to organize a way to get to The Shade and retrieve Sofia while I was still being kept a prisoner at The Oasis, but this was how the Maslens worked, so I had to deal with the situation.

"You're looking like a total babe, Natalie..." I crooned. It sure wasn't my best line, but it was all I could come up with in such short notice. "I never thought I'd be stuck in the same bedroom with you..."

"Shut it, Novak..." She rolled her eyes. She had never responded well to my attempts to hook up with her. She looked around my room. "There have been worse dungeons." Her eyes then fell on me. "I never thought I'd live to see the day when I would find a Novak within the tombs of The Oasis."

"If I remember correctly, *you* delivered the message that brought me here."

"That's because I never thought you'd bite, you idiot." She then bit her lip as if regretting what she had just said. She was about to open her mouth to say something else, but she quickly shut her lips again.

I was surprised by what she had said. It was completely unlike her to voice out her own opinions. She was usually the one who had that infuriating poker face that made everybody wonder what exactly was going through that pretty little head of hers.

"I've never heard you voice a personal opinion about any vampire's decisions before, Nat..."

"Don't call me that." She gave me a long and meaningful gaze. I searched her eyes for judgment or condemnation. There was none. In its place were questions that would never be asked.

Natalie was the ultimate diplomat. She was the one vampire who had the trust of all the covens all over the world. If one coven wanted to deliver a message to another coven, she was the rogue to go to. There weren't many rogues like her—vampires who didn't belong to any covens—but the few that existed were invaluable to all vampires. If anybody messed with a rogue, they messed with at *least* three—if not more—covens at the same time.

Natalie made herself comfortable on one of the Egyptian couches. "Do tell, Novak. Why have you summoned me here?"

"I want you to get a message through to Claudia at The Shade."

A dark brow lifted. "Claudia? Okay...the message?"

"Ask her if there's any way we can get Sofia Claremont out of the island." I took out an envelope from my pocket. "I also want you to hand this over to my father. Make sure he gets it and make sure no one else sees the message it contains."

Natalie stared at me long and hard—almost as if she couldn't comprehend what I was trying to tell her. She eventually nodded her head—slowly and thoughtfully. She took the envelope from my hand and nodded. "I hope you know what you're doing, Lucas."

"Is that you caring about me?"

She shook her head. "It's me caring about Derek."

For the first time since I met her, I found myself fighting the urge to rip Natalie Borgia's heart out.

# Chapter 17: Derek

I took hold of Sofia's hand and was surprised by how devoid of warmth it was. I held it tighter. There was no way of telling how Ashley's body was going to react to the serum that would turn her into one of us. I'd seen many turnings go awry before. It rarely happened, but they weren't the prettiest of sights.

Sofia slowly nodded, acknowledging my gesture of reassurance, but the shaking of her body was only getting worse.

"Let's get out of here, Sofia."

Just as I expected, she shook her head.

*Stubborn little minx.*

Kyle was positioning Ashley again. His eyes found mine as he bared his fangs. I gave him a nod. His one hand rested on her hip bone, while the other clung to the back of her neck to support her. He took a bite. For a moment, he gave in to the urge to drink her blood. I knew it from the way my body reacted negatively to a morsel that was mine being partaken of by another vampire, but the boiling in my blood subsided when he went from sucking her blood to injecting the deadly serum from his fangs into her system.

*The snake has taken a bite.*

None of us could question when the serum began to take effect on Ashley, because the moment it entered her system, she let out an agonized scream.

The blood drained from Sofia's face. She let go of my hand and motioned to run toward her friend. I grabbed her arm to hold her back. When she fought against my grasp, I held tighter. "Sofia, don't. You wanted to see this. This is what happens at turnings. You can't be anywhere near her. She won't have the presence of mind not to kill you."

The mutations were beginning to happen and Ashley's long, slender form was convulsing over the stone slab. She began coughing blood. Sofia once again motioned to step forward. I knew she wanted to do something to help, but at that point, there was nothing any of us could do, so we all just stood by and watched. Kyle was staring at Ashley's form, his shoulders stooped low. We hated the sight unfolding before us, but we all knew that it would happen.

I expected Ashley to stop coughing after a few minutes, but it didn't let up for another five minutes, at which point even I wanted to rush forward to try and do something about it, but I was held back by the knowledge that I had to stand by Sofia. Corrine was powerful enough to protect herself; thus, it left Sofia as the only human being in that room Ashley could possibly attack once the bloodlust took over.

When the coughing stopped, an audible sigh of relief filled the room. Still, Ashley's fingers and toes were twitching—aftermaths of the violent tremors her body had just endured only minutes ago.

When the claws began to grow, Ashley once again screamed in agony.

That's when flashbacks of the night I was turned began to fill my mind.

*I trusted him. I trusted my father. I was supposed to kill him. He was a newly turned vampire, and I was the most powerful hunter there was. It would've been easy to take Gregor Novak down, but he was still my father and as I held that crossbow mounted with a wooden stake, I simply couldn't make the kill.*

*"How could you let this happen?" I asked through gritted teeth. "How could you allow yourself to become one of them?"*

*"You don't know what it's like, Derek," he explained to me as he took a step forward over the creaking floorboards. "The taste of power, the heightened senses…everything becomes a thousand times more beautiful…"*

*I backed away from him, the back of my knees hitting one of the benches in our home's small parlor. "Stop it, Father. I don't want to know what it's like. These creatures killed Mother…how could you…" I drew in a sharp breath. It felt like a betrayal. "How can you live everyday knowing that you're one of them? One of the beasts who killed her?"*

*"Don't talk to me about your mother, Derek…"*

*His words faded away when a surge of panic and fear enveloped me. "Vivienne and Lucas…where are they?"*

*His face morphed from irritation to defensiveness. "You have to understand, Derek…"*

*Breathing began to be quite a task. "No…no…what have you done?" I didn't need to hear what he had to say. I walked past him, trusting that he wouldn't do anything to harm me. I was his son after all. "Vivienne! Lucas!" I threw one of the bedroom doors open.*

*The sight that presented itself to me made me want to vomit.*

*"It was the only way we could all be together. Forever."*

*At that moment, I knew without doubt that my father was a sick, sick man. I stared blankly at the two beds where my brother and sister were lying. Both were writhing on the floor, half-grown fangs were protruding from Lucas' lips. Vivienne on the other hand was doubled over in pain, her hands gripping her stomach. It was clear that whatever she was going through, it was agony.*

*"How could you do this to your own children?" I walked toward my twin sister, longing to hear her speak to me—a pleasure I'd been deprived of since Borys Maslen took her captive. I couldn't hold back a sob as I watched what the turning was doing to her. I wanted to spare her the agony she was going through, but the idea of killing Vivienne was something I knew I would never be able to do. I brushed a strand of her sweat-soaked hair away from her face, whispering, "What have you done?" to my father once again.*

*The moment my hand came into contact with Vivienne, the skin where my finger touched her grew bright red—almost as if she were being burned by my touch. Her eyes—more bright and brilliant than I'd ever seen them before—sparked with fury. Her fangs came out and she glared at me.*

*I withdrew my hand immediately and stepped back. "Doesn't she recognize me?"*

*"She's turning, Derek. She's too consumed by the process." My father was speaking from behind me. I was about to turn around to face him, but to my shock, Vivienne lunged for me, her hands gripping my neck, ready to take a bite. I knew how to take her down, knew what I had to do in order to kill her, but I couldn't do it. She was too precious to me. I shut my eyes as she bared her fangs at me. I had no doubt in my mind that I was about to meet my end by my sister's hands.*

*To my surprise, my father pulled her away from me and threw her right back onto the bed. Vivienne glared at him with a look that was not her own—beastly, menacing, fearsome—nothing like the serene and docile young innocent my sister used to be.*

*"How could you do this?" I spat at my father as he held me down on the ground. "How could you do this to your own children?"*

*"If I don't turn you, they* will *kill you, Derek. Can you really let Vivienne live her whole life bearing the guilt, knowing that she helped kill her twin?"*

*The implications of what he was saying hit me full force. "No…you can't…you won't…" It felt like I was blindsided, because he hit me on the face and everything faded to black. When I came back to full consciousness, it was because of the agonizing pain. Three days of sheer excruciation followed—three days I could barely remember. At the end of the worst seventy-two hours of my life, I woke up to find three unconscious young women surrounding me. To my relief, they weren't dead, but I knew based on the way I was craving them, that I'd had a taste of their blood. Fighting the urge to kill the three innocents—not even bothering to ask how they got to be there, I knew that I needed to leave that place—to get as far away as possible from those three young women before I could do anything I would later regret. It was taking every bit of my will power and self-control not to hunt them down.*

*Until the Battle of First Blood, the battle that secured us control over The Shade, I prided myself on never killing a human being—something Vivienne was also able to accomplish. As for my father and brother, I never dared ask. One thing was for certain though: after the Battle of First Blood, many humans had since died in our hands.*

Mine was a fate I was determined not to let Ashley repeat, but it was going to be an uphill battle and I knew it.

I gripped Sofia's hand tightly until she gasped in pain. I wanted her to know that I wasn't about to be questioned or defied. "We're leaving. You've seen enough."

Tears moistened her eyes. "Is there no way we can help her,

Derek?"

I shook my head. "She's made her choice. Now, she has to live—or die—with the consequences."

# Chapter 18: Sofia

I sat on the red velvet couch in the living room area of my quarters in The Catacombs. It'd been three days since Ashley's turning and I hadn't been able to visit her. Derek simply wouldn't hear of it.

"Sofia," he said through gritted teeth, "I will post guards to keep watch over you if I have to. You are *not* to go anywhere near Ashley. Not now. I should never have allowed you to see her turn. I..." He licked his lips and shook his head as if to wade off whatever demons were plaguing his conflicted mind.

My heart softened at how torn he was by the whole matter and I nodded. "You don't have to do that, Derek. I won't go if you really don't want me to."

He looked at me with blue eyes glazed, expression tender. I had to catch my breath at the way his eyes were set on me. I knew he loved me. I had no doubt about that, but I wasn't sure he understood enough just how much I loved him. That bothered me, because as far as I knew, I'd already given him *everything*. It felt like I had nothing else left to give in order to prove my love.

The tender look in his eyes was quickly replaced with a heated, smoldering one and I knew without a doubt that he wanted me. I wanted him back, so I found myself frustrated when he stepped back, bit his lip and said, "I have to go."

My shoulders sagged as I watched him leave. He'd been true to his word. Since he told me that he would pursue me, he never once made a move to touch me beyond the kind of affection a brother would give a sister. He wasn't as he was before—always hanging a possessive arm around my waist, freely touching me wherever and whenever he pleased. His caresses were soft and tentative, his kisses chaste and gentle. Whenever he was around me, it was almost as if I was a fragile, porcelain doll he was afraid to break.

For the first time since I met him, I hadn't the slightest clue how to deal with him. What came to me instinctively before in matters that concerned Derek Novak eluded me the moment he got this idea that he needed to romance and pursue me. I wanted to reassure him, longed to let him know that I was his and would always be his, but I didn't know how to do that without losing my own self-respect.

Whether he knew it or not, as far as our relationship went, he was calling all the shots, and all I could do was go wherever he chose to take us.

Sitting there that afternoon, my mind was torn between the constant ache in my chest over how I felt for Derek and how anxious I was over Ashley's predicament. Seeing her turn triggered memories of my childhood that I long since buried, memories that I wished could've remained buried. After Ashley's turning, it haunted both my dreams and my every waking moment.

*The fever raged for more days than my nine-year-old self could remember. I kept tossing and turning on my bed, calling for Mommy, but she didn't come like I wanted her to. I couldn't remember anything that happened before the fever. Only Daddy was there to make sure I was alright. I hated looking at him, because he had the saddest eyes whenever he looked at me. It felt like I did something wrong, but I didn't know what it was. When I woke up one night, my entire body was so hot, my skin felt like it was about to burn up, I found Daddy crying, his face buried in his palms as he sobbed. I wanted to complain about how hot I felt, but I felt too sorry for him. That's when I realized that something bad happened. I wished that I knew what it was.*

*Seeing Daddy cry, I couldn't fight back the tears myself. Every part of my body hurt, but not as much as the pain I felt inside as I wondered what could've made my wonderful father cry. I tried to hold it back, but I could no longer stifle a sob. Daddy heard it and he looked at me.*

*"Hey, baby..." he whispered, his voice hoarse and dry. "How are you doing? Why are you crying?" He walked up to me and touched my forehead. He withdrew his hand in surprise. A bad word came out of his mouth. I never heard him talk that way before. "You're burning up, Sofia."*

*He looked angry. It made me feel bad that my body was so hot. I couldn't understand what was going on. I was in so much pain, with no idea how to let him know, so I just let the sobs rack my small body.*

*"Hush..." he whispered in an attempt to comfort me, but he too was in pain I could tell. After I recovered from the fever, I realized why Daddy was so sad. Mommy was gone. Daddy told me that she went off to another home, where they could take care of people like her—people who'd gone crazy.*

*When Daddy left me with the Hudsons, I cried myself to sleep for weeks. Only Ben saw me crying.*

*"Why do you cry every night?" he asked me once.*

*I heaved a sigh and stared into the distance. "My mommy went crazy.*

*Do you think my daddy left me because he thinks it's my fault?"*

*Ben stared at me for a few moments, his blue eyes wide and thoughtful as he tried to comprehend what I had just said. In response, he shrugged and squirted his water gun at me.*

At that memory of Ben, I couldn't help but smile. He always did have a way of making heavy situations feel a lot lighter than they were. I looked around me and held back tears as I realized how much The Shade had changed him—how much it changed me.

"What's with the weird half-smile, half-frown expression on your face?"

I looked up to find Gavin leaning against my doorpost, arms crossed over his chest. His tousled red hair and the boyish smirk on his face were enough to lift my spirits.

I smiled. "I just remembered my best friend…Ben. The memory of him makes me both happy and sad at the same time."

Gavin's brows rose in surprise as he strode toward me. He then plopped himself on the couch beside me. "Wow. So there were actually other men in Sofia Claremont's life before the great Derek Novak."

"Just Ben."

"He must be quite a guy to compete with the likes of the prince."

*He tried to compete. He failed miserably.* My smile was bittersweet. "I miss him." *Or at least the version of him before The Shade destroyed him.*

"Does Derek know that? I might have to report you for dreaming about other men while he's so enamored by you."

I rolled my eyes. "Much as I love the banter, Gavin, what exactly are you doing here?"

"You've been in The Catacombs for more than three days. I'd given you all the time to rest and adjust. It's time to get your ass to work. Contrary to Derek's opinion, you're no princess of The Shade." He paused and raised his brows as he gave his last statement some thought. "At least not yet."

Gavin saw the frown in my face before I could conceal it. "What? Don't tell me that you thought you'd be sitting pretty here all night long…everyone in The Catacombs works. You have to earn your keep, and considering how glorious your keep is, you'd better be good at what you do."

"It's not that I don't want to work. I just…" I heaved a sigh. My stay in The Catacombs wasn't exactly one that received a warm welcome. I'd already made attempts to make friends with some of the Naturals, but though they were all polite and treated me with respect, I couldn't help but sense their resentment. "The idea of having to face the Naturals…"

"What's wrong with us?"

"Nothing…it's just that I can't help but feel like I'm resented…"

Gavin spread his arms, gesturing at my quarters. "Can you blame them?"

"No…still, it doesn't feel good to be treated with a superficial respect, only because of what I have with Derek."

At that, Gavin scoffed. "You think anybody here cares that the prince is professing undying love to you? Vampires are fickle creatures. It's only a matter of time until you bore him, especially considering how you didn't allow him to turn you into one of them." He gently tapped his palm over my thigh. "You poor, clueless thing."

I frowned at him in question.

He quickly explained, "My point is that no one's really threatened by Derek's pronouncement that he will wreak havoc on the lives of anyone who touches you. We live every single day knowing that it could be our last, knowing that any vampire out there could freak out and destroy our lives at any given moment. If anything, the prince's love for you makes you tempting for some Naturals to mess with—especially Naturals who are tired of living the way we are. You know—ones who have a death wish, and trust me…there are many of those."

"If what you're saying is true, why hasn't anyone messed with me yet?"

"Because of Corrine." Gavin shrugged.

"Corrine?"

"Yes, Corrine. The only reason anybody here treats you with any respect, and not pure disgust, is because the witch seems to think highly of you. Corrine's opinion is deemed valuable in The Catacombs. If she says you're okay, then you're okay. Still, people resent you because of Derek and this extravagant display of love for you." Gavin once again scoped our surroundings. "I still can't get over how great this place looks."

"You guys can move here if you want…you, Lily…the kids…you can have the master bedroom and I can move in with the girls…"

"Yeah, right…Derek's going to love that."

"It's *my* home. I can do whatever I want."

"Uh-huh." He placed both his palms over my face and said, "If you want to last in The Catacombs, my dear innocent, realize that nothing here is yours. Everything you are, everything you own…the vampires can take away anytime they please. For your own good, Sofia, don't make decisions regarding this place without Derek's consent. Nobody knows what could possibly set off his fuse and make him turn off his conscience."

What Gavin was saying was beyond anything I could bring myself to comprehend, much less accept. I pried his hands off my face. "How can you guys live this way?" *Always in fear. Always looking behind your backs for the next time a vampire loses its mind?*

Gavin shrugged. "One day at a time. Now, are you going to work or not? I mean, seriously...do you really care what anybody here thinks of you? Just suck it up and make yourself useful, lazy."

"I'm not lazy."

"Well, good then." Gavin stood up. "The Catacombs is no place for lazy people. It's no place for the sick or the weak either, for that matter."

"Why's that?"

Gavin gave me a long, thoughtful look as if wondering if I ought to know what he was about to tell me. "For us normal humans at The Shade, we have to work hard to prove our worth on this island. If you prove useless, you might die in a culling."

I didn't want to hear the answer to my next question, but I asked it anyway. "A culling?"

Anger sparked in his eyes as he explained, "They drain the blood out of humans they deem worthless for storage and future consumption."

My face paled at the idea. "That's a massacre."

"If you haven't noticed, Sofia, death is a pretty common thing on this island."

"How many times has this happened?"

Gavin's fists clenched before he shrugged. "As far as I know, once, and hopefully it will never happen again."

# Chapter 19: Derek

Whenever I wasn't at the Penthouse or The Catacombs with Sofia, or at the Crimson Fortress getting The Shade's army prepared for war, or conducting drills in case of an attack, I was at Vivienne's home, maintaining her greenhouse. She loved that place. It was her sanctuary, the same way the lighthouse was mine. If only to honor her memory, I made sure it was well-maintained and that all the plants were still blooming with life. Liana often came to help me out.

That day, however, I was alone, marveling over the pure white roses that had just begun to reach full bloom. I missed my sister, I missed her wisdom and serenity. I missed how understood I felt when she was around.

I plucked a rose, careful not to get pricked by its long, thorny stem. Brushing my fingers over its petals, I couldn't help but let my mind speak to my beloved twin, part of me still hoping against all hope that she was still alive.

*Viv, you put yourself at risk in order to get Sofia back to me. Now, I'm afraid I'll lose her. How could a beauty like her ever remain true to a beast like me? What if she realizes that she's better off living her life as a normal human being, marrying a man worthy of her? A man not plagued by this curse…*

Before I could once again lose myself in my own melancholy, my ears tingled as I heard the sound of footsteps on Vivienne's hardwood floor.

"Your highness? Are you here?" A familiar voice came from outside the greenhouse.

"Sam?"

The door to the greenhouse creaked open and an uncomfortable-looking Sam peered through it.

"What happened?" I asked him. "Is there something wrong with Ashley?"

"Ashley is recovering quite well, but she is craving human blood desperately. She almost attacked one of the Naturals when Kyle brought her back to his home, but we were able to hold her down. It wasn't easy. The adrenaline rush is making her strong." Sam paused and gave what he was saying some thought. "She's not why I came here though."

Panic surged within me as I stepped forward. "Sofia?"

Sam quickly shook his head. "As far as I know, Miss Claremont is perfectly fine, though I doubt she's going to be very happy about the news I'm about to give you."

I was growing impatient. "Just spit it out, Sam."

"Three young women were brought into your penthouse. A gift from your father. Three new slaves to replace the ones you lost."

"*Slaves*?" I already knew the answer to my next question, but I asked it anyway. "And where did these girls come from?"

"Your father has once again allowed human abductions."

"Unbelievable!" I hissed, storming past Sam, my blood pounding with so much fury. "Does he have any idea how much risk he's putting The Shade in by doing this?"

"Their reasoning behind it is that we've been doing it for years without getting caught." Sam was trailing behind me, knowing fully well how against abductions I was.

"Pure dumb luck!"

"What are you planning to do, sir?"

"Stop this."

I headed straight for the Great Dome, a large, round hall located at the Crimson Fortress. The large space at the topmost level of the fortress' west tower was the site of all governmental, judicial and military strategic gatherings at The Shade.

The dome was one of the places on the island that was close to my heart, because just before she was taken by the hunters, it was the last place Vivienne had re-designed and modernized. She did a wonderful job and being there still reminded me so much of her.

Since my father's return, however, there hadn't been much reason for me to visit the dome. He never really did ask for updates on how the military trainings were going and he never summoned me for any of the council meetings with the Elite either.

After what Sam had just told me, that's exactly what I found myself walking into—an Elite council meeting. The moment I pushed the large double oak doors open, it was my father who I first saw. He was seated on the throne at the front end of the room, on the balcony, towering three feet above ground—above everyone else.

At the center of the room, the round stage that served as the stand was occupied by Eli, the island's resident scholar, and Felix, a vampire I mistrusted to say the least.

The hushed whispers and nervous glances that went around the amphitheater-styled hall made it clear that I'd just walked in on something very important—something that they would rather keep hidden from me.

"What's going on?" I demanded, my eyes glued to my father as I marched right up to the stand.

All eyes shot toward Gregor, who had a bored look on his face. He was looking at me like I was just one of the many annoyances that he had to bear with in his life. "Good of you to pry yourself away from your redhead and join us, Derek," he drawled.

"Could someone explain to me why we're once again abducting people? Did I not make it clear that this has to stop?"

"I overturned your decree," Gregor shrugged. "I'm king of the island, Derek. Learn your place."

An audible gasp came from all present. Never before had my father challenged me in that manner. He may have been king of the island, but he wasn't a fool who would underestimate how much sway I had over the citizens of The Shade.

"Why?" I asked, trying to reel my anger in. Ripping my father's heart out wouldn't really do anyone any good. I found myself longing to have Vivienne there even more. She was always the bridge between us Novak men. Without her, we would've killed one another a long time ago. "You realize how much risk you're putting The Shade in whenever you bring these teenagers here, right? And for what?"

"I am under no obligation to explain my decisions to you, son."

I hated the patronizing tone his voice took on. I knew then that it was a challenge. Every single person in that room was watching me for a reaction. *Was I going to fight back? Was I going to defy the king?* There was no doubt in my mind that should I defy my own father, more than enough vampires would side with me. I could've easily taken Gregor Novak down many times before, but I chose not to. I chose to honor him because he was my father, but at that moment, I was never more tempted to take him down.

"You're going to regret this," was all I could manage to say.

Gregor smirked. "Sure I will. Until then, enjoy the lovely young ladies, Derek. I'm sure you'll appreciate them the moment you get tired of ravishing your freckled redhead."

At that callous jibe once again thrown at Sofia, I lost all control of my temper. I sped forward right to his level, lunging toward him with so much force, the recliner he was seated on went crashing to the ground as I pinned him down.

The tension was electric as screams and nervous mutterings burst out around the hall. I was certain that much of the commotion was over a certain level of confusion over whom they were going to help—their savior or their king.

I didn't really care. I was too busy relishing the terror in my father's eyes. He might have been a vampire longer than I was, but I was far more powerful than he was. Cora had made sure of that.

"Understand this, Father," I said in a voice loud enough for everyone to hear. "If you ever touch Sofia or put her in danger or even *dare* speak of her in my presence again, you can be certain that I *will* take your throne. Without hesitation."

"How Vivienne would roll over in her grave if she saw what you've become! Have you forgotten who your family is, Derek?"

"Vivienne sacrificed her own safety, her own life in order to get Sofia back to me. She would *never* do that for you. That's *how important* Sofia is, Father. I'm pretty sure that if you asked Vivienne now who she would rather spare, she would choose Sofia."

A bone-chilling silence followed my statement as everyone let the words sink in.

"Why?" The voice was Claudia's. I had no doubt about it. "Why is the little freckled redhead so important?"

I rose to my feet, letting go of my father as I did. I slowly backed away from him, finding pleasure in the mixture of fury and fright in his eyes. After reaching the stand, now unoccupied by Eli and Felix, I addressed Claudia's question.

"Sofia is the girl Cora prophesied who would help me find our kind true sanctuary. Without her, I *cannot* accomplish the prophecy."

"Nonsense. You already accomplished the prophecy when you brought us to The Shade and secured it with Cora's protective spell," Gregor spat.

At that, I scoffed. *How blind could he possibly be?* "Don't be a fool, Father. The Shade isn't a sanctuary. It's a nightmare."

Gregor straightened to his full height, his eyes fixed on me. Unable to say anything in response, he looked at the council surrounding us, every single one gawking at the sight that had just unfolded before them. "I want Derek Novak arrested for high treason. His punishment will be discussed at the next council meeting."

I couldn't help but smirk at how delusional my father was. *He really thinks that he holds the power.* I didn't know what he was expecting to happen after his announcement. *Does he really expect the council to pounce on me to make the arrest? Does he expect me to panic and make a run for it?* Apart from Felix making one hesitant step forward, no one else moved. I was certain that it was one of the most awkward moments the Great Dome had ever stood witness to.

My father's breaths were coming in pants, infuriated by the fact that nobody bothered heeding his command.

"Why isn't anyone moving?! Your king has given a command! Arrest him!"

After a few moments of stunned and motionless silence, Claudia burst out laughing. Claudia was one of the most twisted and demented people I'd ever met. She was certainly not an ally and there was no doubt in my mind that she hated my guts, but she was no fool either.

"I have no love for his highness, the prince, my dear king," Claudia managed to say after her laughter subsided, "but no one here will ever be foolish enough to imprison Derek Novak. The only way you can get that man inside a prison cell is if he goes in willingly. Otherwise, a lot of blood will be spilled, and we love our immortality too much to see it end so quickly."

Knowing that I had all the leverage I needed, I glared triumphantly at my father. "The abductions *will* stop. Understood?"

"All right," Gregor said through gritted teeth, the expression on his face making it clear that he was admitting defeat. "This only means one thing then."

"And what would that be?" I asked, suddenly growing anxious.

Eli stepped up nervously. "Even you knew that this would be inevitable since we put a stop to the abductions...we won't have a supply of human blood forever."

I was filled by an overwhelming sense of dread, knowing what my alternative to the abductions were. "You're talking about a culling."

The rest of the meeting flew right over my head, as the council discussed what had to be done to get the culling in order. My father kept glaring at me. I knew then that I just made an enemy out of him, though I wasn't entirely sure if he ever truly was my ally.

Vivienne was the Seer of The Shade. She had the premonitions, but at that moment, I had a premonition of my own. And it wasn't one that I liked.

*Blood will be shed.*

Two things stayed at the forefront of my thoughts: how to protect Sofia and how to keep her mine. I was once again afraid of losing her, because I doubted she could ever forgive me if a human culling actually took place.

After the council meeting ended, my first urge was to immediately locate Sofia. I knew that after the stunt I pulled, she wouldn't be safe from my father. I knew Gregor Novak. He wasn't just going to just sit there and take that kind of humiliation without striking back. It was clear to see that striking Sofia would be equivalent to striking me where it hurt the most. Upon reaching The Catacombs, I found her wearing muddied-up clothes. She was laughing over something the Natural boy, Gavin, said. A pang of jealousy hit me, but I shoved it away.

I cleared my throat to catch her attention.

She looked my way and a brilliant smile formed on her face. "Derek!" she exclaimed before throwing herself at me in an exuberant embrace. "I had a great day. How was yours?"

"Can we talk in private, please?" I eyed Gavin warily. I wasn't thrilled about what I had to reveal to her.

Worry traced her green eyes as she pulled herself away from me. She turned toward Gavin and smiled sheepishly. "Thanks for everything, Gavin."

The boy nodded his head toward her and curtly bowed his head in my direction. "Tomorrow again, Sofia," he said. "If you're still alive by then."

She snickered at the statement, so I figured it was some sort of inside joke they had between them—an idea that grated at my nerves.

I was relieved when Gavin was finally gone and I had my girl all to myself, but any pleasure I felt in her company was overshadowed by the news I carried with me.

"What's wrong, Derek?" she asked pensively as I held her hand and pulled her to a seat on the couch.

"My father reinstated the abductions..."

"What?" Her alarm was immediate. "But why? I thought..."

"I have three new girls at my penthouse. I have no idea what to do with them. I'm thinking of sending them here with you. They'll be more comfortable with you I think..."

My suggestion seemed to go way over her head. "Why would your father do this?"

"We don't stand on the same ground when it comes to these things, but after I found out, I went to the dome and found them having a council meeting. I made sure that there would be no more abductions from here on out."

Sofia sighed with relief as she brushed both hands against her auburn hair. "Still...those poor girls..."

That was a hard blow to my gut. *Of course she feels sorry for them...they have to live through what she lived through under my hand.* I caught myself before sinking any further into my wallowing. *Since when did you become such a dismal sap, Novak?*

She must've noticed the look on my face. "Thank you for putting a stop to the abductions."

I forced a smile, but I swallowed hard at what I was to say next. "Not having abductions may mean something worse..."

The color from her face drained away and I could sense that she already had an idea of what I was about to say.

"They're discussing another culling."

"Oh dear heavens..." She gasped, clamping a palm over her

mouth as she furiously shook her head. "No....no! Derek, no...you have to do something. There's got to be something you can do..."

How was I going to tell her that it was me who originally proposed the possibility of another culling? "I don't know if there's anything I can do about this, Sofia...if I could..."

"You're *Derek Novak*! Of course there's something you can do!"

"My father is king, Sofia." I hated giving out that reason, because after what just happened, it was clear to me and every other member of the Elite that my father's position meant nothing when held against me. "Standing against this would mean civil war. We do need to survive, Sofia. We *need* human blood."

"I can't believe I'm hearing this. Are you actually *defending* the need for a culling, Derek? Seriously? Don't give me that reason, Derek. You don't *need* human blood. You *crave* and *prefer* human blood. There are plenty of beasts in this island for you vampires to feed on. I was just at the farm! There's an abundance of animal blood coming from the livestock there..." Desperation marred her beautiful face. "Derek, there's got to be *something* you can do to stop this."

"Do you fully understand what you're talking about, Sofia? Going against this would mean me waging outright war on my own father."

Sofia was unmoved. Calming down and giving me the sternest look I'd ever seen coming from her—or any teenager for that matter—she made her stand clear. "A culling is a cold massacre. It is wrong and you know it. I *will* fight tooth and nail against this, Derek Novak."

I knew that she meant every word and that she would stand true to them. I hated the thought that began eating at me at that point. *Could the blood that had to be shed be Sofia's?*

# Chapter 20: Ben

*This isn't right.*

I stared at Zinnia's sleeping form on the bed next to mine. The guilt was killing me. *What's wrong with you, Hudson? It's not like you haven't had girls in your bed before...*

I turned to my side, wanting to rip my brains out if it would help me get some sleep. I knew, however, that sleep would provide me no escape. Ever since my first mission, sleep either eluded me or attacked me with an onslaught of nightmares. Sofia, Vivienne and the first vampire I killed haunted my dreams and my every waking moment.

All it took was one mission for me to realize that Sofia had been right all along. Vengeance wasn't the answer. Killing a vampire was nothing like Zinnia told me it would be. There was no sense of satisfaction or glee. In its place, there was just this aching guilt, knowing that a life had been taken by my own hands—a life that, for all I knew, could've been entirely innocent.

I wondered then if Vivienne was innocent. Sofia, after all, had once called the princess of The Shade her friend.

Since we returned to the headquarters after the mission, I began comparing everyone around me to Sofia—especially Zinnia. I realized then that Sofia was nothing like Zinnia or the hunters—and neither was I. I felt like I was surrounded by remorseless people who'd totally lost hold of their consciences. I longed for more of Sofia's compassion and gentleness. I missed my best friend badly and no matter what I did to try and fill the void that she used to occupy, nothing worked.

This was my lowest point. I actually slept with Zinnia just to forget Sofia, only to miss my dear Rose Red even more.

*Is he taking care of you, Sofia? Did I get it all wrong?*

These same thoughts plagued me the next day when Reuben called Zinnia and me to discuss if there was any progress in finding The Shade.

"Ben, are you listening to me?" Reuben demanded.

I blinked my eyes several times and shook my head. "I'm sorry. I barely got a wink of sleep. Nightmares."

Reuben and Zinnia gave me worried glances, but shrugged it off quickly. It was easy to surmise early on that hunters weren't very sentimental people. They just really wanted to finish what had to be done.

"Pay attention, Ben. You're too much of an asset not to understand what's going on." Reuben sounded impatient.

I couldn't help but wince at the mention of me being an asset. It was on the mission that they realized how valuable I was to them. After I killed my first vampire, another attacked me, clawing through my back. I didn't feel a thing. I went through that entire mission, back bleeding, without once feeling the pain. That's how damaged I was by the torment Claudia put me through at The Shade. That's how callous my body had become. I managed to fool myself for a while that I was just as callous inside as I was outside. I was wrong. I wondered if I had fooled Sofia too.

"I'm paying attention," I assured Reuben, though I doubted I had enough presence of mind to go through the plans he was laying out.

"We've had scours of our teams worldwide checking out every possible island known to mankind. Nothing checks out. It's like this island never existed."

"It was hidden by the protective spell four hundred years ago. The spell hiding it is powerful. I believe even cellphone signals can't get past the protective wall the spell creates. There's no way to locate it," I told them.

"No!" Reuben slammed his hand over the table. "There's got to be a way. There's *always* a way."

"What do you even plan to do when we find the island? Attack it? The Crimson Fortress walled around the whole island will give the Wall of China a run for its money...don't underestimate them."

"Don't you think I know that?" Reuben hissed. "The Novaks rule the most powerful vampire clan for a reason. Whoever ends their coven will cripple *all* vampires permanently."

"You didn't answer my question. What do you plan to do when we find the island?"

"Get my daughter out of there and then blow the whole island into smithereens."

I shot a look at Reuben, wondering if he was serious. He clearly was. "There are thousands of innocent human slaves living on that island. If I'm not mistaken, The Shade is self-sufficient and runs on the backbone of these slaves. You'd willingly kill them?"

Reuben gave me a careless shrug. "They were as good as dead the moment they were taken captive by the vampires."

I couldn't help but stare at him, wondering how on earth someone as kind and as compassionate as Sofia could possibly be related to him.

For the first time since I arrived there, it felt like joining the hunters had been the biggest mistake of my life.

# Chapter 21: Derek

I knew it would happen, but it still hurt that it did. After our discussion about the culling and my admittance that there was nothing I could do to stop it, Sofia avoided spending time with me. I knew her well enough to know that she had the tendency to do this when she needed to think things through.

She needed space and I willingly gave it to her. I did, however, station guards to keep an eye on her and update me on what she was doing. I couldn't risk leaving her unprotected because of the recent bout I had with my father. Despite the regular updates, however, I still found myself missing her sorely. I spent most of my time at the training grounds, focusing my energies on the military training I knew The Shade was in desperate need for.

I'd just finished a rather tough fight with one of the best fighters we had—Xavier Vaughn—when a familiar face showed up at the training grounds.

*Ashley.* I hadn't dared visit her since her turning, but I'd kept up-to-date with her through Kyle and Sam. It was strange seeing her and not getting that intense craving to feed on her. She looked incredible as a vampire, her brown eyes having a far more brilliant sheen than they used to.

"Hey, baby vampire," I greeted her, ignoring the irritated look on her face.

"New harem girls, Derek? Really?"

Xavier, while still trying to catch his breath from our fight, raised a brow at her. He usually skipped formalities and called me by name, but as far as he and the rest of the citizens of The Shade were concerned, a new vampire had no business calling me by name.

I gestured toward Xavier to tell him that it was alright. "Let's take a walk, shall we, Ashley?"

"Why can't we have the conversation right here?" She animatedly planted her hands on her hips, her long blonde ponytail sashaying with her every move.

Xavier's eyes grew wide with interest as he whispered, "Feisty girl..."

Ashley squinted her eyes at him. "I heard that."

She was causing a commotion and the other trainees were now gathering around. I chuckled dryly as I turned around to leave.

"Where are you going?!" She ran after me.

"Somewhere we can talk without you getting yourself killed."

Her face paled, realizing how much trouble she'd gotten herself into only moments ago. "Oh shoot...I keep on forgetting that you're some sort of legendary royalty here at the Shade."

"You're a vampire now. You can't forget that."

We began to walk through the forest, aimlessly traveling along the stony terrain, past the giant redwoods that filled the island.

"You didn't even bother to check on me," she said with a pout after a long silence. It was a reminder that in spite of her newfound immortality, she still was a seventeen-year-old teenager. "I mean, I can understand if *you* don't, but Sofia?"

"Didn't either Kyle or Sam tell you that I forbade her to go see you?"

"Well, yeah…they did, but since when did you forbidding Sofia to do something keep her from doing it?"

I changed the subject. "So is it what you thought it would be…being a vampire?"

"Let's just say that I wished I had listened to you the night of my turning."

I bowed my head, truly feeling sorry for her.

"Did you choose to be turned?" she asked.

I shook my head. "My father turned me. He took me by surprise. He did the same thing to Vivienne. As for Lucas…well, I never really got the complete story about how my father managed to turn him."

"Does the craving ever disappear?"

I let out a dry laugh. "No, Ashley. It's in your nature to be a predator now. You need to learn control. It's possible. Vivienne did it. She never once drank human blood. Ever."

"And she just lived on animal blood? I can't stand it! Compared to human blood…"

I grabbed her by the wrist in surprise. "You've had human blood?"

"Yes…I…"

"You've killed."

She shook her head, her eyes showing how nervous she was. "No. I drank blood from the chilling chambers."

The mention of the chambers only reminded me of the culling and the reason behind Sofia's avoidance of me.

"There isn't enough left to sustain The Shade...we consume too much blood. There are too many of us now. The Naturals are in constant danger of a vampire losing it and going after them, but we can't go on with the abductions either..."

"And yet there are still three girls in your harem now."

"I didn't want that. I had them sent to Sofia to help her out in The Catacombs. I haven't seen them since."

"So you haven't been seeing Sofia?"

My silence was enough of an answer.

"Why?"

I told Ashley about the culling, about why I thought it was necessary. "If I let the culling happen, do you think Sofia will ever be able to forgive me?"

Ashley was quiet for quite some time as we walked on. "She's been able to forgive you for a lot. I don't even think she'll blame you, but I think it will definitely wreck her. Gwen's death was something that she took quite heavily. For months, she had to spend every day having those psychological treatments with Corrine in order to get through that. Imagine what a murder of that scale would do to her."

"If I stop the culling, what happens? How do we survive?"

Ashley grew silent once again. As we walked on, she eventually admitted, "I don't think I can live on animal blood, Derek."

My jaw clenched. "I don't know if I can either."

We continued to walk in silence, allowing ourselves to mull over what was about to come and what we ought to do about it. It didn't take long before we bumped into Cameron and Liana, holding hands. Liana was laughing over something Cameron whispered in her ear.

I always did envy the couple from the moment I met them. Both of them had been turned not long after Liana gave birth to their second child—a daughter. Their firstborn was a son. They spent the first decades of their lives as vampires securing a future for their children, while still being away from them. They couldn't risk losing control around the kids, so they had to leave the children with trusted friends. To that day, they still knew and kept track of their children's descendants spanning centuries upon centuries of beautiful, loving families.

Whenever I saw Cameron and Liana together, I couldn't help but wonder what it would've been like to fall in love before I had become what I was.

*If Sofia would just agree to become a vampire, we could be like them.*

I shook the thought away. I once again chastised myself for still entertaining the notion. I shifted my focus back to the couple whom we were quickly approaching.

Liana's face broke into a smile at the sight of us. Still, I didn't miss the hint of concern in her eyes. Even Cameron was looking at me worriedly. They were two of our family's closest friends and most loyal allies. Next to Sofia and Vivienne, they knew me better than most vampires at The Shade.

"So this is the newest addition to our coven..." Cameron eyed Ashley knowingly. "How do you find being a bloodsucker so far?'

"It's a lot like starving." Ashley nodded resolutely. "Every minute of the day."

Liana chuckled. "You'll get used to it."

"You mean it's always going to be like this?" Her eyes grew wide with horror.

Cameron and I nodded in an attempt to scare her. "Uh-huh," we both said.

Liana rolled her eyes. "No. It gets easier the older you get...don't listen to them." She then eyed me and Ashley. "Where's Sofia?"

"On the farm with Gavin, I suspect."

"Have you told her about the culling?" Liana was never really one to beat around the bush and with Ashley being one of us, there wasn't much sense in keeping things confidential.

I nodded.

Cameron shuffled uncomfortably on his feet. "How'd she take it?"

"Her exact words were, 'I will fight tooth and nail against this, Derek.' "

Cameron let out a low whistle as his hand protectively snaked around Liana's waist. "What are you going to do?"

"I don't know," I admitted.

"You explained that it's necessary?" Liana pried.

"How do you justify something that she sees as a bloody massacre?" I couldn't help but scoff. "You can't tell someone like Sofia that murder is necessary."

No words were spoken. We'd been trying to reconcile the past culling with our consciences and we all knew that no matter how much we tried to bend the rules of what's moral and what's not, what was done was exactly what Sofia called it—a massacre. None of us could justify it other than that we needed it to happen in order to survive.

*The strong prey on the weak. Survival of the fittest. Is that not what people laud as the law of nature? If they survive, we don't.*

I let out an exasperated sigh, unable to hide how torn I was over the whole thing. I ran a hand over my hair, longing to once again be in Sofia's good graces. "She hasn't spoken to me in days," I complained. *I miss her so much.*

Liana gave me a long, meaningful look. "Vivienne saw it immediately. I didn't."

"See what?" Cameron and Ashley asked in unison before giving me an odd look.

"You've changed, Derek. With her in your life, you're a different man."

I studied her, wondering what she was getting at. "Is that a good thing or a bad thing?"

"We'll have to wait and see, won't we?"

For some reason, the fact that she would imply that Sofia could have a negative effect on me grated on my nerves. "You are the three vampires in this island who ought to value human life more than anyone else. You." I pointed at Ashley. "Because you were still human barely a week ago. And you two." I then pointed at the couple."Because you have generations of human descendants whom you love deeply."

"That's different..." Cameron began to stand in defense.

"Why is it different? Is a human less human just because he was born at The Shade?" I shook my head, angrier at myself than I was with them. I knew Sofia was right. What we were about to do was a massacre. I couldn't justify it. Nobody could, but it felt like I had no choice. The Elite might have stood with me against the abductions, but how on earth could I possibly make them agree to cutting off their only supply of human blood? "I can't stand this. I need to be alone."

I sped forward, brushing past the couple before any of them could come up with a response. I had no idea how far I'd gone or how long I'd been moving, but I eventually reached a clearing that led me to the Vale. Just as I emerged from the woods, Sofia and Gavin were coming out of the town.

They were laughing with Sofia rolling her eyes as she playfully chucked Gavin's jaw with her fist. The fact that she'd barely looked my way whenever I visited her, combined with her stupid excuses for not spending time with me, made seeing her with Gavin infuriating.

Jealousy reared its ugly head and I wasn't able to hold myself back. I just saw red and all I wanted to do at that moment was snap the Natural's neck in two.

# Chapter 22: Sofia

It all happened so fast, I could barely catch up with what was going on. One minute, I was exchanging jokes and witty banter with Gavin. The next minute, he was lying on the ground, staring defiantly at Derek. One look at Derek's blue eyes was enough to let me know that he was more than ready to make a kill.

"Derek..." I had meant to shout, but his name came out in a breathless, choked whisper.

Derek's hand coiled around Gavin's neck. "So this is why you've been avoiding me? To be with him?"

It was as if Derek wasn't there. His blue gaze seemed vacant and deadly in a surreal way. Gavin was choking but there was no fear in his eyes—just resignation. I, on the other hand, was panicking.

"Derek..." I held him by the arm, wondering if this was one of his blackouts. He didn't even seem to feel my touch. "Come back to me."

He let go of Gavin's neck and for a moment, I thought that I'd succeeded in getting through to him, only to find myself completely knocked out of breath when Derek pushed me to the ground, away from him. He then held Gavin down by the shoulders and stared, as if wondering how he wanted to kill him.

I was about to approach Derek again, but Gavin glared at me. "Don't come near, Sofia. He's out of it. He doesn't have control. You'll only get yourself hurt."

I shook my head. "No…I can get through to him. I know I can." And I did it the only way I knew how. I tentatively approached and placed a gentle kiss on Derek's lips. I was surprised when one hand gripped my arm painfully while the other found my neck.

He pulled his lips away from me and growled before pushing me away again. Within a couple of seconds, he was kneeling over me, straddling my hips, as he pushed my head to one side, clearing my neck for a bite.

I recalled the times in the past when this had happened between us—with him threatening to hurt me and me talking him out of it. This felt different. It felt like the man I loved wasn't even there for me to speak to. It was as if the curse was in control of Derek. For a moment, I was tempted to accept my fate the same way Gavin was about to. I looked at him and knew that he wasn't about to risk his life by doing anything to stop Derek. It was every man for his own at The Shade and in Gavin's eyes, I'd signed my death certificate when I dared to interfere.

Derek's grip over my shoulder and jaw tightened as he moved over me and just as he was about to bite, all I could think of doing was hum. At first, I couldn't even recognize the tune I was humming, but I knew that it was something familiar, a tune I held dear to my heart. A smile formed on my face when I realized what it was. The tune I was humming was the same one that he hummed to me the night of my birthday when he danced with me in the lighthouse.

Tears began to moisten my eyes as I remembered how treasured and special he made me feel that day. Guilt also took hold of me considering the way I avoided him the past few days. He didn't deserve that and I knew it, but I loved him for understanding anyway and giving me the space that I needed. I could feel his fangs on my neck, sinking deeper and deeper. I shut my eyes as he was about to break skin, still humming that song…that tune that played only inside his creative mind, where numerous symphonies must've already taken place.

I bit my lip anticipating the pain that was sure to come. Then nothing.

After a moment's silence, Derek began to swear. "Sofia…" he choked, as he helped me to my feet. "What have I done? I'm so sorry. Sofia, I…"

"I'm alright. I'm not hurt."

He stared at me like I was a precious ornament that he'd just broken.

"Derek…"

Before I could say anything, he had his lips on mine, kissing me like he hadn't in a long time. Demanding. Passionate. Hungry. It's like he poured out every pent up emotion he had into that one kiss. I could feel my knees weaken beneath me, making me lean my entire weight on me, realizing just how much I missed the security of his arms around me.

When our lips parted, we stared at each other for a few moments. I could sense the guilt he was feeling. I knew Derek. I knew that he was beating himself up over what had just occurred.

"I love you," I assured him. "Nothing's changed."

A bitter smile formed on his face as he nodded. "That just makes me feel more like a monster, Sofia. Like I don't deserve you."

He walked away and just as I was about to hold him back, he used his lightning speed to get away from me.

I stood rooted to my spot staring at the direction he went off to for a few minutes, wondering if I should follow him. When I was about to make a run for where I thought he was headed, Gavin held me back.

"Let him go. There's no way you can catch up with him."

"I think I know where he went." *The Lighthouse.* I realized then that I had no idea how to get to the Lighthouse without Derek. There was no way I could make the hundred-foot leap down the fortress without him. I looked Gavin's way. I had actually forgotten he was there for a while. I sighed. He looked nothing like my best friend, but he reminded me so much of Ben and how easygoing things were when I was around him. This time, however, Gavin was looking at me in a different way—like he was in a daze, blinking several times in disbelief.

"I've never seen anything like that," he finally spoke, amazement evident in his voice.

"Anything like what?" I asked.

"*That!* Sofia, the way you get to him…it's amazing. What were you humming? Will it work on all vamps?"

"It was a tune Derek made up on my birthday. We danced to it while were at the…" I caught myself, remembering that no one apart from me and Derek knew about the Lighthouse. I creased my brows at Gavin and quickly changed the subject. "Can't everybody do that? Calm a vampire?"

"*Calm* a vampire?!" Gavin spat the words out like it was the most laughable thing he'd ever heard of. He shook his head profusely as he snickered. "No…not everybody can do that. When a vampire loses it, they lose it. Of all the years I've been here, I've never seen a human survive a vampire attack unscathed or unbitten when the vampire goes into blackouts. The vampire attacks, destroys, ruins. Only their own kind can stop them, and it's usually through bloody violence, but you…" He stared at me like I was the most magical thing he'd ever laid eyes on. "It's like you put a spell on him. How did you do it?"

"I don't know." I shook my head, still feeling the longing ache I had for Derek. "I just matter to him I guess."

"That's really what amazes me. Why do you matter *that* much? What do you have on him?"

*I ask myself the same question every day.* I hated the idea that I could be important to him only because of the prophecy or the fact that Vivienne lost her life in exchange for mine—thus, securing my value in Derek's eyes. "We're in love," was the only answer I could think of that would satisfy my own insecurities and doubts about why Derek wanted me around.

"Yeah? Well, I hope the love lasts. We could use someone among us capable of taming the prince…"

At that, it was my turn to scoff. "Derek isn't some beast that ought to be tamed." I was surprised at my own indignation. The word just rubbed me the wrong way, because it reminded me of Ben calling himself my Prince Charming and me his Rose Red, only for me to end up with the Beast. "Derek is many things, but he isn't a monster."

"Sure. If you say so." Gavin lightly chuckled. He crossed his arms over his chest, both of us still looking in the direction where Derek went off. "Remind me again why you're avoiding him…"

I gave Gavin a long, thoughtful look before deciding that I could trust him with what I knew. "I think this is something we ought to talk about in private."

We ended up meandering along the woods—not the safest place for humans at The Shade—on a long route to The Catacombs. That's where I hesitantly told Gavin about the plan to have another culling.

Most of the walk consisted of a question asked and answered, then immediately followed by a long, tense silence, before another question could be asked. By the time we reached The Catacombs, both of us were heartbroken.

We were already on the level of The Catacombs below where my quarters were when a beautiful young woman with black hair, pale skin and stunning moss green eyes approached Gavin.

"Hi, Gavin..." she greeted shyly as she fidgeted with her fingers.

Gavin's sharp eyes softened at the sight of her. "Hello, Anna...how've you been?" he asked in a manner so patronizing, it was almost as if he was talking to a child.

I then remembered what he told me before when he was talking about Migrates used and discarded by vampires who once professed love to them. *I could introduce you to one. Anna—stunning beauty, but degraded to nothing but a whimpering child.*

I stared at her, suddenly becoming uncomfortable. Gavin was right. She was gorgeous, but her eyes—though beautiful—were vacant of life. I wondered what the vampire could've done to her to make her thus. I also wondered who the vampire who did this to her was. I quickly got my answer.

"They took my doll..." Anna told Gavin. "Felix gave me that doll, and they took it. Felix will get so mad...he always gets mad when I lose things and I get in a lot of trouble for it."

"Forget Felix, Anna. He won't cause you any trouble anymore,"

Gavin assured her. "Now tell me…who took your doll?"

"The guys…"

Fury sparked in Gavin's eyes. "What guys? They were in your cell? Did they do anything to you?"

The thoughts that flashed through my mind at what Gavin was implying made me sick.

"The guys who visited this morning, of course," Anna explained, a flash of fear glazing her wide-eyed and innocent countenance. "They took my doll. I want my doll back."

"I'll get it back, Anna…" Gavin's lips tightened as he nodded in assurance. "I promise."

Anna threw her arms around Gavin and kissed him on the cheek. "Thank you!" she exclaimed happily before skipping off to wherever she spent her time.

Gavin's eyes were glued on her, the expression in his eyes torn. "She shouldn't be living alone, but she refuses to live with anyone else. She has it in her head that Felix will return and she doesn't want him finding her with another guy. She's still afraid he'll hurt her."

"The guys she was talking about…do you think they…"

Gavin shook his head. "Best not to talk about such things. This is what life in The Catacombs is like, Sofia. Get used to it."

"If anyone's abusing her, then something has to be done about it, Gavin."

"She's crazy, Sofia. She doesn't even have a doll. You can't really trust anything she says and to spend our energy on following her around to see if anybody's taking advantage of her is futile. Besides, what do you intend to do if such a thing was happening?"

Tears began to moisten my eyes.

Gavin heaved a deep sigh as he once again looked in the direction Anna ran to. "Sometimes, I think it's better to die at a culling than to live like this. You should've known Anna before she went insane. She was a lot like you. We were actually convinced for a time that Felix truly loved her…he definitely had us fooled. Eventually, he gave in to his nature—blacked out—and turned on her. When he returned her here, the vibrant, kind and beautiful Anna we all knew was gone. All that's left is what you see now—a shell."

I hated to ask, but the words came out before I could stop it. "Do you think Derek could do the same thing to me?"

"I would've said yes if I hadn't seen what happened earlier today, but now I'm not so sure. Maybe you and Derek really are different. For your sake, I hope that's true." He stared at me for a couple of seconds, and turned toward the staircase that would lead to the topmost level where my quarters were. He then shook his head before grabbing my hand and pulling me toward another direction. "Come with me."

"Where are we going?"

"It's time you find out what's really happening here in The Catacombs." He then stopped and faced me intently. "I can trust you, can't I?"

"Of course." I nodded.

"Good, because if you tell a soul—especially Derek—about what I'm about to show you, make no mistake about it, Sofia…I'll kill you myself."

# Chapter 23: Derek

I would've gone to the Lighthouse, but considering all the times I spent there with Sofia, it hardly seemed much of a refuge when what I wanted to escape from were thoughts of her. Thus, I ended up at Vivienne's greenhouse instead, busying myself with tending to the plants and trying to recall lost, but precious, memories I had of my sister.

If gardening was some sort of therapy for Vivienne, it certainly wasn't doing the same thing for me. Everything just reminded me of Sofia and what had just occurred at the outskirts of the Vale.

At some point, I just got frustrated with trying to get Sofia off my mind and miserably failing at it. I returned to the penthouse, head hung low, afraid of what I was capable of doing to Sofia. The darkness had never taken over me while she was here. I thought, and I assumed even Vivienne thought the same thing, that her presence kept the darkness at bay.

That was the first time I realized that Sofia was always going to be in danger while she was with me. I could snap any time and destroy her. How on earth was I going to live after that?

I stepped into my penthouse, riddled with conflicting thoughts, and found Claudia conveniently sprawled on one of my living room couches, waiting for me.

"It took you long enough..." She smiled.

"Claudia? What are you doing here? What do you want?"

"Well, I've been wondering how you were coping after your lovely pet left..." She stood to her feet and slunk her way toward me.

"Don't call her that."

"Always so defensive when it comes to pretty little Sofia...that's what *everyone* calls her, Derek."

"Go away, Claudia." I turned toward the direction of my room, but Claudia wasn't done.

"You're turning the island upside down on her behalf. What do you plan to do when she leaves you?"

"She's not going to do that."

"She's human, Derek. What exactly do you think is going to happen? Would she really want to stay here forever? Age into an old lady, wrinkled and decrepit, still pining for you? Do you really think that little firebrand of yours won't want to accomplish something for herself? Doesn't she have any dreams and ambitions of her own to fulfill? She may be an immature teenager obsessed with you and ready to give in to your wanton needs, but she's going to grow up eventually. You know it. I know it."

I had no idea why I just stood there, allowing Claudia to mess with my mind using her winding spiel, but I did. Claudia was voicing out my own fears and I didn't have an answer to any of the questions she was throwing my way.

"If she wanted to be with you, Derek, she would've allowed you to turn her."

"If she didn't want to be with me, she wouldn't have given up her whole life outside of the island just to come back here to me."

"Oh come on...that doesn't prove anything. For all we know, the only reason she might be here is because she wants to be some sort of hero to her fellow humans."

"She could've done that outside The Shade, Claudia." I felt a spark of triumph as I realized once again just how much Sofia had given up to be with me. "She knows where The Shade is. Vivienne gave her the exact location, the exact coordinates. She could've destroyed us all, but she didn't." *Because she loves me.* I smiled.

"She doesn't deserve you, Derek..." Claudia still tried. "She's just..."

"No. I don't deserve *her.* Yet she is mine out of her own choice and I am hers. You have no idea what she's given up for me and what I'm willing to give up for her. For your own good, Claudia, whatever this is that you're trying to pull, stop before you sorely regret it."

The victory that I felt when Claudia left was inexplicable. I'd been so worried about the future, about losing Sofia, I failed to make her stay at The Shade worth everything she gave up. *Stop acting like a whiny teenager, Novak. Man up and be the kind of man a girl like Sofia Claremont deserves.*

I might not have realized it then, but something clicked inside me. It was at that point that I decided to do *anything* for Sofia—no matter the cost. *I will fight for her.*

# Chapter 24: Claudia

*That didn't exactly work out as planned.* The idea was to drive a wedge between Derek and Sofia, but it seemed all I managed to do was make Derek realize just how much the redhead loved him.

*Of course, the trip wasn't entirely in vain.* My suspicions were correct. Ben was no longer on the island. I couldn't find him anywhere, and based on what Derek had told me, it seemed he'd been gone for quite some time already. *I can't believe I didn't know. I always just assumed that he had my boy hidden somewhere on the island.*

My suspicions were solidified the moment Derek said, "…she wouldn't have given up her whole life outside of the island just to come back here to me."

If my conclusions were correct, Ben and Sofia had already been outside the island after their captivity. *Only Sofia came back.* I knew then the message that I was going to relay to Lucas. I was about to find a scout in order to relay a note to Natalie Borgia, but just as I was about to head off to the port, Yuri Lazaroff showed up.

The same strange mixture of irritation and affection came over me. I owed the handsome young man so much more than I was willing to admit. Though I couldn't relate to Derek and his lunacy over the redheaded human, I could relate to the feeling that I didn't deserve the person I loved. I would rather die than admit it to anyone at The Shade, but I'd always been in love with Yuri, a man I knew I would never in a million years deserve.

"What are you up to, Claudia?" Yuri asked, giving me an irritated glare.

"You're stalking me again, Lazaroff?" I frowned at him.

"I told you I'd keep an eye on you."

"Why?" I seductively purred at him—something I knew he detested. "Are you ready to admit how in love you are with me?"

I expected a wisecrack from him, so I was surprised when he just looked at me with a long, meaningful gaze. "Why do you do this, Claudia? You're no longer a whore. Why must you keep on acting like one?"

"Once a whore, always a whore, Yuri. Do you have any idea why I got out of prison so quickly?" I was recently imprisoned at the Cells for defying Derek during a council meeting. That was before Gregor came back and Derek was still acting like an insane darklord.

Yuri's lip twitched as he obviously steeled himself to what I was about to say. He was the only person in the world that I was certain cared enough about me to be bothered with what I was about to say. "Enlighten me."

"Your noble and valiant prince came to my cell to lay with me. He shortened my sentence right after..."

Yuri's fists clenched. "Claudia...I..."

"Save me your pity and your righteous indignation, Yuri."

"Derek was in a dark place then. I'm sure he didn't mean to offer you payment for..."

"For what, Yuri?" I cut him off. "My *services*?! I can't believe you're defending him!"

"Come on, Claudia...you've done a lot of screwed up things over the years—a lot of which all of us turned a blind eye to and forgave you for. When are you going to stop playing the part of a victim?"

"Of course you'd side with him."

"Well, did he force you to bed, Claudia, or did you willingly give yourself to him like you usually do to all men?"

Before I could stop myself from doing it, I slapped him across the face. Never before had I endured a conversation with Yuri as emotionally charged as this one—not since the night he rescued me from the Duke.

Yuri never did shy away from the truth when it came to me. He never treated me like some fragile flower soiled by the hands of the people who sold me into prostitution as a child. He told me things as they were, told me that I could rise up from my past and be better. The reason we could never be together was because I believed that I was irreparable and he didn't share the same convictions. Being with him meant constantly disappointing him just by being who I was. *A whore with a broken, twisted mind.*

"When will you learn not to mess with Derek, Claudia?" he asked.

I shook my head. "The prince is going to get his comeuppance someday, Yuri. Just wait and see."

"Claudia..." Yuri called after me.

"You're not my conscience, Yuri. Just leave me alone." The moment I said the words, I realized just how miserable my life would be if he actually ever did leave me alone. I then scoffed at the notion. *When have you ever been not miserable, Claudia?* I heaved a sigh and nodded resolutely. Revenge was my source of euphoria. *I'm going to make Derek Novak just as miserable as I am. Misery, after all, loves company.*

Several minutes later, a confidential message was sent to Natalie Borgia to relay to Lucas, perhaps the only vampire I knew who embraced the wicked side of me. My message was simple.

*Ben Hudson is no longer on the island. Find him and use him as an ace against Sofia.*

# Chapter 25: Sofia

Insane was the only way to describe what they were planning to do.

I had no clue where Gavin was taking me when he told me about "what's really happening here at the Catacombs," but I certainly wasn't expecting us to walk into a room—or in The Catacomb's case, a cave—occupied by over a dozen young men and women—most of which couldn't have been any older than I was. All eyes focused on us as we walked in and I began tugging on Gavin's sleeve.

"What's going on, Gavin?" I mumbled.

"Yeah, Gav…" One of the young men nodded. "What's going on? What's the prince's pet doing here?" At the sight of him, the first thing I noticed was the scar that lined his face from the middle of his forehead to his left cheekbone. It was clear to see that he held some sort of authority in the group.

"Relax, Ian. We can trust her. She won't rat us out."

"And I'm supposed to take your word for it?" Ian challenged.

Gavin shrugged and nodded. "Yes."

Ian shifted his focus on me. "Why should we trust you? For all we know, the prince allowed you to live here in The Catacombs to spy on us."

I chuckled dryly. "Yes. That's me. A spy." I rolled my eyes as I made myself comfortable on one of the vacant wooden chairs in the room. "Spying on the humans here in The Catacombs is the last thing on Derek's mind."

"Derek? So you're on a first name basis with him?"

"Yes." I nodded. "How is that a problem?"

"It's not…it's just that the last time I've heard a human refer to a vampire from the Elite on a first name basis was Anna."

My stomach turned at the information I was given, but I turned my thoughts to other things. "What exactly is going on here?"

Gavin leaned back in his seat and looked at our companions. "These fools are planning a revolt."

Murmurs and protests filled the room as the group made it known how indignant they were that Gavin would just blurt their secret out like that.

I was staring at them like they'd gone bat crazy. "A revolt?" I asked, after the murmurs subsided. "Against the vampires? That's insanity."

"That's exactly what I told them." Gavin shrugged.

"Look around you, Red." Ian gestured to our surroundings. "Can you blame us for wanting something better? But of course, you wouldn't understand, would you? You're living in that suite of yours lavished upon you by your lover boy, the prince. You've no idea what it's like to grow up here at The Shade, to live every single day in fear. We've had enough."

It took a moment to register that it was me he was referring to with the name *Red.* Memories of Ben came flooding back, but I shoved them away in place of more urgent matters. "When was the last time an uprising was ever held at The Shade? Do you remember?" I asked, remembering the information I read from Derek's journal at the Lighthouse.

The silence was enough of an answer.

"Of course you don't remember, because the last time there was a human uprising, *all* humans involved were killed. No one lived to tell the story. You don't stand a chance against the vampires. Derek has been going through painstaking lengths to get their military force trained. They're formidable against hunters. What makes you think you can even do anything to scratch them?"

"Is this why you brought her here?" Ian asked Gavin. "She's the prince's spokesperson?"

Gavin didn't respond. He seemed content to let us do all the talking.

I couldn't help but wonder what was going through his mind.

"Do you really think we care if we die, Red?" Ian addressed me after rolling his eyes at Gavin. "We're just tired. We're going to die eventually anyway. We might as well die fighting."

I understood their desperation, but what they were about to do was straight up suicide. "There's got to be a better way."

"There is," one of the girls spoke up—a lovely brunette with violet eyes that reminded me of Vivienne's. "We just have to get Corrine on our side. All she has to do is lift the protective spell over the island and it's over. The sun will do all the killing for us. Nothing makes a vampire more vulnerable than sunlight."

"Word is that you have sway not only when it comes to the prince, but also with Corrine…" Ian eyed me hopefully. "Would you talk to her? Without putting us at risk?"

*And betray Derek by endangering him and everything he's been fighting for?* "I don't think I can do that. I'm sorry. Besides, Corrine has been advocating human rights in this island since she got here. If she wanted to lift the spell, she already would've."

"So you're not going to help us?" Ian asked.

Gavin straightened on his seat. "Sofia, just talk to Corrine. She barely knows any of us and she'd probably just laugh us off if we spoke to her, but if you talk to her, then maybe she can shed some wisdom on all of this, because we all know that a revolt would just get us all killed and I don't want that to happen."

I glared at Gavin, hating that he managed to put me in the predicament I was in. *Why are you doing this?* "I'll see what I can do, but for now, don't do anything foolish. This revolt of yours will be more trouble than you could ever imagine."

They all agreed as long as I promised to have a word with Corrine. When Gavin and I left, I couldn't keep myself from confronting him. "You know how I feel for Derek and how much I love him. Why would you put me on the spot, Gavin?"

"Because I want you to realize that if the vampires proceed with a culling, the humans aren't just going to stand back and take it. They probably don't even realize it, but there'll be more bloodshed than they're capable of handling."

"What do you expect me to do with all this information?"

"Sofia, the prince is practically putty in your hands and Corrine thinks highly enough of you to actually allow him to transform half of an entire level in The Catacombs into your quarters. You're here for a reason. Maybe this is it, Sofia. You have to do something to at least try and avoid all this coming bloodshed."

"How am I supposed to do that?"

"Talk to Corrine."

I huffed at him before walking on. We were nearing my quarters and from the door opening, I could already see Derek waiting in my living room. I missed being around him, but the idea of talking to him after everything I had witnessed and heard of made my mind whirl. It felt like I was betraying him just by knowing what I knew.

Upon seeing me, he stood up from the couch and looked at me with so much yearning that I could almost sense the ache he felt. He quickly shifted his focus from me to Gavin. He began to shuffle on his feet.

I couldn't help but smile. *Is he nervous?*

"About earlier today…" Derek began rubbing the back of his neck with his palm.

Gavin gave me an anxious sideward glance to let me know that he had no idea what was happening.

"I…" Derek cleared his throat. "I didn't know what came over me." He sounded choked. He scratched his head. "I'm…well, yeah…I guess I'm sorry."

"You guess?" I asked.

"Well, no…I really am…sorry…"

"Have you never apologized to a human before?" I raised a brow, amused by the sight of Derek being so uncomfortable.

"Of course I have…" Derek widened his eyes at me defensively.

"Well, what do you have to say to that?" I turned my head toward Gavin.

"Uhh…I'm supposed to say something?" Gavin frowned.

"Do you accept his apology?" I shrugged my shoulders in emphasis.

"Do I have a choice not to?" The redhead boy grimaced. He looked just about as comfortable with accepting Derek's apology as Derek was when making his. "What have you done to him?" he mouthed at me.

I chuckled. "You two are ridiculous."

"Fine. I accept the apology. This is so weird."

Derek nodded in agreement. He then peered at me through his long, dark lashes. "I was hoping to have a word with Sofia. In private."

My gut clenched. How was I going to stay alone with Derek and not give in to the urge of blurting out everything I knew? Talking to Corrine suddenly seemed like the most desirable recourse at the moment. "I'd love that, Derek." I grabbed Gavin's arm when he began to turn to leave. "But I have to go talk to Corrine. I miss you…it's just…"

"When are you going to stop avoiding me, Sofia?"

"I'm not avoiding…"

"Yes, you are." Even Gavin breathed the words out.

I glared at my so-called friend. *How dare you. Traitor.*

I faced Derek, both loving and hating the longing that I saw in his eyes. "Spend time with Gavin here. You two get to know each other." I shoved Gavin forward. "I won't be with Corrine too long." I gave Derek a lingering look. "I'll spend time with you right after. I promise."

"Let me take you there." Derek volunteered.

"No." I shook my head. "I'd rather go alone. I need the long walk to think things through."

I knew I was tearing him apart. I felt the same way, but too much was going on—more than I could handle and being around him was the last thing I needed at that moment. "I'll be back, Derek. Wait for me."

I left the guys to bond, finding their discomfort and awkwardness around each other rather amusing. Still, the amusement couldn't erase weightier thoughts burdening my every waking thought.

*A culling. A revolt. A prophecy.*

*A sandcastle on the verge of collapsing.*

# Chapter 26: Derek

I shifted my gaze from Sofia's hurried, disappearing form to Gavin, who obviously had no idea what to do with the situation Sofia had just pushed both of us into. *She definitely knows how to drive me crazy.*

"Would you rather be alone waiting for her?" he asked, sounding quite hopeful that I would say yes.

"No." I walked forward before nodding toward the direction of the dining area. "I think Sofia's right. You're getting quite close to her. Perhaps it's best we have a talk."

He visibly gulped—something I found strange considering how defiant and confident he was around me before. *Does he have something to hide now?*

"All right..." He nodded.

We headed to the round dark wood table and I sat on one velvet-cushioned chair while he sat on another right across the table from me.

"So what exactly does a Natural like me and a prince of The Shade like you talk about?"

I was impressed by his guts to open up the conversation himself. "The only common ground we have right now, I believe, is Sofia."

"And you want to talk about her?"

"I want to understand her."

"Well then, you're asking the wrong person. Sofia is a mystery to me just as she is to everyone else. It's like she has this thing about her that no one can really peg but you just get this unnatural urge to protect her and keep her safe. Like you'll lose something precious if anything happens to her."

I stared at him, knowing fully well what he was talking about. "She's special, isn't she?" was all I could think of to say.

"After seeing her calm you down the way she did, I'd have to say I agree."

"Sofia was right. You *are* very blunt and honest. Almost guileless. I can assume you'd be very straightforward with me if I asked you to, can't I?"

"It depends." He shrugged. "Do you promise not to kill me in case you don't like what you hear?"

"Maybe."

"Considering that you were going to kill me earlier today, I think I need a better word of assurance than just a *maybe*."

"Fine. I won't kill you, but do tell me…what do the humans really think about my relationship with Sofia?" I gave my question some thought, wondering if I even wanted to hear the answer to it. "What do *you* think?"

"Why does it matter what I, or anyone else, think?"

"It matters to me…because I think it matters to her."

"Okay then…honestly? Nobody here believes that what you have with Sofia will last."

I shook my head in disgust. "I hate hearing that. I'm so tired of everyone saying that—including *her*! You're wrong…all of you…what we have *should* last."

"Will it? When she's a wrinkled eighty-year-old woman and you're still looking like *that*…will you still love her?"

I opened my mouth to answer with a confident "Yes" but was distracted by a guard showing up by the door. It was one of Felix's men.

"The king summons you to the dome, your highness."

I rose to my feet, surprised that my father would call for me. I turned my eyes toward Gavin. I felt a strange sense of dread. "If she returns before me, tell Sofia that I'll be back."

Gavin nodded. "Sure."

Every fiber of my being told me not to go, but I was already in enough trouble with my father. I didn't want to irk him any further. I really should've just listened to my gut feeling.

I was about to find out how grossly I had underestimated Gregor Novak.

# Chapter 27: Sofia

I made myself comfortable in the red loveseat that Corrine had in her study. She was looking through some books when I arrived, black-rimmed glasses over the bridge of her nose as she looked up what was likely to be some ancient spell for another one of her projects.

"To what do I owe the honor of this visit?" she asked as she shut the book she was holding and gave me her full attention.

For the next ten minutes, I poured my heart out to her—my concerns over my relationship with Derek, the culling, the revolt…I told her *everything,* not withholding a single detail, giving her my complete trust.

"I have no idea what I'm going to do, Corrine. The culling is wrong. How could the witch before you have just stood there and done nothing? Is there anything you can do to stop this? I mean, if these people go on with a revolt, they're done for! It's suicide…"

Corrine patiently laid her palms over the top of the wooden desk she was seated behind. “There are some things you can’t change here at The Shade, Sofia. One of them is that the vampires need to feed on human blood. Take that away from them and everything falls apart.”

“So it’s okay for them to massacre the weak and the defenseless?” I spat out.

“Can you think of a better alternative?”

I stared at Corrine with utter disbelief. “Well, yeah! Force the vampires to live on animal blood!”

“Trust me, Sofia. That would cause more chaos than you can possibly wrap your mind around, but if that’s what has to happen.” She shrugged. “Then so be it.”

I couldn’t understand her nonchalance. We were practically talking about genocide and she was just sitting there talking as if life didn’t matter. “I can’t believe it. Doesn’t life matter to anyone here at The Shade?”

“It’s going to be over soon, Sofia,” was the only assurance I got from the witch.

I stood from my seat and began pacing the marble floor. “What does that even mean?” I muttered through gritted teeth.

I could feel Corrine’s eyes on me as I paced the floor anxiously. I didn’t bother to hide my irritation from her. My heart broke just thinking of what a culling could mean for the people I’d begun to care about.

“Do you have any idea why I’m here, Sofia?”

I paused to glance her way. “Yeah. They took you from your university, because the last witch was about to pass away. They need you to keep the protective spell over the island going.”

She chuckled dryly. “I could leave this island anytime I want. Derek knows that. You know that. Why do you think I don’t?”

"I always assumed it's because you want to look after the humans of The Shade, but considering how apathetic you are over this whole culling business, I'm not so sure anymore..." I was surprised by my own bluntness. *Perhaps Gavin has begun to rub off on me.*

"That's one reason, yes. I've tried to do my part in making the lives of the Naturals a bit more comfortable. As for the Migrates, there wasn't much I could do for them. They were trapped prey inside a den of beasts from the moment they stepped onto the island. You weren't supposed to survive, Sofia. You were supposed to get killed like everyone else. Derek Novak's nature dictated that he suck the blood right out of you from the first moment he laid eyes on you, but he didn't. Why is that?"

I pursed my lips, unable to come up with an answer. I recalled the conversation I had with Vivienne when she risked her life—and lost it to the hunters—just to get me back to The Shade.

*"Derek thought he'd already fulfilled the prophecy when we established The Shade. The island, he thought, was our true sanctuary. Cora knew otherwise. She knew that he wasn't done, so without his knowledge, she tacked on an end to her spell. Derek was to wake once it was time to find the girl who would help him fulfill his destiny. It was Corrine who signaled that he was about to wake and she made it very clear that the girls taken on a certain night were to be reserved for him." Vivienne said.*

*"My birthday..." I threw the words out there, remembering the way I felt that night.*

*"Yes...your birthday..." she said the words as if she found it amazing that Lucas abducted me and brought me to The Shade on that particular day. "Derek hadn't fed on human blood for four centuries. You couldn't possibly understand how difficult it was for him not to feed on you. When he slammed you against that pillar, I thought you were done for. But he spared you. I don't know what you told him, but you got to him*

*in a way no other person was ever able to. Not our father or our brother or me or even Cora was able to get through to him the way you did…"*

The conversation I was having with Corrine felt eerily similar to that conversation I had with Vivienne at the coffee shop near the stadium where Ben was having his championship football game. I remembered how I felt back then, how confused I was when Vivienne looked me in the eye and told me that I wasn't just a pawn present at The Shade to keep the board moving. I was "the queen."

I looked at Corrine and answered her question. "I'm the girl meant to help him fulfill the prophecy." That was the moment I snapped out of my denial and actually embraced that what Vivienne told me at the coffee shop could actually be real.

"Exactly." Corrine nodded. "I am the final witch, Sofia. After me, there will be no other. The prophecy has to be fulfilled in my lifetime, or The Shade will no longer have anyone from my lineage powerful enough to keep it protected. I chose to be here because I want to watch it all unfold. To be honest, I doubted the prophecy. I doubted that Derek could bring the prophecy to completion. He seemed too far gone in darkness—like Claudia and Lucas, Felix and Gregor—vampires who have lost all touch of their humanity and conscience. I took one look at Derek's sleeping form when I first came here at The Shade and I scoffed. I saw so much darkness in him. I convinced myself that Cora believed what she wanted to believe about him because of her famed unrequited love for Derek…"

I frowned at that statement. *Cora was in love with Derek?*

"After I saw the way Derek was with you, however," Corrine continued, "I had to believe that there was still goodness in him. He wasn't too far gone." She must've noticed the glazed look on my eyes, because she furrowed her brows and asked, "What's wrong?"

"I just had no idea…Cora and Derek?"

"I thought you knew. Derek was the love of Cora's life. Everything she did for The Shade was out of her love for him. He never did quite return her love though—not the way she wanted to at least. He protected her. She was his best friend, but no…he never loved her, not the way he loved you."

My heart broke for Cora, and yet to be once again assured that I was the love of Derek's life was something that made my spirits soar.

"For a time, Cora thought that she was the woman who would help him fulfill the prophecy. It took years before she realized and accepted that she wasn't and that his heart would never be hers. I think you already know this, Sofia, but Derek has been with countless women throughout his lifetime, but he never did fall in love until you came along."

I opened my mouth to respond, but no words came out. How was a girl to respond to a revelation like that? To my relief, it seemed I didn't need to come up with a reply, because within seconds of her finishing her last statement, Corrine's brown eyes grew wide with utter panic as she stood on her feet, her hands clutching the edge of the desk until her knuckles grew a pale white.

"Corrine?" I asked, my concern immediate.

She swallowed hard. "Something's wrong. Something is very, very wrong…"

Before I could even react, a blow to my head knocked me unconscious and everything that surrounded me succumbed to darkness—a phenomenon that seemed inevitable in a place like The Shade.

# Chapter 28: Derek

Over the past five hundred years, my father had already given me many reasons to hate him, but I never did quite hate him as much as I did that night.

I was intrigued to say the least. I was no fool. I was gearing myself up for a fight—an argument at the least—once I reached the dome, but what greeted me was something that was far beyond my expectations.

The moment I walked through the large oak doors of The Shade, multiple tranquilizer rifles—the same ones used by hunters—were fired at me before six guards jumped at me to chain me up and restrain me from fighting back. I was still able to severely maim one of the guards who attacked me, but I was outnumbered and weakened by the suppression serums the tranquilizer darts injected into my system. It was the same serum used to inhibit a vampire's healing abilities—the same one used on Claudia when she was whipped for her defiance toward me. The serum also worked to suppress a vampire's strength.

Five chains were placed on me—my neck was shackled, my wrists and my ankles. The five guards who jumped on me were holding the other ends of the chains, all of them pulling on opposite directions. It felt like they were trying to tear me apart. The guard I was able to take down was still writhing in pain on the ground, severely wounded, as he clutched a chain that I figured must've been for my waist. I knew them. *Felix's men.*

I glared at my father. "What's going on?" I hissed as I tried to fight against the restraints.

Seated on his throne, my father smirked at me. "How the mighty have fallen…this is just a father giving his son a lesson in humility," he said as he leaned back and crossed his legs, wicked glee evident in his eyes.

"Do you really think you can kill me without the rest of the Elite destroying you for it?" I spat at him.

"Kill you? There are worse ways to make you suffer than just end your life, son."

I pulled against the chains, mainly to gauge just how strong the guards were. I couldn't remember seeing any of them at the training grounds. I wondered then if Felix had been doing training of his own. The guards were strong, perhaps the best he had.

My father rose from his seat and began walking down the balcony to the stand where I was restrained.

I glared at him as he approached. "What do you want?"

"A trusted source of mine revealed to me that some of the Naturals are planning to incite a revolt. The key people are being arrested as we speak. We don't want them to get in our way once we conduct the culling tomorrow."

My stomach turned. *Tomorrow?! How could I have not known that?* "No one told me that plans have been finalized for the culling!"

"Not many knew. We couldn't risk you and those whom we know are loyal to you finding out about the plans and getting in our way. Considering how you're practically bordering on treason on behalf of that human of yours, it's hard to trust you, son. You understand, right?"

I once again pulled at the chains. The guard holding down the chain on my right wrist budged. I smirked, noting a weakness. I shifted my glare back to my father. "I have nothing to do with the revolt. Why restrain me here when you need military force to conduct the culling and take down the inciters of the revolt?"

"Because I doubt you would do anything to punish one of the key people leading the revolt."

Realization dawned on me. *Sofia.* All I could do was scream as I pulled on my restraints, making all five of the guards holding me down tense as they tried to keep hold of the chains. "I swear if you do anything to harm her…" Several curses flew from my lips. "No! What are you going to do to her?!"

"Give her the punishment any rebel deserves. Make an example of the little fool. They're all being hauled to the town square, where they will receive fifty lashes each."

I remembered the way Claudia's back looked after receiving thirty lashes. Despite the suppression serum inhibiting her ability to heal, a vampire was still much more capable of taking that much pain. "There's no way she's going to survive *that* many lashes!"

"Exactly." My father grinned. I could barely recognize him anymore. "Well, I have punishments to see to." He walked out of the dome, chuckles still coming out of his mouth.

I couldn't stand him. At that moment, I *hated* him. I took several deep breaths as I glared at the guards surrounding me. *No…not again…Sofia isn't going to shed any more blood. Enough is enough.*

Gathering up my strength, I let out all my fury with one long growl before pulling on my restraints. The next half hour was spent taking down every single one of the five guards restraining me. I walked out of the dome still holding the beating heart of the final guard in my hand.

I might have underestimated my father, but he had no idea how much he had just underestimated me.

# Chapter 29: Sofia

I was woken by a splash of cold water. The first person I saw was Corrine standing at a distance from me, amongst a crowd of onlookers. I wondered why she didn't do anything to help me. She could've easily rescued me from whomever it was that attacked me. That's when I realized that she wasn't exactly an ally, that she would never meddle with our destinies or interfere with the events that were unfolding. She was an observer. She was there to watch the prophecy unfold. She wasn't there to change it or mess with it. Considering everything she knew, to do so would be dangerous.

I broke eye contact with her and began to try and make sense of my surroundings. We were at the Vale's town square and a rather large crowd had already gathered—many were vampires sending me hostile glares. I saw Liana whispering something to Cameron, a worried look on her face. I could just about make out what she was saying as she nudged Cameron's arm: "We have to do something," she mouthed.

My heart began thumping double its usual pace. *What's going on?* I realized then that my wrists were bound together and I was shivering from the cold water that was now beginning to soak my clothes and seep around my skin.

"Did you do this, Sofia?"

I followed the direction of the all-too-familiar voice and saw Gavin glaring at me with suspicion. "No! I don't even know what's going on!"

"Someone ratted us out," Ian hissed as he tried to break free from the ropes binding his hands. "I was certain it was you, Red. I still think it is."

"If it were me, why on earth would I be here with you?" The look on their faces showed that they were unconvinced. We were lined up in front of a wooden pole—there were five of us, two of the others I recognized from the secret meeting Gavin dragged me to. "I didn't do this."

Ian scoffed. "And we're supposed to just take your word for it?"

"It wasn't her."

The murmurs of the crowd grew silent. Heavy footsteps approached. I didn't really have to look up to know who it was. Gregor Novak. I lifted my head and sure enough, he was standing over me, staring at me the same way he always did—with a strange mixture of hatred and desire.

"My son's redhead didn't rat you out," he clarified. "She's too intent on destroying The Shade and everything it's become to do that. I'm no fool. I have my eyes on The Catacombs, humans who do my bidding for certain luxuries and privileges. I've had her watched from her first day there. I know what a traitorous snake she is. She might have my son fooled, but not me. I know *exactly* why you're here at The Shade, Sofia Claremont."

I gave him the most defiant glare I could muster. "I have no idea what you're talking about."

The back of his hand connected with the side of my face so forcefully, I thought my neck would snap.

"How dare you address me! You little worm!" He grabbed a clump of my hair and yanked me to a standing position. He leaned over my face so closely our noses almost touched. "I know exactly who you are."

He threw me on the ground toward the direction of the pole. I tried to scramble upwards, but two guards grabbed me by the arms and dragged me toward the pole. All I could do was attempt to steel myself against what I knew was about to happen.

"Fifty lashes for the treasonous little wretch," Gregor announced.

The guards unbound my hands, which had been tied behind my back, so that they could bind them on ropes that hung over a hook on top of the wooden pole. I was trembling uncontrollably by the time they started ripping the back of my dress in order to expose my bare back.

"That's right, Sofia." Gregor had a tone of triumph in his voice. "Tremble."

I could hear the whip crack over the concrete ground. I shut my eyes, trying to swallow back my fear. *Derek, where are you? Do something...*

"Stop this! Right now!"

Relief washed over me at the distant, but very much recognizable, voice of Derek as the crowd made way for him.

"Unbind her this instant!" he ordered the guards and they were about to do just that, but Gregor must've done something to make them stop.

"So you really are as strong and as powerful as they said you were, taking down five of Felix's best men all on your own. I'm impressed." There was a tone of amusement on Gregor's voice. Not a single ounce of intimidation or defeat could be found in the way he was speaking. I wondered what ace he was hiding up his sleeve.

"I told you not to lay a hand on Sofia. I warned you." When he saw that the guards weren't about to do as he told them, Derek approached me and unbound my hands. He cupped my face with his strong hands and winced when he noticed the bump on my head where my captors had knocked me unconscious.

"You care for her like she's some fragile little doll, when you don't really even know who she really is. She's playing you for a fool, Derek, destroying everything you fought hard to build."

Derek's chiseled features tensed as he let out a controlled breath, as if trying to reel in his anger. "I warned you, Father. You've gone too far."

"She's Ingrid Maslen's daughter, Derek. Did you know that?"

I saw the flash of confusion that crossed Derek's eyes as he withdrew his hands from my face. I felt the exact same confusion. *What is this guy talking about?*

"Lies." Derek shook his head, but for a moment he looked at me as though I might have been a wholly different person. Desperation began eating at me. I knew how much he hated the Maslens.

"My mother's name is Camilla Claremont," I told him trying to stay calm. "She's been in an insane asylum for the majority of the past decade. You know this. Your father's bluffing, Derek."

"I'm not bluffing. I can prove everything," Gregor said confidently. "I have all the background checks to prove it. Ingrid Maslen was once Camilla Claremont, wife of Aiden Claremont. They only have one daughter—your pretty little redhead right there."

I shook my head. "No. It's not true. Ingrid Maslen is *not* my mother."

"When was the last time you saw Camilla Claremont, Sofia?" Gregor continued to pry. "Did you actually ever even see her in an insane asylum? Or is that just the story you're weaving to cover up your connection to the Maslens?"

"That's not…I'm not connected to the Maslens." My voice was weak, Gregor's words shaking me up. The idea of my mother being anywhere but inside an asylum was already too much for me to even comprehend. The thought that she was a vampire was something I was certain would drive *me* insane if I entertained it.

I kept my eyes on Derek's, wondering what was going through his mind. If Ingrid really was my mother, I wondered if he could ever look at me the same way again. He was slipping away from me and I could feel it and the worst part of it all was that I actually had no clue whether or not Gregor was telling the truth.

Derek gave me a hurt and confused look. "Sofia…is it possible that Ingrid Maslen is your mother?"

"I don't know," I admitted, my heart sinking as I did. "Aiden and Camilla Claremont *are* my parents, but apart from Vivienne's memories, I've never heard of Ingrid Maslen before I came to The Shade. You have to believe me, Derek."

"Why would you believe her, huh? For all we know, the only reason she came back might be because her mother sent her, so that they could destroy The Shade or perhaps even take over. She might be their inside person."

I looked into Derek's eyes, wondering if it were possible for him to actually believe that I would betray him in that way. I couldn't read the expression on his face and the realization made my heart drop. "Derek…" was all I managed to say, searching for some sort of assurance that he was going to side with me, that he loved me still. I found none. All I could see was the blank expression on his face as the wheels inside his mind churned the information he'd just been given, perhaps wondering what he was supposed to do with it.

His hands formed into fists and his muscles tensed at the motion. He took a step away from me and that was all he needed to do to make me feel like I'd totally lost him. Tears began streaming down my eyes as I looked into his eyes, desperate to find words to get him back to me.

"Get her back on the pole," Gregor ordered the guards. "She's guilty of inciting rebellion within The Shade. That's the sentence for rebellion."

"No." Derek shook his head and looked at me. "Did you know about the plan to hold a revolt?"

My heart sank. I couldn't lie. "Yes, but..."

The betrayed expression on his eyes tore me apart.

"Derek...please..."

"She admits her guilt." Gregor chuckled. "You never should've trusted her."

"Her knowledge of the rebellion makes her guilty." Derek nodded. His words were said with a tone of resignation. "The Shade's law dictates that any involvement in such a rebellion is to be met with a punishment of fifty lashes."

"That's it then!" Gregor exclaimed triumphantly.

The guards grabbed hold of me and began dragging me back to the pole. I couldn't control my sobs. I knew that my sandcastle would totally collapse one day, but I never would've guessed that it would be in this way.

They were about to bind my wrists over the pole. I'd completely lost all hope when Derek called out, "Wait!" My heart stopped. "I cannot go against the law, which clearly dictates that she is to be punished for her actions, but the law also states that a citizen of The Shade can volunteer to take on the punishment of another citizen upon himself. I will take on her sentence."

What he said caused such a commotion among the crowd, we were barely able to hear Gregor's angry protests.

"No!" he cried out, when the murmurs of the crowd eventually died down.

I adored Derek too much at that moment to even bother looking at Gregor, but the king of The Shade sounded livid.

"You will do no such thing! A vampire taking on a human rebel's sentence is unheard of. You're the prince of The Shade! You will not do this. I forbid it!"

Ignoring his own father, Derek pulled his shirt over his head and threw it on the ground. "Let's get this over with."

He approached me, giving me a look that made me feel like I was the most precious creature on earth. I still couldn't control my tears as he stood right in front of me. "You had me scared to death..." I confessed.

"Did you really think I could just stand here and let them hurt you?" he told me.

Though relieved as I was being spared the ridiculous punishment the king was meting out on us, the idea of having to watch Derek take on the punishment meant for me was frightening. "I don't want to see you get hurt."

He gently brushed a hand through my tangled hair. "Don't worry about me, Sofia. I can take it. I heal, remember?" He then pressed his lips against my forehead. "Just do me a favor and leave. I don't want you to see this."

I shook my head. "No. You wouldn't have to go through this if it weren't for me."

"The thought of you seeing this will only make the experience more painful, Sofia. Please…"

"I can't leave you. I wouldn't know where to go or how to bear being alone. If you have to go through this, Derek, if there's no other way, then we have to learn to go through things together. No matter how painful…"

He kissed me full on the mouth before finally glaring defiantly at Gregor who seemed to have gone mad, not knowing what to do about the whole thing. He'd already run out of aces against me—against *us*—and he knew it. Derek approached the pole and as they bound him to it, that's when I got a good look at the whip they were going to use.

A lump formed on my throat at the sight of it. When the first blow on Derek's bare back was made, I could barely breathe. I waited for the dark, ugly welt on his back to heal, but it didn't. Another lash was inflicted and still, he didn't heal.

Murmurs and whispers began to float across the crowd as the onlookers were beginning to wonder why he wasn't healing.

All I could think about was that he told me he would heal, and it wasn't happening and with every blow, I felt worse and worse. By the tenth blow, Derek's skin broke and blood was drawn. Every single blow that followed drew even more blood, creating a mess out of the flesh on his back. Halfway through, I couldn't look anymore. At some point, I wanted to throw myself at him and just take the punishment myself, but I knew that doing so would've made all that he was doing be in vain.

It was at this point that Ashley stepped by my side and squeezed my hand. She drew me to her embrace and held me close as I flinched through the sound of every crack of that whip.

After the fiftieth lash was inflicted, an electric silence filled the atmosphere. I wondered what was going through everyone's mind, but no one moved.

"It's over, Sofia," Ashley whispered into my ear.

I pried myself away from her and willed myself to look at Derek. His back was barely recognizable and I noticed the confusion on everyone's faces—especially the vampires. The question on everyone's mind remained the same: *Why wasn't he healing?*

Derek was supposed to be the most powerful vampire of his time, revered by everyone at The Shade. He was practically untouchable, and from Gregor's own proclamation, he was only recently able to singlehandedly take down five of Felix's best men.

However, at that moment, he hung motionless over the pole, unconscious.

I trembled as I approached him. Cameron and Liana following. The guards untied Derek's wrists and he slumped to the ground. Cameron came in time to catch his limp form.

"What's going on? Why isn't he healing?" I asked, unable to keep the alarm from my voice.

"Let's take him to Corrine's," Liana said.

"Not so fast!" Gregor said, menace lacing his words. "There are four other rebels who haven't yet met their punishments."

I drew a breath as I looked at Gavin, Ian and the two other Naturals who were caught with me. If Derek wasn't able to take the blows, then how on earth would they survive?

"They won't be able to handle it. They're going to die..."

Cameron shook his head as his eyes met with Liana's. It was as if they had some sort of telepathic communication, because Liana worriedly said, "Cam..." But then she paused and nodded.

Cameron stood to his feet. "As a show of loyalty to Derek Novak,

I'll take on the punishment of one of the rebels."

Xavier stepped forward from the crowd and nodded. "I'll do the same."

Eli and Yuri Lazaroff followed and so did at least half a dozen others of the Elite. It was clear to see who it was that held the real power at The Shade, and it definitely wasn't Derek's father. My spirits soared on behalf of Derek, but I was more concerned about getting him the medical treatment he so desperately needed.

Corrine approached us. "Let's get him to Sanctuary. I think Cameron, Xavier and the rest of the Elite are more than capable of handling matters here. Let's get the prince taken care of, shall we?"

Sam, Kyle and Ashley were soon by our side as we hauled Derek out of there.

At the Sanctuary, we discovered why he wasn't healing.

"He was administered a suppression serum before he showed up," Corrine explained. "I'm thinking he already had a confrontation with his father even before he came to the town square. Perhaps that's what they were talking about when Gregor mentioned him taking Felix's men down."

"So he knew he wouldn't heal?" I asked, my voice choked. "And yet he still went through this."

Corrine shrugged. "I guess he loves you *that* much."

# Chapter 30: Derek

When I woke up, the first person I saw was Sofia, staring at me with wide-eyed concern. Despite the excruciating pain on my back, I had to smile at the sight of her. "Hey there…" I greeted softly.

She made her way to my side, kneeling on the ground by the bed, so that she could look into my eyes. "I'm sorry, Derek. I should've told you what I knew, but I just…"

"Shhh, Sofia. I understand why you didn't tell me." I tried to look around the room we were in and immediately surmised that we were at the Sanctuary. "We're alone?" I asked.

She nodded. "Corrine's in the other room developing an anti-serum. Liana and Sam went to check on Cameron and the others. Ashley and Kyle went to the chilling chambers to get you some blood."

"What happened to Cameron? And what do you mean 'the others?'"

She told me what Cameron and the rest of the Elite did to show their support toward me and all I could think of was how humbling the whole thing was. At the same time, I sensed the pressure that came with it. The immensity of the prophecy and everything it meant hit me full force. I had no idea if Sofia realized it, but lines had just been drawn. We were at war.

"Don't worry about them for now…" She tried to soothe me. "Just get yourself healed." She squeezed my arm tightly. "They're taking forever. You need blood."

Something sparked in that pretty little brain of hers and she quickly shoved her wrist in front of my mouth. "You can have my blood. It will help you heal, won't it?"

I chuckled wryly. "I'm not going to drink your blood, Sofia."

"Why not?" she insisted indignantly. "You've made me drink yours more times than I can count."

"Do you have any idea how much control I need to have over myself in order not to feed on you? Tasting your blood will be the end of us, Sofia."

*The end of us.* I could remember the desperation in her eyes when she thought that I'd turn my back on her. *Are you thinking about the future at all, Sofia? Do you dread losing me as much as I dread losing you?*

Based on her response, it was as if she was reading my mind. She lowered her wrists, seemingly accepting that nothing she said could ever make me agree to drinking her blood. She gave me a pensive, longing look. "I thought I lost you back there, Derek," she admitted. "I don't know what your father was talking about, Derek, but if Ingrid Maslen really *is* my mother…"

"…it won't matter," I assured her. "I know you well enough to know that you could never have been in league with her all this time.

What we have is real, Sofia…no matter who your parents are."

I couldn't help but wonder what she thought about the possibility of the Maslens' baby vampire being her mother. It didn't even seem to be bothering her at the moment, but I couldn't really blame her. So much was going on. I doubted she had time to let the revelation sink in.

She kissed me gently on the lips. "I adore you for what you did for me back there, and I hate that you're in so much pain because of it."

"I'll be better in no time, Sofia. I'll get a drink blood when Ash and Kyle get here and I'll be as strong as I was before."

"You lied to me. You said that you would heal. You knew that you wouldn't."

"I wanted to assure you that everything was going to be alright, and it will be, Sofia."

She was silent. I wondered what was going through her mind, but I was afraid to ask.

"You love me still, don't you?" I asked instead, longing to hear her assurance before what I was about to reveal to her.

"Always," she assured me.

I believed her, but still, I was afraid of what her reaction would be to what I was about to tell her. "The culling is tomorrow, Sofia."

She gulped. I could see the wheels inside her mind turning as she let the news sink in. "You're just going to let it happen?"

I hated that we didn't stand on the same ground regarding the matter, but all I could do was be honest with her. "I don't know what to say, Sofia. Blood is seen as a necessity at The Shade."

She shook her head. "I understand where you're coming from, Derek, but it doesn't mean I think a culling is alright. You know how I stand regarding this matter."

I was expecting her to look at me like I was a monster, advocating a bloody massacre, but all I saw was a quiet resignation, an acceptance that she couldn't change my mind no matter how she tried. I saw sadness, perhaps even a trace of disappointment, but no less love than there was before. I also realized then that though she wasn't saying it out loud, she was still determined to fight the culling with everything that she had.

"Tell me what you really think, Sofia."

"I think you're better than this, Derek."

"I don't know what to do," I admitted. "I don't know how on earth I'm going to fulfill Vivienne's prophecy. How on earth am I going to provide my kind true sanctuary, bring all the covens together and fight against the hunters when war is brewing right here within The Shade?" I could feel my senses waning as the worrisome thoughts began to take over my consciousness.

As usual, Sofia knew exactly what to say to make me believe that I was still capable of good. Just before I once again drifted into unconsciousness, I could still comprehend her assuring whispers, practically lulling me to sleep, "All the answers to the questions you're asking are right within you. You were meant to fulfill that prophecy and you will. You'll find a way." She paused and gently pressed her soft lips against my forehead. "You're Derek Novak. You'll find a way."

# Chapter 31: Sofia

*The culling is tomorrow.*

When Ashley and Kyle returned with the blood, I felt confident enough to leave Derek's side and entrust him into Corrine's capable hands. I had to warn Gavin and the others about the culling. What they planned to do with the warning was entirely up to them, but whatever they did, I was determined to support them, trusting that Derek would understand my reasons for doing so.

"Where are you going?" Ashley asked when I bade my leave.

"Back to The Catacombs."

She exchanged nervous glances with Kyle, who stepped up and said, "That's probably not a great idea right now..."

"Why? What happened?" I asked anxiously, dread coming over me based on the uncomfortable looks on their faces. That's when I realized that the expression on Ashley's face was beyond discomfort. It was of pure heartbreak. "Tell me, Ashley."

She licked her lips. It was clear to see that she was fighting back tears. "The king was livid after what happened. He hit the only people he could in order to hurt you."

I sucked in a breath steeling myself against what they were about to tell me. "Go ahead."

Tears began to brim Ashley's eyes. "Paige and the three new girls…they're dead. Felix and his men…while everything was happening at the town square…they went to your quarters and killed everyone they found there. By order of the king."

"They planned on doing it even before everything that happened at the town square," Kyle continued to explain when Ashley broke into a sob. "It was their back-up plan in case what Gregor wanted to happen at The Shade—turn Derek against you—didn't push through."

"A last-ditch attempt to hurt me." I nodded with understanding, tears beginning to fall down my cheeks. Gregor definitely knew how to hurt me. "Rosa?" I asked.

"She was visiting with Lily and the kids when it all happened," Kyle said the words reassuringly in hopes of giving me a thread of comfort.

I wanted to break down. I wanted to just crumble and give in to the despair that I felt over the loss of four innocent lives, but even as tears flowed down my face, beyond the grief, what I felt was anger. Paige and the girls had nothing to do with Gregor's hatred toward me. They had nothing to do with what had happened at the town square. If I'd just dragged Derek into a war with his father, at that moment, I hoped with everything that I was that Derek could someday find it in himself to actually kill his own father.

What had to happen now—however—was for the deaths to not be in vain. I shoved the urge to give in to the grief and instead focused my thoughts and energies on making martyrs out of my friends.

Upon my return to The Catacombs, I met with Gavin, Ian and the rest of those who were planning a revolt.

"The culling is tomorrow," I announced. "During the unexpected events that occurred at the town square, they murdered four of my friends here at The Catacombs. Tomorrow, they plan to murder more people."

"Let's get straight to the point, Red." Ian stood to his full height—standing at least half a foot taller than me. Even with his lanky build, he was a rather intimidating sight, considering the fury blazing in his eyes. "Is your prince going to help us stop the culling?"

I shook my head. "He's unconscious. We're on our own on this one."

"We can't just let this happen..." Gavin sat up straight in his chair. "There's got to be something we can do."

It was perhaps the anger I felt over what they did to my friends, over every atrocity that I'd seen happen at The Shade. It was perhaps the righteous indignation I felt over losing Ben and Gwen and Paige and those three young innocents taken from their homes just like I was to become slaves at The Shade. At that moment, however, I didn't care if I lived or died. I wasn't just going to stand back and let them drag the weak and defenseless to their deaths. Not while I was there, not when there were thousands of human beings in The Catacombs capable of fighting back.

I knew that blood was going to be shed. I was also very much aware that the blood could most likely be mine, but I really didn't care anymore. I was tired of running, tired of being afraid. If I was the girl who was going to help Derek fulfill the prophecy, then I was going to do it fighting for what I believed in and hoping that he would someday find it in his heart to forgive me.

At that point, I realized that my return to The Shade wasn't just about Derek and me anymore. It couldn't be. If I was going to be of any use to him, I couldn't remain a love-struck teenager pining over him. I had to come into my own.

Looking into the hopeful and passionate eyes of the people surrounding me, I knew what had to happen. "We are going to do something." I nodded resolutely. "We're going to fight back."

# Chapter 32: Ben

We were on a private plane. Fly, the resident pilot of the hunters, lifted us into the air. We'd just finished another mission. Haunted by the new batch of lives I'd just claimed, I was quiet during our whole trip back to headquarters. It was easier to kill that night. At least I was certain that the ones I had killed had blood on their hands, since I just saw them sucking the life out of a couple of beautiful young girls taken from a human trafficking ring.

In particular, it was these girls that were bothering me, reminding me of the many young men and women that'd been abducted and brought to The Shade.

"What's going on with you, Ben? You seem so out of it these days…" Zinnia sounded annoyed as she plopped herself down on the seat beside mine. She had a bottle of champagne in her hands and she looked ready to celebrate.

I inwardly groaned. "Seriously? Champagne?"

"Don't we have reason to celebrate?"

"We just saw a bunch of young women get murdered by vampires, who we then murdered. Death is not something we ought to celebrate, Zinnia."

Her eyes widened. "Gosh…so touchy…fine…no champagne then…" She was silent for a good fifteen minutes before she eventually blurted out, "What is wrong, Ben?"

"I think I want out…" I finally confessed. It just came out of my lips before I could stop it.

Zinnia's brow rose. "Just like that? You just want to quit being a hunter? After all the work you've put into becoming one, after…"

"I became a hunter to find The Shade, exact revenge on the insane vampire bitch who ruined my life and try and get Sofia back. So far, there has been absolutely no progress in finding the island."

"These things take time, Ben…you can't just up and quit so soon. Give it time."

"It's not just that…" I clutched the armrests of the first class leather recliner I was seated on as I began to shake my head. "I can't do this anymore."

"Do *what*?"

"Kill…devote my life to just killing vampires…it's not like I thought it would be."

Zinnia stared at me. I knew she was trying to understand what I was saying, but I doubted she ever would. "Have you talked to Reuben about this?"

"Of course not."

"You're too much of an asset to the hunters, Ben. I don't think he's going to be thrilled about you leaving…are you sure this is what you want?"

*I want to turn back time. That's what I want. I want to go back to the time when there never was a Derek Novak in our lives and Sofia only had eyes for me. I want to go back to her seventeenth birthday and treat her the way I should've—like she was the most beautiful girl I'd ever laid eyes on, because that's exactly what she was.*

"I don't know what I want," I lied to Zinnia, because I was fully aware that what I really wanted could never be.

"Think this through before you do anything you regret."

*Regret.* That was all I really felt and I had no idea how to make things right again. For the first time, I actually felt like I truly saw Sofia for what she truly was: a treasure—one that I misused and abused and discarded like it was nothing but trash.

I wondered how she was doing. *Is he treating you right? Is he treating you the way I should've when you were still mine?*

For the rest of the plane ride, Zinnia steered clear of me—something I was grateful for. I lost myself in thoughts of what should've been and what could've been, in *what-ifs* and *maybes.* By the time we landed on the headquarters' runway, I was in a world of my own. When my feet hit the tarmac, all I could think about was my desire to go home, because being back in California could perhaps make me feel like I was closer to Sofia.

When I reached my suite at the headquarters, I took out my phone and dialed my mother's number. I knew that they would be asleep at this time of night, but I called anyway. I was answered by my mother, Amelia.

"Hello?" she drowsily greeted.

"Mom?"

"Ben?!" I could immediately hear the mixture of worry, elation and heartbreak in her voice. It was the same tone she had whenever I called to check on them.

"Yeah…how are you doing?"

"We're doing fine. Abby's joined the girl scouts and your father got promoted, but we're missing you, Ben…don't you have any plans to visit? Are you staying well?" As far as my parents were concerned, I'd taken up military training.

Due to Reuben's long-term friendship with my father, Lyle, it was easy for him to convince him that I was in some sort of special training program for the government.

"I'm fine, Mom. It's been fun, but I've been missing you guys too. I'm hoping my superiors will allow me to leave so I can visit you soon."

"I would love that, Ben. I'm sure Abby would love to see you too."

I grinned. My little sister could be quite a brat, but I loved her dearly. "Mess up the midget's hair for me, will you, Mom?"

"I'll do no such thing."

I laughed at the sound of reprimand coming from her tone of voice. When my laughter died down, all I could think about was asking a question that I already knew the answer to. "Have you heard from Sofia, Mom?"

"No."

I could hear the resentment in my mother's voice. She'd never liked Sofia much, and she was often outspoken about it, but I appreciated that she didn't express her negative opinion of my best friend at that point. Perhaps she could sense how much I missed Sofia.

"A friend of yours has been calling though."

I creased my brows in surprise. "Who?"

"A Natalie Borgia. Familiar?"

Strangely, the name *did* sound familiar, but I couldn't quite place who the person was and where I'd heard the name. "What did she say?"

"Well, she just left a number and asked me to tell you to call her."

"Okay. Could you give me the number, Mom?"

My mother dictated the number and I took note. We exchanged a couple of stories before finally calling it a night and hanging up. I stared at the number, still trying to remember who Natalie Borgia was, wondering why she would want to get in touch with me.

Overcome by curiosity, I dialed the number. The phone kept ringing and I was just about to give up waiting when a sultry voice with an Italian accent greeted me, "Hello?"

"Hi. Is this Natalie Borgia?"

"Perhaps. Who's calling?"

"Ben Hudson. You were calling my home, trying to get in touch with me?"

"Finally," she said. "I have a message for you."

"A message?"

"Yes. From Lucas Novak. Does the name ring a bell?"

That's when the name finally clicked. *Natalie Borgia.* She was mentioned in one of our training lectures. She was one of the oldest known vampires existing. She was a rogue, not belonging to any covens. Catching her would make for a king's ransom. Every vampire coven would be clamoring for her. *What on earth did she or Lucas Novak want with me?*

"Hello?" she cleared her throat. "You still there?"

"Yes. Lucas Novak? What does the prince of The Shade want?"

"He wants to help you get to The Shade."

"Why on earth would he do that?"

"He wants to separate Sofia Claremont from his brother. He wants her out of The Shade and he believes only you can help him do that. He will arrange transport for you. Of course, you won't know how to reach the island. Its location must remain protected."

"What kind of fool would I be to trust Lucas Novak? Or *you* for that matter?"

"Lucas says that he knows where your family lives..."

My jaw tensed at this blatant threat. "Look, whoever you are...If Lucas..."

"Hey, Ben..." she interrupted me calmly. "I don't care about whatever it is that Lucas Novak is up to. I'm just a messenger. Don't shoot me. What message do you want me to relay to him?"

I gave it a moment's thought. Before I could completely think things through, I went with my impulse. "Fine. I'll do what he says, but I have my terms."

"And those terms would be?"

"I keep Sofia."

"Interesting. I'll let him know. I'll be in touch with you, Ben Hudson." Natalie chuckled, and then hung up.

The only thought on my mind was whether or not to kill Lucas Novak while I had the chance. And for some reason, I realized that I didn't want to. I wondered why. After the things he'd put Sofia through, I knew he deserved to die. As I mulled over it late into the night, I realized the reason behind my willingness to spare his life.

Lucas Novak was the only chance I had to get to Sofia.

# Chapter 33: Sofia

What we were doing was suicide and I knew it, and I think every other human insane enough to join in on our "stand" knew that they could die for what they were doing, but we did it nonetheless.

On the day of the culling, the whispers of our stand passed on through word-of-mouth like wildfire across every single one of the thousands of cells within The Catacombs. The message was simple: *Tomorrow, there will be a culling. Make a stand against this and guard the entrance to the Black Heights.*

Gavin visited my quarters earlier. We exchanged glances and gave each other a weak smile.

"You sure you're up for this?" he asked.

"I've never been more certain of anything in my entire life," I told him.

"What's the prince going to think?"

"I think he will love me still."

After I returned to my quarters from the meeting with the rebels the night before, I found Ashley waiting there for me. We shared an embrace and a couple of tears. She apologized for not having visited sooner. She was afraid of her own cravings and what she could possibly do to me and the girls. She wished now that she'd come earlier. Rosa arrived with Gavin. She remained silent, visibly shaken. She and Paige had been very close. I found myself at a loss for words when it came to trying to console Rosa. It seemed Ashley felt the same way.

I eventually asked how Derek was and Ashley assured me that he was recovering, though he was still mostly unconscious. I wondered what he would think if he found out what I was up to. I asked Ashley to let him know that I loved him.

"Do you want me to let him know what exactly you're getting yourself into?"

I gave it a moment's thought and nodded. "I think he knows where I stand. I think he knew that, by telling me about the culling, something like this would happen. We love each other, but I guess this is just us fighting our own battles."

"You really are a piece of work, Sofia Claremont."

The next morning, as Gavin and I made our way to the opening of the Black Heights, I wasn't exactly feeling like "a piece of work."

"What if nobody shows up?" I asked Gavin.

"Ian will." He shrugged as we descended one of the ladders.

I had to chuckle. "So that makes three of us?"

"Nah..." Gavin assured. "People will show up, Sofia. Don't worry your pretty little head over nobody showing up. Give the Naturals more credit than that."

I wanted to ask him how he was so sure, but I figured it might just be him trying to reassure himself. When we reached the entrance to the Black Heights, it seemed our fears were unfounded, because thousands of Naturals already stood at the cave entrance, in silent protest against the culling.

We didn't have any weapons, no means whatsoever to fight against the vampires—who were in every way more powerful than us, but winning wasn't our objective. We didn't have any delusions about actually being able to stop the culling. It was just the Naturals coming together to make a stand against a blatant massacre of their own loved ones.

We saw Ian approaching us. "I can't believe this many people showed up…" I confessed, still stunned by the sheer number of people standing there, protesting the culling.

"Did you really think you're the only one crazy enough to stand for the lives of people you love?" Ian teased before his eyes fell and lingered on a lone figure coming out of the Black Heights—Anna.

From the way he was looking at her, I knew immediately that they had an untold story—most likely too tragic and heartbreaking to hear. I gently brushed a hand over his shoulder.

"She was beautiful," Ian said breathlessly. "She still is, but it wasn't just physically. She was one of those rare beauties who are just as beautiful inside as they are outside. She was a gentle soul who loved people and who loved life. She was vibrant, smart and kind…"

"Many have been destroyed by The Shade," I muttered, my own thoughts on Ben, Gwen, Paige and the many innocents ruined by the island.

From just one look at the young men I was with, one could already easily surmise that the embers burning within them were now a full-on fire, ready to set ablaze anything that came in their way. They'd had enough and it seemed thousands of others shared their sentiments.

A sense of tension and excitement filled the atmosphere, but more than that, it was an overwhelming sense of unity that overtook us all. Still, whatever elation we felt was short-lived because we were well-aware that we had a great battle ahead of us—one we had no chance of winning.

When the vampires arrived, it was clear to see that we outnumbered them, but we knew that meant nothing. We would be lucky to even take down a handful of the vampires who arrived under Gregor's command.

Gavin, Ian and I were still standing at the back of the crowd, by the cave entrance. The collective hush that swept over the crowd was enough to tell us that trouble was brewing. Gavin and Ian began to push through the crowd in order to make way for me. I was surprised to find that every time someone saw that it was me they were making way for, they quickly stepped aside—almost as if in reverence. At some point, they were already making way of their own accord, and all Gavin and Ian had to do was stand on either side of me as some sort of protective gesture.

"Why are they looking at me like that?" I muttered under my breath at Gavin when I finally had enough of the way people would look at me and nod their heads in a show of respect.

"You're a legend, Sofia. What happened at the square last night was unheard of…the prince of The Shade thought of you highly enough to take fifty lashes for you—even knowing that he'd just been administered a suppression serum. That's a big deal. The fact that other vampires took on the same punishment for the rest of us, it gives a lot of us something that we thought we could never have."

"Oh, and what's that?" I asked as we finally broke to the crowd and reached the frontlines.

"Hope," Gavin responded before we both took a deep breath in order to peruse what we were up against.

"We definitely need that now…"

About a hundred fully-armed vampires were standing before us. We might've outnumbered them ten to one—perhaps even more, but I was no fool to believe that we could possibly stand a chance against them.

"You…" Gregor sped my way, stopping a couple of inches away from me. "You did this?"

"You're going to have to kill a lot more than just the weak and defenseless if you want to proceed with the culling," I told him, sounding far more confident than I actually felt. "Are you really willing to cripple The Shade by murdering off a good chunk of its loyal human population?"

"Yes, you little fool. I'm willing to do exactly that." He smirked at me and I knew then that he was made of pure evil. I couldn't help but wonder how on earth he could be related to Derek and Vivienne.

I wanted to falter, wanted to run away, but this was my war now.

"You're going to die, Sofia Claremont." Gregor nodded. "I'll make sure of it."

"I know you're immortal, Gregor Novak, but know that we all pass away eventually. At least I will pass away with dignity."

Infuriated, he was about to lunge right for me, but a commotion within the vampires' camp caused him to turn around. I froze when I saw Derek, towing along a good number of the Elite behind him, pushing through the vampires' lines.

He still looked weaker than normal, but definitely a lot stronger than he was when I left him at the Sanctuary. He gave me a look and bowed toward my direction. I wondered if he meant it as a show of deference.

"There will be no culling today or anytime soon," was all Derek said.

Every single soul present stared at him in shock. None of us—myself included—could believe what he was saying.

Gregor stood his ground, fists clenched, staring his son down. "I am king of The Shade, Derek. You answer to me."

"You became king of The Shade out of my respect for you, out of my desire to heed to Vivienne's wishes and keep our family intact. This time, however, I realize that I can no longer serve you. If I'm to fulfill my destiny, then I must rule The Shade." Derek took several steps forward, looking more imposing and authoritative than I'd ever seen him before. "I am commander-in-chief of The Shade's army, father. Consider this our coup d'état. I doubt you'll find many vampires brave enough to go against me in this."

One look at Gregor's face was enough to tell us that he knew what Derek was saying was true. I sincerely thought that it was the first time he realized that the only reason he ever held any real power at The Shade was because of the respect the kingdom had for Derek—not for him.

"You can't do this." He shook his head, still in denial.

I could see in Derek's eyes that the situation was tearing him apart. Gregor, after all, was still his father, but he was doing what he thought ought to be done. My heart went out to him as Derek smiled bitterly. "I just did, Father. You're no longer king of The Shade. I am."

*Awkward* was the only word I could think of to describe what happened next. Gregor walked away and Felix's small contingent of men followed after him. Derek informed everyone that there wasn't going to be a culling and that everyone ought to head back to their normal daily activities. As the crowd dispersed, he reached his hand out to me and squeezed.

"Thank you," I said.

He nodded, but I could see how torn he was. I could only imagine the weight that now fell on his shoulders. He instructed Cameron and Liana to gather up the Elite for a meeting at the dome. The couple nodded and went off to do as instructed.

Xavier lingered, waiting for instructions from their new king. Still clutching my hand, it seemed Derek was in a daze. I wasn't sure if he even fully understood the immensity of what had just happened.

"Are you sure you know what you're doing, Novak?" Xavier asked, giving me a quick glance, as if he were wondering if I had anything to do with what had just occurred.

Derek shook his head. "I haven't got a clue what I'm doing or what I ought to do, but I figured it's time I did what was right—no matter the cost."

At that, I had to gaze up at him in wonderment and admiration. In my eyes, he never stood taller than he did at that moment.

"I've never lied to you, Derek. Not once in the past five hundred years..." Xavier stood to his full height, the features of his handsomely chiseled face taking on a very serious expression.

Derek nodded at his statement, his hand tightening over mine to prepare himself for what his friend was about to say.

"Not everyone will stay loyal to you up to the very end. This will get worse before it gets better—especially if you are unable to secure a supply of human blood for the vampire population."

"I know that, but what I really want to know is whether I'll have your back to the very end—yours, Cameron and Liana's, the Lazaroffs..."

Xavier was silent, weighing his words very carefully before finally nodding. "We started The Shade together. If we have to see it crash and burn, we'll still do it supporting you."

Derek smiled. "That's all I needed to hear. Let's get to that council meeting, shall we?"

"I'll return to The Catacombs." I volunteered, bowing my head and pulling my hand away from him.

He held on tight as he shook his head, pulling me back to his side. "No. As king of The Shade, I want you to become part of the Elite—you, Corrine, Gavin and the other rebel leaders. It's time we brought the humans in when it comes to matters regarding how we're going to run the island."

Both Xavier and I stared at him in surprise. Things were changing fast. Though I felt a sense of accomplishment and pride over what was happening, I also couldn't help but shudder at what was to come, because I knew without a shadow of a doubt that somewhere along the line, Derek was going to pay a very high price for the decisions he was making.

At that realization, I swore to myself that through it all, I would always be by his side.

*Let the sandcastle collapse. In its place, I will build a fortress—one that the waves of nature and time could never destroy.*

Just because he was the only man I knew deserving of it, I was determined to give Derek my forever.

# Chapter 34: Derek

To say that the vampires were adjusting to the new setup we had during council meetings was a huge understatement. The presence of Sofia, Gavin and Ian during council meetings was definitely making it hard for them to concentrate—especially Claudia who'd already had a taste of Gavin's blood.

Even I had to admit that Sofia's presence often made my mind wander off to multiple far off directions when it should have been concentrating on matters concerning The Shade.

Corrine wasn't as much of a temptation, considering how most of us feared her too much to crave her, but she rarely ever attended the council meetings either.

I had already taken the place of my father as king of The Shade and occupied what used to be his seat at the dome. My former place was reserved for him as a show of respect, but he never showed up to any of the meetings either. As far as I knew he kept himself cooped up inside his penthouse, perhaps planning how to take me down.

Sofia took Vivienne's seat. Though I could sense some resentment from several members of the Elite when it came to this move, they kept their mouths shut. After all, no one could question just how much of a voice Sofia had at The Shade. The fact that she was able to inspire a showing of protest the likes of which had never happened before, proved that she had a lot of sway among the human population—thus making her a force to be reckoned with on the island. After all, the fact that the humans greatly outnumbered us was a reality that wasn't lost on any of The Shade's vampires.

Gavin and Ian didn't seem to have any issues or qualms taking their newly assigned positions as ambassadors for the Naturals. It was mostly the vampires that were finding it difficult to be around the two virile young men.

I couldn't help but smile whenever I caught Claudia licking her lips every time she caught sight of Gavin. I could practically imagine the amount of self-control she needed to keep herself from devouring the lad.

During a particular council meeting, I was particularly finding amusement in Claudia's discomfort after Gavin chose to sit right beside her. I was so distracted by it, I was barely paying attention to what Eli was saying as he took the stand.

It wasn't until he cleared his throat and I saw Sofia looking over her shoulders at me that I finally snapped back to attention.

"What? What were you saying?" I asked, forcing myself to focus on Eli.

"I was saying that the chilling chambers are nearly empty of human blood," Eli announced. "If we don't get replenishments soon, we might just end up with another coup—this time, to overturn *you*."

The Shade's blood supply was, of course, the main point of contention at The Shade. I hated discussing the matter, because it felt like something I was incapable of finding a solution to. But it was an issue I couldn't escape.

"Well, we've gone through this matter so many times before. Has anyone been able to offer up a solution?"

The silence was irritating.

"There must be a way," Sofia spoke up to break the silence. "There are thousands of blood banks across the world. Could we not tap into that supply?"

"How, Sofia?" I snapped, sounding harsher than I intended to be. "How on earth are we going to do that?" I bit my lip when I saw a pensive look glaze her eyes. I didn't mean to throw all my negative energy on her, but the pressure was on me and I was definitely feeling it.

I stared longingly at her, hoping to be able to steal some time away with her. Since the day of the coup, I'd hardly been alone in a room with her. In fact, we saw each other mainly during council meetings—to discuss matters of The Shade. The rest of the time, I was either overseeing military trainings, making sure that Gregor and Felix and all other vampires suspected to be loyal to my father were kept under close surveillance, verifying Sofia's genealogical background and generally making sure that my rule at The Shade was secure. It helped that Corrine backed me up by making it known that should anyone overthrow my rule, she would break the spell keeping The Shade hidden.

Sofia, on the other hand, took on her new role as champion of the humans of The Shade in strides. With Gavin and Ian acting as her advisers, she was able to quickly get the pulse of the people in The Catacombs, and get a sense of what they needed. She was also kept busy by making sure that Paige and the rest of the people killed in The Catacombs were given proper memorials.

We were quite a team—Sofia and I, but the demands of the world around us was keeping us apart, stealing time we barely had to begin with away from us.

At that point, with her looking up at me, I found myself keenly aware of how much I missed her, how much I longed for her presence. Without really thinking about it, acting on mere impulse, I stood up and leapt over the steps landing on her level at the dome's balcony. She looked up at me in surprise.

I grabbed her hand before looking at Eli, who was still in his place at the stand. "Eli, look into the possibility of tapping into blood banks' supplies. I expect everyone to give Eli all the support he requires."

"Of course, your high…" Eli paused mid-nod. I'd already requested that they stopped using the royal titles on me. King or not, I much preferred to be called by my own name. Only my father and brother really ever felt the need to use the titles in the first place.

"Sofia, come with me."

"Where are we going?" she asked.

I couldn't help but smile when I heard the hint of breathless excitement in her words. I knew without a doubt that she was excited to be with me too.

"Off to where I can have you to myself."

I didn't need to tell her where that was. We were off to the lighthouse.

# Chapter 35: Sofia

It felt like forever since we'd been in the lighthouse together, and though I was surprised by his impulsive urge to leave the dome and run off to the lighthouse with me, I was thrilled he did it. I missed him so much.

Before he could whisk me off to the Crimson Fortress and make the deadly hundred-foot leap that would lead us to his only sanctuary at The Shade, I requested that we make a stop at my quarters in The Catacombs. It'd been so long since I had Derek all to myself. I really wanted the next few hours to be special.

I wore a green, sleeveless dress that Ashley used to tell me highlighted my eyes. With it, I wore the necklace Derek gave me for my birthday.

The smile that lit up his face when he saw me was enough indication that he appreciated the gesture.

"You like it?" I asked timidly. I felt awkward asking the question, surprised that I was secure enough to believe that he would like me just the same if I were wearing an oversized t-shirt and pajamas.

"Yes," he said. "Very much, but you know you don't have to dress up for me, right?"

"I know, but I want to…I want to look good for you."

He caught his breath and I couldn't keep the smile from my face when he gently laid his hands on my waist and drew me closer. He'd been treating me like a fragile piece of porcelain ever since he told me that he wanted to do things right this time around, to treat me differently than he did the other women in his life. I missed his touch and I knew right then that I wanted to be with him. I wanted what he wanted—for us to find a way to stay together forever.

He kissed me on the forehead, then on my temple, on my cheekbone, on the corner of my lips, before claiming my mouth once again—wooing, alluring, coaxing. He was intoxicating me.

Tears came unbidden. I couldn't stop them. When Derek realized I was crying, he immediately stepped back, afraid that he might've crossed some sort of boundary.

"I'm sorry. Sofia, did I…" He was doing a careful inspection of me, wondering what he could've done wrong.

I chuckled as I shook my head, tears still streaming down my eyes. "Just kiss me, will you, please?!"

Relief replaced the anxiety in his countenance. He was about to once again hold me and draw me close when confusion marred his features. "But why are you crying?"

I grinned as I wiped my tears away. "Please don't force me to say something corny." I giggled as I bridged the gap between us by lifting up on my tippy toes and letting my weight fall on him. I reached forward to press my lips over his, but he pulled his head back.

He scrutinized me before a smirk formed on his lips. "Something *corny*? Like what?"

I rolled my eyes. "You know…the usual sappy stuff…I'm crying because I'm so overcome by joy." I mocked an overdramatized version of typical romantic flicks I'd seen before. "I couldn't hold back the tears because I'm so in love with you…"

He wrinkled his nose. "You're right. That really is corny."

I pouted, then shrugged. "Doesn't make it any less true though, does it?"

He responded with a kiss. By the time our lips managed to part, we were both breathless.

"Let's go to the lighthouse, shall we? Before I end up doing something I'll regret…"

At first, I wondered what he was talking about. It wasn't until after we took the leap down the Crimson Fortress that I realized what he meant. He was going to stay true to his word. He wanted our love chaste and I knew without a doubt that he would never dare take me to his bed again until he married me.

After everything he'd done for me and all the times he stood up for me and fought for me, that was the first time it really sank into me just how much Derek Novak truly loved me. I felt like I'd given up everything for him. I realized that he was willing to do the same for me if he needed to.

Thus, that night, standing in the middle of the lighthouse's octagonal top floor, dancing to the music in his head which he shared with me by humming, my heart leapt when he once again whispered in my ear the same heartfelt plea he gave me on my birthday.

"Marry me, Sofia."

I wrapped my arms around his neck and buried my face against his chest, breathing in his scent, adoring the way his heart was now thumping at a quicker pace than normal. I couldn't even remember why I had hesitated before, because the most sensible thing to respond with was a simple: "Yes."

# Chapter 36: Derek

I couldn't believe my ears. I asked her out of a wishful whim, expecting her to once again decline my request, telling me that what we had could never last forever and that we needed to accept that. I expected her to look at me with those lovely green eyes of hers and tell me that she loved me, but that she was sorry, because she couldn't marry me. She simply couldn't.

But no…what she responded with was something that sounded strangely similar to the word "Yes."

"What?" I asked her, stepping back, so that I could look at her and make sure that she wasn't joking. "Did you just say what I thought you said?"

She laughed at my reaction. "I'm not sure…" She tilted her head to the side, her long auburn locks falling over her shoulders. "What did you think I said?"

"It sounded like you were agreeing to marry me."

She paused and wrinkled her nose before shuffling on her feet. When she heaved an anxious sigh, I was already certain that I was just hearing things.

But then a huge smile broke into her face. "Then you definitely heard right."

I stood there stunned, letting the news sink in, taking in that moment and how stunningly gorgeous she looked in that green silk gown that clung to her curves in just the right places. I wanted to remember every single detail of that moment, because I wanted to treasure it forever.

"Derek, say something..." she said breathlessly.

I had no idea what to say. Was I supposed to thank her for making me the happiest man alive? Was I supposed to once again profess my love for her at the risk of her accusing me of being corny? What was I supposed to say? How was I supposed to express what she made me feel when she agreed to trust me enough to marry me?

"I don't deserve you, Sofia Claremont," were the words that I eventually blurted out. "But I will spend every single day of my life making up for that. I'm so in love with you." I cupped her face with both hands and once again crushed my lips against hers, breathing her scent in, tasting her sweet lips, committing every bit of that moment into my memory.

At some point during the kiss, she began laughing. "We're so corny..." She began shaking her head, before biting her lip and nodding. "But...I'm so in love with you too."

As much as I wanted to fully enjoy that moment and hopefully freeze it so I could live in that moment forever, I couldn't deny that something felt amiss. We were ignoring the fact that I was immortal and that she wasn't. I would forever be eighteen and she wouldn't. I knew I could love her still even if she was already that old woman walking around with a cane, but what kind of life was I offering her?

"Sofia…" I couldn't hide the hesitation and sadness in my tone. "Are you sure you want to do this?"

"Yes, Derek. I wouldn't agree to marry you if I wasn't entirely sure," she assured me, then hesitation sparked in her green eyes. "Are *you* sure?"

"I feel like I'm being selfish with you," I admitted. "Is this really the life you want? I mean, you're this beautiful, vibrant person, strong and wonderful in so many ways…you should be able to find a husband who can give you a normal life, let you have kids, support you and allow you to fulfill your dreams…I want to be with you, but I feel like I'm taking all that away from you."

Every word she said next broke down all my weak attempts to resist the idea of a marriage with her.

"But you're giving me so much more, Derek. *You're* the man I love. *You're* the man I want to be with. I don't want a normal life, Derek. I want to live a life with you."

I didn't know how we were going to make the marriage work. I didn't know how any of it would work out. All I knew was at that moment, we had each other, and that was really all that mattered.

We didn't leave the lighthouse until the next day, determining to just enjoy each other's company and stay away from all the issues that we knew would assault us once we returned to the kingdom. Holding hands with her as we practically skipped our way—like love-struck teenagers—back to The Shade, I wished we could've just stayed at the lighthouse and locked ourselves up in there for as long as we could.

We'd just left the Crimson Fortress when Xavier approached us, worry traced in his eyes.

"What's wrong?" I asked him.

Xavier shifted uncomfortably on his feet. “Ben Hudson is back.”

# Chapter 37: Sofia

I was struggling to wrap my mind around what Xavier had just said.

*Ben's back on this island?*

At first, I was worried for my best friend. Why was he back? Was he alright? With him back, would Claudia be able to keep herself from tearing him into shreds?

When I saw the reaction on Derek's face, however, I realized that we had greater issues to contend with. Ben had joined the hunters. Did he now know how to get back to The Shade? How did he find out? Was he going to compromise The Shade by letting the hunters know? Was he with the hunters now? Should we be gearing up for an attack?

My heart went out to Derek. He already had so much on his plate, so many issues to deal with…I knew that the additional burden of wondering whether or not The Shade was still safe with Ben back was something he didn't really need nor want.

I squeezed his hand to let him know I was there for him. "Everything's going to be alright," I assured him.

He held my hand in a firm grip and looked me straight in the eye. "With him back, does it change anything?"

I narrowed my eyes at him. "I can't believe you'd even ask me that question, Derek. Nothing's changed," I assured him.

Xavier was staring at us like we'd gone mad. "We're holding him at the port," he informed. "We had no idea what to do with him. We weren't sure if you'd agree to have him brought into the island. I've sent scouts around the island, and as far as we aware, he arrived alone."

Derek nodded. "I'll go to the port to speak with him. You coming, Sofia?"

He gave me a look that was practically begging me not to go, but I wasn't going to miss out on seeing Ben. He was still my best friend, someone who mattered dearly to me, so I nodded. "Yes. I'm going."

Derek didn't bother to hide the disappointment in his face, but understood me enough to know that he could do little to dissuade me from going.

Once we reached the port, an underwater facility that contained cells where new arrivals were held before they were allowed to enter the island, we were immediately brought to the cell where they were keeping Ben.

The moment we arrived, he stood up from the cot where he'd been seated. His eyes first fell on Derek and I watched him for a trace of the usual hatred he had whenever he looked at the prince of The Shade, but there was none of it. Ben just looked from Derek to me and once his eyes were on me, they stayed there.

Derek stared for a while before shaking his head. "I can't stand this. I'll be speaking with you in a while and I expect you to answer all my questions truthfully, but for now, before we get into the nitty-gritty of your sudden appearance here, I'm going to leave Sofia with you. I know that you two will want to spend time alone."

Ben seemed sincerely grateful. "Thank you."

Derek just grunted and nodded before leaving us on our own. I knew how Ben's presence was eating at him. Ben, after all, was the reason I'd decided to leave The Shade before. I couldn't blame him for being threatened that Ben was back, but I was also peeved. I'd just agreed to marry him. Was that not assurance enough that I was his?

Derek kissed my cheek. "You'll be alright?" he asked.

I smiled and nodded. "I'll be fine, Derek. We'll call if we need anything."

Derek and Xavier left, shutting the door behind them.

The moment I was finally alone with Ben, all I could think to do was stare at him. It felt like an eternity since I'd last seen him. His blonde hair was now shaved. He looked a lot more buff, stronger, bigger. He also appeared to have matured in likeness. Still, he was just as handsome as I remembered him to be.

It took me a while to finish studying him. When my gaze fell on his blue eyes and saw them moist with tears, I was taken aback. I had no idea what to say to him or even how to conduct myself around him.

"How've you been, Ben?" I managed to croak out. I hated the awkwardness we had between us. It was never this way before.

"I've been better," he admitted, his fists clenching as he said the words. "And you? Has he been treating you well?"

"Derek?" Just saying my fiancé's name put a smile on my face. "I just agreed to marry him. I guess that should answer your question."

I expected a violent reaction from my best friend, but apart from the spark of surprise in his eyes, he just nodded with resignation and said, "I'm happy for you."

His reaction was enough for me to realize that something had changed in him and I wondered what could have happened to bring about such a change. "Why are you here, Ben?" So many questions were whirling in my mind regarding his return to The Shade and I had no idea where to begin. "How could you have possibly known how to get here? Ben, please...you can't give away the location of The Shade to the hunters..."

"I really just wanted to see you, Sofia, find out if you're alright, if he's treating you the way you deserve to be treated." The longing that I saw in his eyes as he stared at me made my heart ache on his behalf. "I missed you so much."

No matter how much I tried to harden my heart against him, to try and figure out why he was at The Shade out of instinct to protect the man I loved, Ben still mattered too much to me, and I couldn't help the tear from running down my cheek as my shoulders sagged. "I missed you too, Ben."

He spread his arms in a welcoming gesture and I quickly responded by running to him for an embrace. I sobbed as I nuzzled my face against his neck. "I thought you'd never be able to forgive me for leaving."

"I did too," he admitted, "but you're Sofia. You'll always be my Rose Red and I couldn't bear the idea of always being resentful of you. I realize now that you were right to leave. It seems Derek Novak deserves you far more than I ever will."

I could sense the sincerity in his words and despite all the qualms I had over his sudden appearance at the island, I could honestly say to myself that I was glad to have Ben back.

# Chapter 38: Derek

I was anxiously pacing the floor right outside the cell where I'd left Sofia and Ben.

"You just left them there?" Xavier asked. "Without even bothering to interrogate the lad?"

"Shush," I snapped at him.

He was my second-in-command when it came to all military matters at The Shade and I was expecting him to question my judgment over why on earth I would leave Ben—an obvious risk to the island—to have a grand reunion with Sofia, who in truth was also a risk to the island. Despite what Xavier might have been thinking, however, I hadn't gone entirely mad. I still had my protective instincts toward The Shade completely intact. I wanted to listen in on every word coming out of both Sofia and Ben's mouths. I felt bad not trusting Sofia and eavesdropping on her conversation with her best friend, but I couldn't help but give in to the temptation to do it.

If I was to be completely honest with myself, I knew that my reasons for eavesdropping on them weren't purely because of my desire to keep the island safe. Ben was the only person who had ever posed a real threat to what I had with Sofia. The fact that he would just suddenly show up at The Shade right after Sofia became my fiancée rubbed me the wrong way.

Beyond that, the onslaught of fears that came with his appearance was something I could not deny.

Of course, whatever fears I had completely washed away when Sofia made it known to Ben that she had agreed to marry me. I was expecting the young man to react with anger. He had never liked me after all, but I was surprised—and made suspicious—by his reaction.

I couldn't believe my ears when he told Sofia that he thought I deserved her more than he did. *Why exactly is this man back here? Risking his life to return "just to see Sofia" seems too good to be true.* Unable to hold myself back, I barged inside the room in time to see them withdrawing from an embrace. The idea that he was touching Sofia—much more hugging her—made me sick with jealousy.

*Rein yourself in, Novak. Don't do anything you'll regret,* I reminded myself as I tried to look unbothered by their embrace. I kept repeating in my head that they were best friends and that it was perfectly normal for them to hug each other after being apart for so long.

"Derek?" Sofia cast me a questioning look. "We were just talking and…"

I shook my head. "You don't have to explain. I understand. You understand that I do need to interrogate, Ben? I know he's your friend, but the threat he poses to the island is too great to ignore."

Sofia nodded. "Of course."

I shifted my attention to Ben, expecting to find the usual haughty and defiant expression on his face. Instead, he just seemed…exhausted and somewhat jaded by the time that had passed since he last stepped foot on this island.

I gestured toward a small wooden chair in one corner of the small room. "You may take a seat."

He shook his head. "I prefer to stand, thank you."

I leaned my back against one of the walls. From the corner of my eye, I could make out Sofia taking a seat on the edge of the cot. Xavier was leaning against one post of the open door. All attention was now on our unexpected visitor.

"I understand that you're a hunter now?" I asked as I crossed my arms over my chest.

Ben nodded. "Yes. That's correct."

"That makes you a threat to us. Do the hunters know about the location of The Shade?"

"No one knows I'm here."

"And I should just believe you?"

"I don't care what you believe or don't believe, Novak. Prepare for a hunter attack for all I care, strengthen your defenses, put everyone on alert if you must. I'm telling you that it's a waste of time. If the hunters knew about the island, then it would have been blown to pieces by now. They don't care about all the humans you have here. They just want you dead."

That they wouldn't think twice about blowing up the island was something I could believe. *It's what I would've done if I were still a hunter.* It was how the hunters operated. Collateral damage and the loss of human life were acceptable as long as they fulfilled the mission of wiping out every single vampire from the face of the earth.

"How did you make your way back to the island, Ben? How could you have known how to return here?"

"Your brother, Lucas, sent me," Ben said flatly.

"Why on earth would Lucas Novak risk his own neck to contact a hunter and make him come here?" I narrowed my eyes, trying to understand what my older brother's motivations could possibly be.

"He wants Sofia out of here. He was threatening to kill my family—my father, my mother and my little sister. Although that was a bluff. I'm sure he's aware that the families of hunters are always closely monitored; he'd be a fool to come within a mile of our house. He got in touch with me through Natalie Borgia. He sent me here to coax Sofia out of the island."

He said every word with such blunt honesty, it felt like a huge blow to my senses. "So all this time, my brother is still after Sofia."

# Chapter 39: Ben

"He doesn't trust me," I told Sofia as she laid a plate of stir-fried vegetables on top of the wooden table inside her quarters in The Catacombs.

"Of course he doesn't." Sofia shrugged nonchalantly. "Why on earth would Derek trust you? Nobody here trusts you, Ben. No one has any reason to trust you."

"Not even you?" I asked, swallowing back my hurt, knowing how much truth rang in her words.

Loose strands of her auburn hair fell to her face as she sat across the table from me. "I want to trust you, but I have so many questions running through my mind. I just…am I really supposed to believe that you had a complete turnaround and are now willing to protect The Shade?"

"I have no desire to protect The Shade, Sofia," I clarified. "I still want to have my vengeance on Claudia. I still want to see her die for what she did to me. The only reason I'm here is because I want to make sure you're alright. I want to make sure that he's treating you right. Lucas was the only way I could get to you. If I was going to betray The Shade, I already would've done that."

"Well, now that you're here and you've seen me, I guess you can see that I'm perfectly fine, that Derek has treated me well. Now what?"

I stared at her in wonderment. After Derek released me and allowed me to go to The Catacombs with Sofia—under close surveillance at *all* times—Sofia, Ashley and Rosa had updated me on what'd been happening at The Shade since Sofia's arrival. I was saddened by the news of Paige's murder, shocked by Ashley's choice to get turned into a vampire and moved by the stories about the culling and how Derek stood up for Sofia at the town square. More than anything, however, I was stunned by what Sofia had been able to accomplish at The Shade.

"She's practically the princess of The Shade now," Ashley had said proudly, as she cast an affectionate gaze toward Sofia.

"She's about to become the queen." Rosa smiled as she fingered the ring on Sofia's finger. Derek had given it to her shortly after he released me from the port.

The sight of the ring made my heart ache with a sense of loss as I wondered what could've been if I'd done things differently, if I had been the one who treated Sofia the way she deserved to be treated.

Every time I looked at Sofia, I couldn't help but regret how things turned out between us. I felt the same way as I had supper with her.

"Stop looking at me that way, Ben," she said as she took a sip from a spoonful of soup.

"What way?" I asked.

"I don't know…you look at me a certain way, Ben. Like you've somehow lost me…"

I cleared my throat. "Am I that transparent?"

"I just know you, Ben. That's all. You feel like if you don't get something you want, you did something wrong. The fact that I'm with Derek right now has nothing to do with you. You couldn't have done things differently and expected things not to turn out as they have now. Some things are just meant to be."

"And you think you and Derek were always meant to be?"

She nodded. "Yes. He's the love of my life."

The words stung and she knew it, but I appreciated her honesty.

"You saw me when no one else did, Ben. You took care of me all throughout high school and you made the worst nine years of my life livable. I love you, Ben."

"But not the way you love him."

"Why do you keep on tormenting yourself?"

I needed to change the subject. I debated with myself then whether or not to tell Sofia that her father was running the hunters' headquarters in the USA. I had no idea how she would react. I decided not to tell her just yet. *Not now, there will be time later.*

Sofia kept quiet as she finished her meal. When she was done, she laid her spoon over her plate and looked straight at me.

"I can't explain how great it is to see you again, Ben, but your presence here terrifies me, because the man I love is fighting to keep this island protected. You're a threat to him and that makes you a threat to me."

I looked straight at her, surprised that I meant every word when I said, "If you're on his side, Sofia, then so am I."

# Chapter 40: Derek

We were at my penthouse. I was leaning back over the edge of my living room couch and Sofia had her back leaned against my chest. I absentmindedly played with the ends of her hair, my thoughts occupied by Ben and the recent reports from Eli about the possibility of tapping into the supplies of blood banks.

"Do you trust him?" I asked Sofia. It'd been three days since Ben's arrival.

She nodded her head. "I want to. If he's still anything like the Ben I knew, then he seems sincere…but Derek, I'm worried about his family…little Abby is the sort of girl Lucas would love to sink his teeth into. Ben is convinced Lucas poses no threat to them, but you know how scheming your brother is."

"I know you see them as family, but I'm not going to risk losing you on their behalf." My hand tightened around her waist, fearing that she'd act on a whim and do something stupid.

"What are we going to do then, Derek?"

"I think we have no choice but to trust Ben and trust that the hunters are fully capable of keeping his family safe."

She licked her lips, worry evident in her green eyes. "I have a very bad feeling about all this, Derek."

"So do I…but what I know for sure is that you cannot—under any circumstances—step out of this island. If Lucas is out to get you…" The thought sickened me. After everything Lucas had already put Sofia through, losing her to him was something that I could never allow to happen. "I think it's best to have you stay here at the penthouse with me for now?"

To my relief, she agreed. "I think that's best for now." She paused. "I'm scared, Derek."

I couldn't deny the truth. "So am I."

# Chapter 41: Lucas

I was staying at a hotel in Cancun, a place I detested. I hated how sunny and full of life it was, but it was one of the coasts closest to The Shade. It was also the same place where I'd found Sofia, so I figured it just might bring me some luck.

I couldn't wait for evening to come, and when it did, I immediately prepared myself to go out on a hunt for some lovely young women I could feast on that night. I was about to leave the room when I heard a knock at my door.

I opened the door and smirked. *Natalie.*

"Seems you can't get enough of me these days, Natalie..."

"Not my fault messages for you keep on coming." She brushed right past me and went straight to the bar and poured herself a glass of wine. The lovely Italian vixen then retrieved an envelope from her purse. "From Claudia."

I raised a brow. I wasn't expecting any correspondence from

Claudia. I ripped the seal off the envelope and took out a short note. An onslaught of curses flowed from my lips as I read the message: *It looks like your boy, Ben, has now joined Derek and Sofia's bandwagon. Your brother is now king of The Shade, and is about to make your pretty redhead his queen. He overthrew your father as king with a coup.*

"You don't look very happy," Natalie commented. "News from home not that good?" She took another sip from her wine. "But wait a minute…where's your home exactly, Lucas? Is it The Shade or is it The Oasis?"

I grimaced. *I'll have no home if I don't get Sofia out of The Shade and into The Oasis. In fact, I won't need a home, because Borys Maslen will have my head.*

Things were definitely not going according to plan, but it was clear that I now had two allies at The Shade: Claudia and my father. I had been certain that Ben would side with me, but it seemed that wasn't the case. *I never should've underestimated Derek's powers of persuasion, but then it probably wasn't his charm that turned Ben. Sofia really is a cunning little minx.*

"Do you have a message you want me to bring to Claudia?" Natalie asked, finishing off her wine. "This is awful," she commented, wrinkling her nose. The Italian was known to have grown up in vast and lush vineyards. She definitely knew her wines.

I, on the other hand, still could not fend off the annoyance I felt toward her—especially when I found out about the fondness she had for my brother. Still, Natalie Borgia was necessary to my existence and I knew I couldn't mess with her.

"Well?" she asked, tapping her foot on the carpeted floor impatiently.

"Give me a couple of minutes." I took out a piece of paper and began scribbling a simple message on it. I folded the paper twice and handed it over to Natalie. "Make sure only Claudia and my father see this."

Natalie stared at the piece of paper as if she were afraid it would morph into a viper. I knew that was exactly how she saw me: a snake. Still, it wasn't her job to interfere or condemn. Her job was to bridge the gap between vampire covens. It was clear to see that she didn't like the idea of helping me, but she really didn't have a choice. Interfering would compromise her position as the rogue vampire whom everybody could trust.

I smirked as I watched Natalie take the paper, nod and leave. I was nervous about what was to come, but at the same time, I found myself full of anticipation. The thought of once again having Sofia Claremont in my grasp was all the encouragement I needed.

*If everything goes according to plan, Sofia will be in Borys Maslen's hands by the end of the week and once she's at The Oasis, she'll be within my reach and far from Derek's.*

# Chapter 42: Sofia

*Pulse quickening, heart thumping, I kept on running through pitch-black darkness with no idea where I came from, where I was or where I was going. All I knew was that I had to run, because this overwhelming feeling of dread told me that if I stopped at any point, it would be the end of me. Thus, I kept running. When I saw light shining from a distance, slowly lighting my blackened surroundings, hope surged within me. I was just about to reach the light when a small voice called out to me.*

*"Sofia..." the voice said—small and frail, "you're back."*

*I turned around and saw a little girl standing a few feet away from me. Her green eyes and knotted red hair eerily reminded me of myself. "Hello," I greeted her. "What are you doing here?"*

*She walked toward the light and I gasped when I realized that she was me.*

*"I'm scared," she told me.*

*"Why?" I asked. "Why are you scared?"*

*Her lips began to quiver and her hand moved toward her neck before letting her fingers fiddle with a pendant hanging under a golden chain around her neck. I walked closer to this smaller version of myself, wondering what was bothering her.*

*"You don't have to be scared..." I told her.*

*She shook her head. "No. I should be afraid. Very afraid." She let go of the pendant and I realized that it was mine—the diamond one that Derek had given me for my birthday.*

*"Who gave you that necklace?" I asked her.*

*"It's mine." She pouted.*

*"Yes, but who gave it to you?"*

*"It doesn't matter now." Tears began streaming down her face as she shook her head. Suddenly, the diamond pendant changed into a large heart-shaped ruby red pendant.*

*I could feel the blood drain from my face as I heard a piercing scream fill the air, followed by the sound of glass shattering. I then saw a glimpse of Vivienne running from light to darkness, screaming, "How dare he! How dare he!"*

I sat up in bed. I was breaking into a cold sweat and trembling uncontrollably. The alarming sense of fear was taking over all of me. The little girl in my dream—the little girl whom I was sure was a younger version of me—was still etched in my mind.

I could remember clearly the significance of the ruby red pendant based on one of the memories Vivienne shared to me—one of Xavier handing her a velvet pouch, telling her that it was a gift from Borys Maslen. When Vivienne retrieved the heart-shaped pendant from the pouch, she was livid. I'd always known Vivienne as this calm, collected person who sometimes seemed cold and heartless, so to see her so hot with fury was hard to forget.

"Sofia?" A voice came from the other side of the door after a timid knock. "Are you alright?" The door creaked open and someone peeked in. I was hoping that it would be Derek, but it was Ben.

I must've looked frightened out of my senses because he immediately stepped into the guest room and climbed on the bed next to me.

"What happened?" he asked, gently brushing his hand over my hair.

"It's nothing. I just had an awful nightmare..." I pulled my knees up, embracing them against my chest. I gingerly looked at him. "What are you doing here?"

"I came to visit you... I kept on knocking, but no one was answering, so I just let myself in. Rosa told me that you spent the night here. I could hear you screaming from outside..."

I hated how much I doubted him, wondering if what he had told me was true. I wondered if Claudia even knew that he was around. I hadn't seen the crazy, blonde vampire since the last council meeting.

It then dawned on me. *Where's Derek?* If Ben was knocking, Derek would've heard it. He was a very light sleeper. *If I'd been screaming because of my nightmare, he would've heard.*

"I need to go find Derek..." I motioned to get off the bed.

"Wait." Ben grabbed my wrist and held on tight.

"Ben?" I actually felt nervous. Suddenly, being alone in the same bedroom with my best friend didn't feel safe. "Let go of my wrist."

He looked surprised, and even hurt, by my reaction. "I'm sorry. I don't mean to be rough. You're obviously shaken." He got off the bed and stepped away from me. "I just wanted to tell you that just as I crossed the walkway leading to your bedroom, I saw Derek's father enter the penthouse. He's in the living room, and I don't know...something's not right. I don't trust him, Sofia."

I laughed wryly. "Yeah? That makes two of us." I had no idea what was going on, but I was sure about one thing: Ben was right.

Something was wrong.

Something was *very* wrong.

# Chapter 43: Derek

*Clad in a glowing white dress, Sofia held a bouquet of white roses as she marched across the aisle. The only ornaments that graced her were beautiful pearl earrings and the diamond necklace I had given her. She was a vision to behold—just as I imagined she would be on our wedding day.*

*Her smile was enough sunlight to brighten up the darkness that had been my life. She was my life and she was about to become mine, bearing my name, making it known to the world that we intended for our love to last far longer than they ever gave it credit for. However, it seemed fate had other things in mind.*

*She was halfway down the aisle when she suddenly stopped, panic evident in her eyes. Blood began to trickle from two small holes in her neck and she began to breathe in pants as she held on to her neck.*

*I immediately ran toward her the moment I saw the bouquet of flowers fall onto the ground. To my horror, the diamond pendant she was wearing morphed into a heart-shaped ruby red one. I didn't understand what it all meant, but I didn't have to. It was clear that something wasn't right.*

*When I reached Sofia, she looked at me, her eyes wide with terror. She swallowed hard as tears began to run down her face. "I'm scared, Derek."*

*And just like that, she was gone.*

Eyes still shut, I tossed and turned in my bed, half-asleep and half-awake. The terrified look on Sofia's eyes still etched into my brain. I knew that something was wrong and that I had to do something about it, but I was still in a state of limbo, trapped in the place between wakefulness and dreams. I knew I was mumbling something even as I shifted on the bed, but I couldn't quite make out what I was saying.

Then a feminine voice said my name. "Shh…everything's going to be alright, Derek. Relax."

I could feel the bed shift and I knew then that I wasn't alone. Warm lips began to press against mine and I found myself breathlessly saying the name of the girl in my dream. "Sofia…"

"Yes…Sofia…"

I was conscious enough to know that the woman in my bed wasn't her, but it all still felt like a dream. I wanted to snap out of it, but it was almost like I was trapped in that state, unable to get out. When the lips pressing against mine pulled away, I forced my eyes open.

Blinking several times until my vision cleared, seeing who was lying on my bed was like a blow in the gut. *Claudia.*

She smiled and before I could even react, she stabbed a large syringe right into my veins. "I'm sorry, Derek, but you made a big mistake the day you treated me like your whore."

The last thing I could remember was the crazed and manic look on Claudia's face as I drifted off into unconsciousness. Just before I completely faded away, I could hear Sofia's voice croak out the same way she did in the dream, "I'm scared, Derek."

And by instinct, I knew that when I woke up from the sleep that Claudia had put me in, Sofia would be gone.

# Chapter 44: Sofia

At the sight of me, Gregor stood up and slightly bowed his head. He had a smile on his face—calm and unnerving. All I wanted to do was get as far away from him as possible.

"Derek's not here," I told him. "I haven't seen him since I woke up."

Gregor looked at Ben, who was standing right behind me. "Is he aware that you're with your lover boy over here?"

"What do you want, Gregor?"

He smirked. "I want you out of this island, Sofia. What else would I want?"

"Well, I'm here to stay."

"No, darling. You're not," a feminine voice from behind me spoke up. I didn't need to turn around to know who it was. *Claudia.*

Before I could even react, Gregor lunged for Ben, and Claudia had already tackled me to the ground, her hands around my neck.

"Derek!" I screamed.

"Your king is back to sleep for the moment, Sofia." Claudia grinned before stabbing me in the neck with a syringe. Panic took over as I watched Gregor do the same thing to Ben. A sob escaped my lips as complete dread took over every fiber of my being. I tried to struggle against Claudia, but I knew that there was nothing I could do. I just drifted off into unconsciousness, dreading the thought of Derek waking up to find me gone.

When I came to, it was clear to see that I was no longer at The Shade. I was lying in the middle of a king-sized bed with soft white linen sheets. I looked around the torch-lit room and was relieved to find it empty.

*Where am I?* I sat up on the bed, my head feeling rather hollow. I cringed when I realized what I was wearing—a one-shoulder white dress that went down to my knees. The fabric was so thin, it was practically sheer. The intricate beading it had, however, spoke of the richness of the material. I trembled to think of where I was and what my purpose was for being there.

It seemed I was about to get answers to the questions filling my mind, because the door swung open and Lucas stepped in.

"You're awake!" he exclaimed delightfully.

"Where am I? What have you done to me? What are you going to do to me?" I spluttered.

"Always so many questions, huh, Sofia?"

I glared at him in response.

He rolled his eyes. "You're at The Oasis. If you don't know what that is, it's the home of the Maslens. We're in the middle of the desert now, Sofia."

*The Maslens...* Tears began to brim my eyes. The thought was horrifying.

"What have I done to you?" He smirked. "Well, the question I think should be what do I *want* to do with you, but I'll spare you those details? Sadly, as much as I wanted to have my way with you, I had to bring you to Borys Maslen unscathed. He wanted you to remain a virgin until the night of your wedding to him. Now, for you final question, I'm about to take you to your betrothed, Sofia."

I was finding it hard to take in the information that I'd just been given. My mind was whirling. "Why would you do this?" was all I could manage to ask.

"You ruined my life, Sofia. I'm about to ruin yours." He lunged forward, pushing me down on the bed, and letting his weight fall on top of me. He then whispered right into my ear, "Make no mistake about it, Sofia…after your wedding night, I *will* have my way with you. I still remember how sweet your blood is. I would've taken a bite during the journey back here, but there was no way I could have hidden the scars from Borys."

I trembled beneath him as I began to get a better picture of the life I was about to lead should things go the way they planned. "Derek's going to come for me."

He laughed. "Oh baby, that's exactly what we're counting on."

He got off me and none-too-gently yanked me upward out of the bed, forcing me to stand up on my feet. He looked at me from head to foot.

"We're going to have to do something about the hair. It's a mess. Otherwise, you're good to go."

He clapped his hands and several women stepped in.

"Prepare her," Lucas ordered, a smirk on his face, as he stood back and watched as they began to fix my hair and straighten out my clothes. I could feel his eyes on me, raking over my body. I shuddered at the thought of being in the same room with him, remembering all the torment he put me through when we were still at The Shade.

Still, it seemed Lucas was the least of my worries. I'd never met Borys Maslen before, but Vivienne's memories told me enough about him to know that he was bad news. I couldn't wrap my mind around the idea of being his "betrothed." *Why would he even want me?*

I then remembered Gregor's revelation back at the town square. After everything that happened following the whipping at the square, I'd barely given his pronouncement that Ingrid Maslen was my mother any thought. I thought the whole while that he was just bluffing. Since Derek never brought it up, I just assumed that I was right.

*I guess I'm about to find out.*

Once satisfied that I looked good enough to present to Borys, Lucas waved everyone off and walked toward me. "You ready?"

"No."

He just laughed. "Well, it's not like it matters if you're ready or not..." He held the small of my back and pushed me forward. "This is going to be fun."

We walked through eery torch-lit corridors surrounded by dusty brick walls. We weaved through hallway after hallway until we stopped in front of a large, arched door.

Lucas pushed the door open and led me into a large courtroom. A lone figure could be seen in the middle of it. He was seated on a tall black throne, made up of what looked like human skulls. At the sight of me, he stood on his feet, his dark eyes lighting up as he licked his lips.

I immediately assumed that he was Borys Maslen. He didn't look like I thought he would. I'd expected him to look like the Novaks. He had muddy brown hair, and a stocky, wide, muscular physique.

He looked like he could crush me with his bare hands if he wanted to.

"So this is *my* Sofia." He smiled as Lucas pushed me forward, forcing me to approach the throne. "It's about time you came to me, my dear betrothed."

"I'm *not* your betrothed," I spat out. The notion was sickening.

"Actually, Sofia," a feminine voice came out through the deep burgundy curtains behind Borys' throne, "you are his betrothed." A beautiful woman emerged from behind the curtains and it was clear to see who she was. *Ingrid Maslen.*

Tears began to flow down my eyes at the sight of her. *Gregor was telling the truth. It's my mother.*

"She looks so happy to see you, Ingrid." Borys tilted his head to the side.

I couldn't even bear looking at him. My eyes were glued on my mother as questions began to flood my mind. "Mom?"

"Yes, Sofia." She smiled at me. "It's me. Your mother. I gave you to Borys a long time ago. You are rightfully his."

I had no idea how to cope with all the information being thrown my way, but two things I was still certain about: my mother was indeed crazy and there was no way that I belonged to Borys.

I managed to pry my eyes away from Ingrid, or whatever she called herself nowadays, and look at the man who was claiming me as his. I felt nothing but disgust toward him. I gathered all the courage I could muster and smirked at him. "You're too late." I raised my hand and showed them the ring Derek had given me. "I'm already married to Derek Novak."

It wasn't a difficult lie to tell, because it was almost true. Derek was already my fiancé and it was him whom I belonged with.

Borys' face colored into a deep, beet red. He lunged forward, until he was standing right in front of me, grabbing my jaw. "You lie!" he accused.

I kept the smirk on my face. "You can check if you want. He's already taken me to his bed. Many times." At least that part was true. I could almost sense the surprise coming from Lucas. I wondered why he thought Derek would never take me to his bed and realized that Lucas knew that I was different from the beginning, knew that Derek never touched me while I was initially at The Shade.

To my surprise, Borys took out his frustration on Lucas. He let go of my jaw and threw Lucas against a wall. "How dare your brother touch what is mine! First, he takes Vivienne away from me, now he has soiled my betrothed!"

I winced when he grabbed a clump of Lucas' hair and hit him right across the face.

"Borys, my dear, that's enough." Ingrid sounded almost bored. "You're scaring my daughter."

Borys hit Lucas one more time before turning his attention toward me once again. He grabbed my waist and pulled my body against his, yanking me like a rag doll. His free hand began groping me roughly as he pressed his lips against my cheek. I screamed with pain and terror when his claws came out of the hand that was touching my thigh, sinking into my skin as he scratched my thigh upward and drew blood.

Once satisfied that he had drawn enough blood, he used both his arms to wrap around me so tightly it felt as if he wanted to crush my ribs. He whispered into my ear, "Derek might've already had you before I could, but I still want you, Sofia Claremont. Don't worry. I'm going to make him pay for what he did to you, for taking you away from me. Once I make a widow out of you, you're going to be mine, Sofia—just as you were always meant to be."

He then let go of me and pushed me to the ground. Delight sparked in his eyes when he saw the blood trickling down my thighs. I knew then that I was facing one sadistic man, and I could only shudder to think of all the horrors that Vivienne had to go through under his rule.

"Heal your daughter," he instructed Ingrid. "I'll see to it that everyone prepares for my wedding." A spark of glee showed in his eyes. "We have to make sure that Derek Novak gets an invitation."

# Chapter 45: Ben

When I opened my eyes, the first thing I felt was a sharp pain in the right side of my head. I tried to remember what had just happened, and could recall Gregor Novak hitting me on the head with a hard object. After that, everything was a daze. I sat up, feeling slightly dizzy, and noticed that I was lying on a couch, my wrists cuffed behind my back.

I looked around the room and immediately saw Sofia, sitting over the edge of a large bed, her hand cuffed to the bed's railings. It was clear to see from the tear stains on her cheeks and her swollen eyes that she'd been crying.

"Sofia? What happened? Where are we?"

She shook her head. "I'm not sure. Lucas says that we're in Egypt, a place called The Oasis."

I drew a breath. The Oasis was the stuff of legends. It'd been one of the hunters' main quests to find it, because it was rumored to be the Maslen coven's hideout. I wondered then why on earth Gregor and Claudia would bring us to the Maslens. That's when what Sofia had said fully registered in my mind. *That would mean they'd been working with Lucas all along, and Lucas had been working with the Maslens?*

"Why would they bring us here?" I asked Sofia. "The Novaks and the Maslens are known enemies…"

"I don't know why Lucas would work with the Maslens after what Borys did to his sister, but he's a twisted, sick man… so I can't pretend to try and understand the way his mind works."

I studied Sofia and noticed the blood stains on her dress. Panic gripped me. "What did they do to you? Sofia…"

"It was Borys Maslen. He clawed through my thighs. He has this notion that I'm meant to be his, that I'm his betrothed…" her voice hitched. "They're going to force me to marry that sick, sadistic bastard, Ben. They're sending Derek a wedding invitation."

"Derek Novak isn't a fool. He knows that you love him. He's not going to believe that you're in this wedding out of your own will."

"I know that," she assured me. "They're using the wedding—using *me*—to trap him. I think the Maslens want to take over The Shade." She began to sob uncontrollably.

I wanted to run to her and pull her into my arms, assure her that everything was going to be okay and that all would work out fine, but I couldn't do that. I wasn't sure about what was happening or what was going to happen.

"Ben, I don't know what I would do if anything happened to Derek," she managed to say in between sobs. "I wouldn't know how to live with myself. I'm terrified."

I stared at her, my heart breaking on her behalf. I wondered if she'd ever cried for me the way that she did for him. I remembered all the times that I'd caught him looking at her and the way she'd looked at him. As I sat there watching my best friend break down over the man that she loved, I couldn't help but be amazed over the amount of sacrifice Derek and Sofia were willing to make for each other.

It was the first time I truly began to accept that Derek and Sofia were meant for each other, and I knew then that nothing in the world could keep Derek Novak from storming The Oasis to get Sofia back.

"Derek is known to be the most powerful vampire alive, Sofia. If he comes, he's going to put up a good fight and considering that it's you who's involved, I think it's the Maslens who have reason to tremble. Don't underestimate the man you love, Rose Red."

She looked at me with hopeful eyes. It seemed the words were enough to console her.

"Everything's going to be okay, Sofia. I know it." As I said the words, I realized that I now meant every word. It gave me a sense of resignation, but also a sense of fulfillment, to know that she was in good hands, that my best friend really had found her true love in the person of Derek Novak.

Though I was still filled with dread over what she might possibly go through at The Oasis, a part of me was happy for her, knowing that unlike me, she would live her life knowing that she loved and that she was loved in return.

# Chapter 46: Derek

Since Sofia's disappearance, I'd been turning The Shade upside down trying to find her. It helped that she was so loved by the citizens of The Shade, because their full cooperation was immediately given to me the moment news that she was no longer on the island came out.

During a council meeting called specifically to discuss what to do in order to find Sofia, I found myself losing hope.

"She most likely eloped with the boy." Felix leaned back on his seat, not bothering to hide how bored he was by the entire thing.

At that, Gavin scoffed, earning himself Felix's ire.

I shook my head. "No. She wouldn't do that to me."

"Then maybe your father was right. She's in league with the Maslens and she's probably now at The Oasis cavorting with her mother and their king. We all know she has a taste for royalty." Felix eyed me pointedly.

"For crying out loud, Felix," Cameron interrupted in his distinct

Scottish accent. "Will you shut up for a moment? Do you not think before you speak?"

I was trying to reel my temper in, and was thankful that Cameron butted in on behalf of me. "It is true that Ingrid Maslen is Sofia's mother. Eli's background checks have already proven this as true, but I know Sofia. I know for a fact that she had no idea that Camilla Claremont became a vampire. I believe her father tried to protect her from the knowledge."

"We know Claudia has something to do with their disappearance, obviously, since she's the one who tranquilized Derek," Liana spoke up. "And I suspect Gregor is involved too. It's too much of a coincidence that they would both disappear the same time Ben and Sofia did."

"My thoughts exactly," Gavin agreed. "Sofia is far too loyal to The Shade or perhaps more to *you*." He gestured toward me."To leave The Shade out of her own accord."

"The arrival of the human boy…this friend of hers…changes everything and we know it." Felix frowned. "He might have been working with Lucas all along and they might have been communicating with Claudia and Gregor."

"You're Gregor's right hand man, Felix," Gavin butted in. "Don't you know what he's been up to?"

Felix frowned. It was clear to see that the fact that my father made a move without his knowledge wasn't something that he was entirely pleased with.

"Why would Claudia turn her back on us?" Xavier spoke up, ignoring Felix entirely.

"I know Claudia has several scores to settle with you," Yuri spoke up, looking at me with a hint of accusation. "You took Ben from her, you had her punished simply for defying you, then you shortened her sentence after sleeping with her. Does that sum up all the things that would give her a reason to hold a grudge against you?"

I grimaced. Claudia may not be the most shining example of a good-hearted vampire, but I had to admit that neither was I, and it was true that I'd wronged her in the worst possible way when I visited her cell and ended up sleeping with her. I knew immediately that I'd made a mistake when I told her that I'd shorten her sentence. I regretted it, and I regretted never apologizing to her properly for it.

I looked Yuri in the eye. "I never intended to sleep with her. It happened, and I offered to shorten her sentence without thinking it through. I should've apologized."

"Well, it's too late now, isn't it?" Yuri narrowed his eyes at me.

"I wronged Claudia and I'm sorry for that, but make no mistake about it, Yuri, I will make her pay for what she has done."

Yuri's eyes saddened. He'd always stood as Claudia's protector for as long as I could remember. I always wondered if he actually held true love for Claudia. I knew him well enough, however, to be secure that his loyalty to me far outweighed whatever feelings he held for the beautiful blonde.

"Regardless of Claudia's reasons for betraying Derek and thereby, betraying us all, the fact still remains that we have no idea where they are," Liana butted in. "Besides, that's not the point. If Sofia was taken against her will, then yes, we really do have to find her, but if she went out of her own accord..."

Cameron straightened in his seat, clearly bothered as he finished his wife's sentence, "Then finding Sofia is the least of our worries. There's nothing stopping Ben from betraying us to the hunters and having The Shade blown up."

"Sofia did *not* leave out of her own choice. I'm certain of it." I tried to push back any doubts. I hated the feeling of not trusting her.

"Well then, we're going round in circles. Truth of the matter is that I think they're at The Oasis." Xavier shrugged. "Where else would Lucas run off to? I think they sought sanctuary there."

I thought about what Lucas could possibly be putting Sofia through and I found myself fighting the urge to break someone's neck. I fought back tears, sickened by the idea of my beloved being in any kind of pain. The additional thought that she could be within Borys Maslen's territory was even worse.

A knock at the dome's large oak doors momentarily interrupted any responses anybody present could've given to Xavier's statement.

The doors swung open and I could make out Sam standing outside the dome. "Sir, Miss Natalie Borgia is here," he announced.

I straightened up in my seat. "Let her in."

The beautiful diplomat strode inside with grace and dignity. "Natalie," I acknowledged as she took the stand.

She swallowed hard as she nodded her head toward me in response. She didn't seem comfortable with the message she was about to give me. "I have a message for Derek Novak from Borys Maslen and Sofia Claremont."

Murmurs were exchanged throughout the dome. I gulped as Natalie left the stand and climbed up toward the balcony in order to hand me the letter.

"I'm sorry," she said quietly before turning and once again taking her place at the stand.

I stared at the envelope, dreading what it could possibly contain. I swallowed hard as I opened it. No words could explain what I felt upon seeing the wedding invitation. I let out a deep growl.

"Derek..." Natalie knew me well enough to know when something was tearing me apart. We'd had our fair share of memories together. She heaved a deep sigh. "I was told to let you know that you are to go alone. Any vampire from this coven seen stepping anywhere near the desert will be shot down. Only *you* are to go there if you want to see her."

"What is it?" Xavier rose to his feet, taking a place at the stand. "What's going on?"

"See for yourself." I threw the invitation his way.

He caught it with both hands. His eyes widened. "Oh my…"

"What? What is it?" Gavin asked as everyone looked curiously at the message.

Xavier looked up at me. "It's an invitation for one to Sofia and Borys' wedding."

"Derek," Liana spoke up. "You realize this is a trap, don't you?"

"It doesn't matter." I shook my head. "If Sofia is in the Maslens' hands, I have to go to her. There's no other way."

"But what about The Shade?" With all the noisy murmurs and mild commotion going on, I didn't even recognize who was asking questions anymore.

"Cameron, Liana, Xavier and Eli are more than capable of working together to run the island while I'm away."

"Derek, you're seriously considering this?" Xavier seemed apprehensive.

"You of all people are aware of what Borys is capable of," I told him. "You know what he did to Vivienne. Borys will break and ruin Sofia."

"Sofia is stronger than we've given her credit for," Cameron spoke up and I knew immediately that what he was saying was true. "Maybe she will find her way out of there by herself and back here."

I smirked. "Yeah…maybe…maybe she can, but I'm not going to hang the fate of the woman I love on *maybes*, Cameron. I'm not going to just sit here and allow that shameless brute to have his way with Sofia."

"So you're actually going to The Oasis?" Liana verified.

I nodded. "I wouldn't miss Sofia's wedding for the world."

# Chapter 47: Sofia

It felt like days since I was brought to The Oasis. I hadn't seen Borys since our first meeting—something I was immensely grateful for. The only vampires from The Oasis I'd seen then were the two guards they sent to keep watch over me and the women who came to take my measurements and do the fittings for my wedding gown.

To my relief, they kept Ben inside my room, but he wasn't supposed to talk to me much, and the guards strictly warned us that he was not to touch me. Apparently, Borys made it some sort of law that no man would be allowed to lay a hand on me until the day of our wedding.

"He wants you pure," the guard explained.

I couldn't help but wonder what kind of a demented lunatic Borys Maslen really was.

"Doesn't the idea of marrying him just make you sick?" Ben wrinkled his nose, as he sat on the edge of the bed next to me. He said the question in a low voice so that the guards wouldn't hear.

"All I can think about is escaping. I haven't even really let the possibility of being his wife sink in. It's too horrible a thought to be with anyone other than Derek." I bit my lip, wondering for a moment if I was being insensitive toward Ben, knowing how he felt toward me.

I was relieved to find him nodding as he eyed the guards warily. "Yeah…I've stopped thinking of you ending up with anybody else other than Derek, but…I can't see how we'll escape this place alone. We're hundreds of feet below ground, and these two nuts are always around."

I blew out a sigh as I eyed the two guards standing nearby. During the time we'd spent there, we'd gotten more information—mostly from the women dolling and dressing me up—about what exactly The Oasis was. I tried chatting the two guards up, but I quickly found out that they were thoroughly lacking in personality—completely unlike Sam and Kyle, who'd always been more than willing to exchange witty banter.

Their presence made both Ben and I uncomfortable because of the way we would catch them staring and licking their lips whenever they laid eyes on me. They weren't subtle in showing how much they were craving me, and based on the way I saw Derek black out and attack Gavin, I knew that if these vampires suddenly flipped out, neither Ben nor I had any defense against them.

I suddenly heard a knock at the door. My stomach fluttered when I realized who it was. *Ingrid.* I still couldn't wrap my mind around her being my mother. Questions whirled within my mind, questions I wasn't even sure I wanted to hear the answers to.

The guards quickly made way for her and she walked into the room with grace and elegance. She stopped near the end of my bed and gave Ben a pointed look.

"So it's you that my daughter has been hiding with all these years."

Ben sneered at her. "So it's you who abandoned Sofia all these years. For what? So you could become Borys Maslen's baby..."

"You're going to regret saying that, boy." She tilted her head to the side. "You obviously mean something to my daughter, so I'll let that go for now." She walked toward us—toward me and stopped right in front of me. She used a finger to lift my chin so she could take a good look at me. I turned my eyes away from her. I found myself recoiling from her touch.

"I did not abandon you, Sofia. Your father kept you away from me. I've been looking for you all these years."

"And why exactly were you looking for me? So you could give me to Borys as a bride?" I realized that I didn't even know how to address her or what to call her. *Do I refer to her as Ingrid or as Camilla?* Calling her Mother didn't feel right.

She brushed her thumb against my cheek. "You have your father's eyes, but you don't have his build, I'm glad to see...fragile, weak, breakable..."

I glared up at her. *Was she insulting me?*

She withdrew her hand from me and raised a brow at Ben. She addressed the guards, "I want time alone with my daughter. Have the young man brought to the little blonde vampire from The Shade. She could use some company."

My blood began to pound as alarm rose from the pit of my stomach to the top of my head. "No..." I immediately saw the fright in Ben's eyes. "Please...no...not her...not Claudia...Mother, please."

Surprise sparked in Ingrid's eyes the moment I called her Mother.

She raised a hand toward the guards who were already approaching to take Ben. "Wait. What did you just call me?" she asked me.

"Mother..." My lips trembled as I spoke. I grabbed Ben's hand, not knowing whether I was trying to comfort him or draw strength from him. "Isn't that what you are? My mother?"

"Yes. That's right, Sofia." She smiled, but I saw only insanity in her eyes. "I'm your mother. That means you do what I say, right?"

Terrified on Ben's behalf, I nodded in attempt to humor Ingrid. "Of course."

"So you're not going to cause any trouble tomorrow, yes?"

"Tomorrow?" My grip on Ben's hand tightened.

"Yes. Tomorrow. Did you not know? You're to be wed to Borys tomorrow."

"Why? Why would you do this? Why would you force your own daughter to marry that brute?"

She began brushing strands of my hair away from my face. "You just don't know him, Sofia. Borys deserves the best and you, Sofia, are the best. Why wouldn't you be? You're my blood, my beautiful, perfect little girl. You belong to Borys."

Chills ran down my spine as she straightened to her full height. "I've changed my mind," she announced. "Leave the boy here. The Shade's little blonde vampire can have him after the wedding. Right now Borys is requesting the presence of his blooming bride. Have my daughter brought to his chambers."

It was as if everything stood still. I could make out Ben trying to put up a fight as the guards took me away. I knew what was happening, but I couldn't understand it. I couldn't comprehend how such a vile creature like Ingrid Maslen could ever be the mother I remembered that I had.

By the time I reached Borys' chambers, I was in tears. I was pushed inside, with Ingrid following shortly after me. Borys was pouring alcohol into a bronze chalice. He turned and frowned at the sight of me. "Why is she crying?"

My stomach turned when I realized that he was wearing nothing but a loincloth to cover his bulking frame. His gaze quickly went from my face to my body. I wasn't even sure if he heard Ingrid's explanation that I was just nervous to be presented to my bridegroom.

"Leave us," he ordered, his eyes traveling the length of my body. Ingrid gave him a nod. I grabbed her hand before she could move. "Please…don't leave me…"

"You'll be fine, my love. He won't take you to his bed until after the wedding. He's a gentleman that way."

*A gentleman.* I almost laughed at the thought. *How could she call him that after what she had witnessed him do to me?*

Ingrid shook my hand away and quickly strode out of the room. "Enjoy getting to know each other, children!" she chirped before closing the door behind her.

Standing in the middle of the room, I couldn't control the way my body quivered as Borys slowly approached. He began circling me like a vulture, his eyes taking in my form, violating me with mere looks.

I shut my eyes and tried to remember Derek. His eyes. His smile. Of all the times that Derek had overstepped his boundaries, threatened to hurt me, threatened to take me, he never made me feel the way Borys did at that time. Derek had many times over made me feel vulnerable and fragile under his touch, but he never made me feel like he would enjoy breaking me and hurting me.

Even on the first night I met him, with him throwing me up a post and threatening to suck at my neck and drain me of my blood, I could sense goodness and light in Derek. I feared him, but he was never without hope.

The way I felt around Borys was different. He made my blood run cold in a way even Lucas and Gregor were never able to accomplish. Whenever he looked at me, it felt as if he was finding delight in all the cruel things he planned to do with me.

He reached for me and I flinched. He laughed at my reaction, but reached forward anyway. He began to thumb the necklace I was wearing—the one Derek gave me for my birthday. "Beautiful," Borys complimented. "Who gave it to you?"

"Someone I love dearly."

He scowled. "I don't like it. Remove it. I never want to see you wear it in my presence again."

I stood still, not knowing what to do.

"Remove it!" Borys growled right into my ear and then reached behind my neck and unclasped the necklace and threw it on the ground. He then grabbed a clump of my hair and said, "The next time I tell you to do something, you obey immediately. Do you understand that, Sofia?"

I nodded, knowing that defiance toward him would only lead to more pain. He brushed his lips over mine and I felt as though I was about to throw up. I found everything about him absolutely revolting.

"You're shaking," he sneered. "I like that. Vivienne shook the same way when she first came to me."

The fact that he would brag about what he had put Vivienne through made my blood boil and it was taking all my self-control not to attack him. "What did you do to her? She was a broken spirit by the time Derek took her away from you."

He let go of me and turned away. "I had fun with her. That's all.

Of course, that husband of yours always was a party pooper. I still hate that he's soiled you already." He began rummaging for something inside a desk drawer. "But you're the immune, Sofia. I can't help but want you." He took out a velvet pouch.

My heart almost stopped beating at the sight of it. I knew what it contained. Vivienne's memories and my recurring nightmares were enough to let me know that the item he was retrieving from the pouch was a necklace—a heart-shaped, ruby-red pendant.

He approached me, the necklace dangling in his hand. "I want you to wear this every time you're in my presence, Sofia. Do you understand?"

*Was this what the nightmares were warning me about? Does this mean that I will really lose Derek forever and be Borys' toy instead?* He put the necklace on me, taking liberties by tracing his fingers down my neck and shoulders as he did so. "It looks beautiful on you, does it not?"

"Why do you want me? What do you mean, I'm 'the immune?'"

He chuckled. "Don't you remember?" He forcefully twisted me around and threw me on the bed. I would've screamed but the surprise knocked the breath out of me.

"What are you doing?" I gasped.

He approached the bed and quickly climbed on top of me. "Your blood, Sofia…it's like a siren call. I wonder how any vampire could ever resist it. Especially after having tasted you already…" His fangs came out and he forcefully yanked my head to the side.

The sight of his fangs etched itself in my mind. And it triggered a memory—an image of him, wearing a different outfit, standing over me, fangs bared. I found myself confused—not sure whether the memory was mine or Vivienne's, but at that point, it didn't matter. Borys Maslen was about to feed on me.

I screamed when his fangs sank into my neck. His hand clamped over my mouth to silence me as he fed on me. Tears were streaming down my face as my mind begged for him to stop, his weight crushing my much smaller frame beneath him and making it difficult for me to even breathe. When I heard the door swing open and a voice I recognized as Ingrid's called out his name, relief washed over me.

"Really, Borys?" Ingrid groaned. "I thought you said you'd only feed on her after your marriage?"

Borys continued to suck on me for a couple more seconds before pulling his fangs away from my neck, sneering down at me as my blood dripped from his lips. "I couldn't help it. She's too sweet and enticing." He turned toward Ingrid. "What do you want now?" he asked through gritted teeth.

Ingrid seemed annoyed and even slightly concerned for me, but she soon seemed to brush away the fact that her king was draining the blood from her own daughter. "Our special guest has just arrived."

A fearsome grin formed on Borys' face as he shifted his gaze back to me. "Did you hear that, my lovely Sofia? Derek Novak has come for you." The hand he had clamped over my mouth tightened as his other hand gently brushed over my hair. "Maybe he really does love you, huh? Do you want to go see him?"

I nodded furiously, wanting nothing other than to once again be in Derek's arms, and find comfort in his strength.

Borys leaned over and whispered into my ear, "I will enjoy watching the reaction on your face when you see him die."

# Chapter 48: Ben

Soon after Ingrid had left with Sofia, the guards dragged me out of the room. I wasn't entirely sure if they were going against Ingrid's orders to keep me there for Sofia's sake or if she just allowed me to stay in order to appease Sofia into being compliant about the idea of being brought to Borys. Either way, it didn't matter. My best friend—still very much the love of my life—was in the arms of a monster and there was nothing I could do about it. Without my hunting weapons, I was useless against the vampires. I was just another weak human being they could prey on.

"Where are you taking me?" I demanded.

One of the guards smirked. "To the little blonde vampire."

Terror filled me. "But Ingrid just said..."

The guard hit me on the face, making my surroundings dim and blur. "You are not to call her by name. She is your superior in every way."

I gritted my teeth as I fought to stay conscious. One guard had already grabbed me by the arm. That's when an adrenaline rush took over. I wasn't going to be handed to Claudia on a silver platter. No. Not again. Not without a fight. Summoning all my strength, I managed to tackle him to the ground. He fell with a loud thud. The only way I knew how to kill one without a stake or a UV gun was to rip their hearts out, but I doubted I had enough strength to do it.

Thus, with one vampire down and the other still in shock that a human would dare fight back, I made a run for it. Of course, I was no match for the vampires' speed and agility, so I didn't get far before they hit me on the back of my head and forced me unconscious.

When I opened my eyes, my stomach turned, because I was sprawled on a large bed, with Claudia looking down at me.

"Hi, Ben." She smiled. "I missed you."

I thought that I would be terrified at the sight of her. I was expecting to feel fear and dread over what she was going to put me through, but there was none of that. Just hatred, hatred the likes of which I'd never felt for anyone or anything before.

I sat up on the bed and backed away from her. She reached out for me and I flinched when her fingers brushed over my shoulder. I glared at her, expecting to see the same glint of manic glee in her eyes—the same look she always gave me when she held me captive at The Shade. Instead, the look on her eyes was soft and pensive—practically moist with tears.

"Do you love her, Ben?"

"Love who?" I practically spat the words out. I was sickened by the way she was acting. I felt as if someone like her had no business talking about love.

"Sofia..."

I stared at her incredulously. She didn't have the right to talk about Sofia and I had every right not to give her a response. "And if I do?" I managed to say.

She shrugged one shoulder. Her head bowed slightly, a mass of curls falling over her shoulders. "I love someone too. I didn't realize how much until I got here. I never should've left The Shade. I need him."

I practically gawked at her. I had no idea who I was facing at that moment. Gone was the evil, sadistic vampire who made my life a living hell. In her place was this broken young woman looking for love. *Does she really expect me to sympathize with her?*

"Why are you telling me this?"

She began pacing the room as she scratched her head. "I don't know...because you're here. I promised Lucas I would help him, and in return he arranged for me to have you. I thought perhaps you could get rid of this longing I have for Yuri, but when they brought you here...just when I was about to feed on you, all I could think about was what Yuri would think of me if I once again tormented you for things you did not do."

"Just let me go, Claudia. I can't stand the sight of you. I can't stand being in the same room with you. When I look at you, I really just want to kill you." I was probably crazy for saying those words out loud, because they could only get me into more trouble. Still, the truth remained. I didn't care about this soft side of Claudia any more than I cared for her wicked villainess act. I just wanted to get as far away from her as I could.

I was expecting her to slap me in the face and put me in my place, remind me that she was my mistress and I was her slave, but she just stopped pacing and looked at me with a bitter smile.

*What on earth is going on in her mind? Is this for real? Is this*

*Claudia having a heart for once?*

I searched myself for some sort of compassion, any form of empathy for her, and I found none. I still wanted to see her pay. I wanted to kill her myself. Fury was still burning in my veins over what she did to me, over how she ruined the life that I knew. However, deep inside me, I knew that I couldn't do it. I wouldn't be able to kill her if I had the chance. My time with the hunters had completely eradicated my thirst for vengeance, because I knew without a doubt in my mind that no matter how tempting the notion of killing Claudia was, seeing the life drain out of her would not satisfy me.

*Sofia knew the way all along. No matter what she'd been through, she was never a captive. She'd always been free to love and trust and accept others. She never built walls around herself to protect her from what others could put her through. She remained ready to forgive and to embrace the things that actually mattered in life.*

At that moment, it felt like I understood Sofia completely for the first time. It was the fulfillment of Vivienne's prophecy about me.

"What do you want from me, Claudia?"

She sank over the edge of the bed and buried her face in her palms. She was the abject picture of dejection and I had no idea how to handle it. "I don't know what I want. I still want to taste you. That much is true, but I want Yuri…I want Yuri more than anything."

I didn't even know who Yuri was. "Then why the hell are you here at The Oasis when whoever this guy you're pining for is way back at The Shade, where your home is."

"I can't get back to The Shade, not after I betrayed Derek, not after I brought Sofia here."

"Derek might not be able to forgive you, but I know Sofia will." I couldn't believe the words coming out of my mouth.

She scoffed in response. "Sofia hates me. After what I did to you…after what I wanted to do to Gavin…"

I shook my head. "You don't know Sofia. If you're actually sincere in what you're saying, I'm sure she'll find it in her heart to forgive you." I scoffed. "Assuming that you're sincere, of course…I still think you're playing mind games with me."

"Maybe I am…" she said softly.

"Are you?"

She shook her head. After a rather awkward silence, she then spoke up, "I want to go back to The Shade."

"I don't." I grimaced. "I don't get it…just go back. Who the hell will care?"

"You don't understand. If I go back, I don't think Yuri will ever be able to forgive me. He is fiercely loyal to Derek. Unless I get back in Derek's and Sofia's good graces, he would never take me back."

I stared at her. I was still wondering who Yuri was and why he was so important to Claudia. I had a vague recollection of a guy paying her a visit once in a while. She never let him in her home. It was as if she was afraid that he would see what she was doing. She always was in a better mood than usual after spending time with him. *Maybe that's Yuri.*

"Will you help me get back there?"

"How on earth am I supposed to do that?"

"I know Derek will come here. He loves Sofia enough to come here alone. He won't stand a chance against the Maslens. Not on their turf. I'm going to help you out of here, but you have to call the hunters. I'd call the vampires and help them get in unnoticed, but they're too far away and they don't have the means to get here quicker than the hunters will. If I help Derek and Sofia get out of here alive, knowing that I helped you and that you got the hunters to destroy the Maslens, then Yuri might be willing to give me a second chance…if they die, I've lost him. Perhaps forever."

I stared at Claudia unbelievingly. I was still waiting for a catch, some cruel twisted thing she had in mind in an exchange for what she was proposing. I narrowed my eyes at her. "If the hunters come, I might not be able to stop them from killing you. I'm not even sure I would want to stop them."

"If I can't go back to The Shade, back to *him*, then I might as well die." She sighed with resignation. "Just make sure that Derek and Sofia make it out of here."

I blinked my eyes several times to make sure I was hearing right, but I chose not to question her. I chose not to pry. I had to take advantage of Claudia's momentary lapse of insanity—if this was what was going on. I didn't have to understand her. I just needed to get Sofia out of here.

I knew what Reuben would do once I revealed the location of the Maslens' coven. He wouldn't hesitate to destroy the place. I knew that Sofia would be spared, but I wasn't so sure about Derek and I couldn't help but wonder if Sofia would ever be able to forgive me if anything happened to Derek. That's when I realized that more than anything, I wanted Sofia to be happy, and I knew that wouldn't be possible if she had to live a life apart from Derek. I completely let go of any hopes that I could still be with Sofia.

*It's time to let go of my Rose Red and help fight for her to get her happy ending.*

# Chapter 49: Derek

I knew that it was crazy for me to walk into The Oasis alone. I knew that it was possible that I could be walking toward my own death, but it felt like I had no choice.

Standing in the middle of the throne room, surrounded by dozens of guards, who were well briefed on my strength and capabilities, I felt vulnerable in a way that I never had before. However, it didn't matter, because all I could think of was Sofia.

Thus, when Borys stepped into the room, dragging her beside him, his hand clamped around her arm as she held her bleeding neck, every muscle in my body tensed. I knew right then that there were no peace talks on the horizon. I was going to draw blood—if only to avenge Sofia.

Borys let go of her and the moment he did, she ran into my arms, tears streaming down her face. I held her tight, unwilling to let go, sickened by the thought of what she'd been through since she arrived at The Oasis.

I didn't need to ask if she was alright or if they hurt her. It was clear to see that she wasn't. It was obvious that they had.

"Get me out of here, Derek," she sobbed against my chest. "He's going to destroy me. Everyone here is insane. Especially my mother..."

*She knows.* I shut my eyes, trying to find words to soothe her, wondering how on earth I was going to get her out of there. I could smell the blood on her neck. My mouth watered at the scent, but I was too horrified by the idea that Borys had already tasted her blood to even start craving her. "Sofia, I'm so sorry," was all I could think of to say.

She shook her head. "You didn't do this."

"I've failed to protect you so many times..."

"Don't do this, Derek. Just don't. We have to get out of here—you, me and Ben. Staying here will be the end of all of us."

Borys cleared his throat. "Much as I hate to break up this sweet reunion between husband and wife, I have to interrupt."

*Husband and wife.* I creased my brows in confusion as I reluctantly let go of Sofia. Ignoring Borys, I bit into my palm to draw blood and coaxed Sofia to drink the blood so that the bite on her neck would heal. The moment the skin on her neck closed, I glared at Borys. "I demand the life of whomever it is that has tasted her blood."

"You're king of The Shade, Derek Novak." Borys frowned. "But I'm king here. *I've* had a taste of your wife. Do you demand *my* life?"

"Yes."

"You insolent fool!" Borys smirked. "She is my betrothed, offered up to me by her own mother since she was a child. She is *mine.* You never should've touched her in the first place, and because you did, because you spoiled her for me, I've invited you a day before our wedding so I could make a widow out of her."

Sofia's hand found my arm and she held on so tightly, it felt like she was trying to break my arm. "Derek…you can't possibly take on this many men…"

"I don't have a choice, Sofia." I pushed her out of the way and the fight began. One vampire after the other attacked me. I was able to rip several hearts out, but I didn't stand a chance. Though a lot of Borys' men proved to be ill-trained and a lot weaker compared to the vampires at The Shade, I was simply outnumbered.

The moment they had me subdued and bound on the ground, I was sure that it was the end of me. I cast a desperate glance at Sofia who was being held back by Borys, delight evident in his eyes as he saw me fall.

"Kill him!" Borys gave the order, his eyes fixed on Sofia.

Sofia took one look at me, tears streaming down her beautiful face. She began shaking her head and I knew how difficult it was for her to do what she did next. She knelt in front of Borys to plead for my life. "Please…don't do this…I will do *anything* you want me to do. *Anything*. Spare his life."

Borys sneered as he gestured for the guards to wait. "Anything?"

"No, Sofia!" I yelled.

Sofia nodded and all I could think of was the horrors her agreement would put her through.

"Very well then." Borys nodded. "Take the king of The Shade to level seven."

I didn't need to ask what level seven was. The terrors done within the walls of The Oasis' dungeons were no secret to vampires.

"What are you going to do to him?" Sofia croaked.

"Whatever it takes to punish you for daring to bargain yourself in exchange for my enemy's life, my beautiful bride." His voice was cold and merciless. "You'll soon find, my love, that there are fates far worse than death."

# Chapter 50: Sofia

Borys pushed me into my chamber, a wicked grin on his face. Ingrid stood beside him, staring at me with blank disappointment.

I tumbled backward, attempting to balance myself from the force of his push. I eventually tripped and crashed to the ground, tears streaming down my face as I glared up at Borys. "What's in level seven? What are you going to do to Derek?"

I groaned in pain when Borys leaned over and once again grabbed a fistful of my hair. "You'll find out tomorrow on our wedding day, my love. Don't worry about him. I'll take care of him. Just get some beauty sleep so that you can be the bride that I deserve."

I choked on my tears. "Please. We're not actually married. We're just engaged. Let him go. I'll do everything you want. Please…" I sobbed.

"Kiss me, Sofia."

I sealed my lips, sickened by such a horrible thought. "Please…" I whimpered.

"You let *him* touch you and you respond to his every touch, his every kiss, his every caress, don't you? You shall not refuse to do the same with me—especially not after you've said your vows and surrendered to the inevitable. The *immune* will be my wife and you will show me that you enjoy everything I do to you." He grabbed my jaw. "Do you understand?!"

I was staring pure madness in the face and all I could do was tremble as I nodded, wondering to myself how on earth I could survive even just a night with him without completely losing my mind. Everything about him revolted me. I couldn't help but recoil with even just the thought of his touch. To even pretend and act the part of a blushing bride who found pleasure in his presence was sheer torment.

"Now, respond..." He pressed his lips against mine—painfully, his fangs came out and drew blood from my lower lip. For a moment I thought about forcing myself to return the kiss, but I found that I couldn't. I simply didn't know how. Every part of me was just wishing for it to end. It didn't seem to matter to him, because the blood on my lips quickly shifted his attention from forcing me to kiss him back to his craving for my blood.

His mouth quickly left mine and found my neck, and he once again sunk his fangs in and drank my blood. I was trembling uncontrollably as his arms clamped around my body, crushing my chest against his. I tried to push him away, but found that I couldn't. I stared up at Ingrid, who was still standing by the door watching everything that was happening and I wondered how she could do it. *What kind of mother do I have? How could she just stand there and watch him do this to her own daughter?*

She looked at me blankly, her arms crossed over her chest.

"Please…make him stop…" I mouthed at her.

She rolled her eyes and sighed. "That's enough, Borys. You're going to drain her of blood before you marry her."

Borys withdrew his mouth from my neck. "I love how she trembles. Your daughter is so beautiful, Ingrid. Untouched." His eyes darkened. "Except for that brute, Derek Novak." He let go of me and stood up, looking down at me as I curled into a ball on the floor. "I'm going to make him pay."

"Please don't hurt him…" I begged. For that, I got a kick in the gut.

As I coughed, he looked at me coldly. "Your pleas only make me want to hurt him further." He then turned and brushed past Ingrid. "Put a bandage on the bite mark," he instructed her before leaving. "I don't want it healed. I want to see the scars tomorrow. It will be a sign that she's mine. Make sure she's a stunning sight tomorrow. Make me look forward to our marriage bed."

The door closed and I was alone with my mother. That's when I realized that neither Ben nor the guards were in the room. "Where's Ben? What did you do to him?"

"Your best friend is fine. Don't worry about him. I instructed Claudia to be gentle with him. We need him to be presentable for the wedding tomorrow. He's the best man after all." She walked past my still curled up form on the floor. "Get up, Sofia. Why must you be so stubborn and pathetic?" She began to rummage through a drawer in one corner of the room.

"What kind of mother are you?" I managed to say in between broken sobs. "Your king is about to kill the man that I love."

I shuddered when she sped my way and threw me onto the bed. "Understand this, Sofia," she hissed. "The man you love is Borys Maslen, not Derek Novak. The Shade's prince has obviously brainwashed you..."

Despite my tears, I laughed wryly. "It's *you* who's been brainwashed, Ingrid...or maybe I ought to call you Camilla...is there still any part of her left in you? Dad was right about you. You *are* insane. You left your own family to blindly serve this villain of a king."

"You have no idea what you're talking about. You don't know what my life was like. I loved Aiden. He was everything to me, and then you came along. I never wanted you, but I gave in to his requests for a child, because I loved him. You stole him from me." She was saying the words calmly, her eyes set on the bite marks on my neck as she proceeded to tend to the wound.

The spite every word contained mixed with the calmness and affection by which she expressed them made her one of the scariest people I'd ever met. I couldn't begin to fathom how broken a creature my own mother was. I was certain, however, that even though I had been born of her womb, she was now a complete stranger.

No more words were exchanged until she was done. As she turned to leave, I couldn't help but cry out, "Please...help Derek. Help Ben. They are dear to me. I love them."

She stopped right by the door. She didn't bother to face me as she shook her head. "No, Sofia. You love Borys. He's the only man you're allowed to love from now on."

That's when I accepted that my mother was completely gone. Camilla Claremont wasn't just insane. She was dead and her body had been replaced by Ingrid Maslen.

# Chapter 51: Sofia

The silence and solitude was driving me crazy. It'd been more hours than I could count since Ingrid left me. I had no way to track time, nothing to take my mind off of Derek and Ben and what torment they were most likely going through. I couldn't stop crying. At some point, I just crumpled myself up on the bed, knowing that there was no way I could escape that bedroom, hoping that sleep could provide me with an escape from the tormenting thoughts and emotions coursing through my mind and soul.

I could still feel the stabbing ache of the bite marks on my neck. My lips felt swollen from the cuts caused by Borys' sickening kisses. The heaviness in my chest made it difficult to breathe.

I'd never felt more helpless and distraught than I did at that moment. I lay there for hours, sleep eluding me. My stomach was already grumbling. No one had bothered to bring me food since Ingrid had left. I wondered if it was some sort of punishment.

When my eyelids began to get heavy and sleepiness began to overtake me, I gladly gave in, hoping that when I woke up, I would find that The Oasis was my nightmare and The Shade was my reality. The Shade had its own horrors, but though firelight flooded the tombs of The Oasis, to me, it would always be darker than the island Derek spent a hundred years establishing and fighting for.

I had no clue how long I'd been asleep, but disappointment washed over me when I woke up to find that The Oasis was still the reality I was being forced to inhabit. I couldn't help but sob when I realized that maids were milling around my chamber. A dress that was far too revealing for my taste was laid out on the bed beside me.

"You're awake!" an elderly woman exclaimed. "The wedding is in a few hours."

The mention of the wedding once again turned on the waterworks. "Please…help me out of here…"

She sighed and smiled. "There's no way out of here, beautiful." She paused as if to give me time to let the words sink in before clapping her hands together. "Now, get up and let's take you to the shower. You look awful and we can't have that, because the king wants his bride to be stunning. Right now, you're an absolute mess. Did you not get any sleep at all?"

I ignored her question. "What's in level seven?"

She gave me a sorry look. "Darkness…things a bride shouldn't be thinking of on her wedding day."

"The man I love, the man I want to marry…he's in level seven."

"Then you best forget him and love the king instead." She heaved another sigh—now more exasperating and impatient than kind. "Come, come…hurry."

I was pulled out of the bed and from that point on it felt like my body wasn't my own. I went where they led me, did what they told me to do. I sat when they told me to sit and stood when I was instructed to stand. They stripped my clothes off and dressed me. They adorned my hair with pearls. They dabbed makeup on my face. They tried to chat with me and lighten my mood as they went about the process, but they knew that I was an unwilling bride and sometimes, I would catch them giving me sorry looks. They knew that my plight was not one any woman would envy.

The whole time, it felt like everything was happening to someone else. By the time they were done, the elderly maid pushed me in front of a full-length mirror.

"I would've chosen another dress, but the king picked this himself," she explained apologetically.

When I saw my appearance in the mirror, I fought back tears. Derek would've been horrified. The neckline was too low, stooping down almost to my navel. The back of the dress also showed a lot of skin. The dress clung to my curves like a glove. I wondered what the dress was intended for—whether it was meant to reveal or conceal. I clenched my fists. I knew the maids had done their best to make me look as decent as possible. They chose to keep my hair down instead of pull it up in order to have my long locks cover at least some skin. Still, I thought I looked more like a whore than a bride. The heart-shaped ruby red necklace adorning my neck only added insult to injury.

I was about to break down into tears when the door creaked open and Borys stepped in. I didn't even dare look at him. I didn't want to see the grin on his face.

I asked him the one question on my mind. "Where's Derek? I want to see him."

The atmosphere immediately tensed. The maids began to exchange nervous whispers as Borys slowly approached me. My entire body tensed when he stood right beside me. He didn't seem to mind how rigid I was against his touch, because he took all the liberties he had as both his hands and eyes roamed my anxious form.

"You still *dare* mention him to me?" he said in a low voice, his breath cold against my ear, his lips so close they were almost touching me.

"Where is he? What have you done to him?"

I could feel his anger. He didn't like my defiance. He didn't like that I was holding my head up. He wanted me to whimper and beg. He wanted me to cry. I'd already done that and I was determined to no longer give him this satisfaction.

"Do you still love Derek Novak, Sofia?"

This time, I turned my face toward him, looking him straight in the eye. I smiled. "I will *always* love him."

Fire burned in his muddy brown eyes as the muscles in his face tensed. I realized at that point that Borys could've been a very handsome man if his features weren't so marred by his brutality and blatant wickedness. When he grinned, I braced myself for what was to come. A smile coming from Borys Maslen was never a good thing. "Very well then. I will show him to you."

He wrapped his arms around me and pulled my body against his as he sped out of the room and along the corridors. We went up several flights of stairs—I could barely keep track of the places we passed. He was going too fast. I was out of breath and slightly dizzy when we stopped in front of a wooden door. He twisted me around so that my back was pressing against his chest, his arms clamped around my waist, keeping me in place. The corner of his lips pressed against my cheek as he said, "When you see him, I'm sure you'll beg me to kill him. If only to end his misery…"

My heart broke at his words. *I'm so sorry, Derek. This never would've happened to you if it weren't for me.* I steeled myself for what I was about to see, but nothing could've prepared me for it.

We entered the dungeon—and all my resolve not to cry was gone at the sight of Derek. He was hanging by his wrists, held by thick metal chains. He was unrecognizable. He was just a mass of blood and flesh hanging from the ceiling.

Borys chuckled when I began to struggle against his embrace. "Is this what you wanted to see, Sofia?"

"Sofia?"

My heart leapt at the sound of Derek's voice. It was weak and broken, but it was his. *He's alive. My Derek is alive.* Still, as I tried to break free from Borys' grasp, I wondered if it would be better if Derek really did die…if only to escape this.

Finally, still chuckling, Borys let me go. I hurried toward Derek, tears still streaming down my face. "I'm sorry. I'm so sorry." I wanted to touch him, but I was afraid it would only add to his pain, so I just looked up at him, hoping that I could do something to ease his pain. "Who did this to you?"

"I did," Borys answered, sounding very much proud of himself. "Although I can't take all the credit. Lucas helped a lot too."

Derek forced his swollen, bloodshot eyes open in order to look at me. "I love you," he mouthed.

I wanted to respond, but I was too overcome by sobs to form coherent words. The thought that Derek's own brother would do this to him shattered my heart. I knew that despite everything that had happened between them, Derek truly did hold affection for Lucas. He never would've done anything like this to his own brother.

"So you've seen him." Borys began to approach after closing the door behind him. "Are you satisfied now, Sofia?" He stopped behind me and stared up at Derek with delight, as if admiring his handiwork. "Is this what you wanted to see?"

I stepped away when Borys began to run his hand down my shoulder. Borys responded by using one strong arm to grab my waist and pull my back against him, holding me in position so that he could touch me any way he pleased right in front of Derek.

I kept my eyes on Derek's, wondering if things would really end this way. I was grasping for any thread of hope. I wanted to be strong for Derek, but I had no idea how to do it. We were both too weak, too broken.

When a soft knock interrupted Borys' shameless display, I could hear Derek sigh with relief. "What?!" Borys screamed. A guard entered. He looked terrified.

"Your highness..." His voice trembled. "The boy...Ben...he escaped with the blonde vampire. They both left The Oasis...they haven't yet returned."

I could feel Borys' breathing suddenly get heavy. His arms clamped around me so tightly, I thought he wanted to snap me in two. Instead, he pushed me to the ground and marched toward the guard. He grabbed the guard's neck. "How long have they been gone?"

The guard stuttered as he replied, "More than fifteen hours, sir..."

Borys growled and ripped his heart out. The guard's body dropped to the ground and Borys sped out of the dungeon, shutting the door behind him and locking it from the outside.

My jaw dropped open. *What just happened? He's leaving just like that? Did Borys really just lose it?* I snapped to attention. *Who cares? Do something.* I rushed toward Derek, doing the only thing I could think of. I offered him my wrist.

Upon seeing it, he gave me a weak smile. All he said in response was: "No."

# Chapter 52: Derek

"I'm not going to drink your blood, Sofia." I shook my head—or at least tried to. I wondered if she could even understand what I had just said. To me, it all just sounded like a raspy mumble of words. Every part of my body was in agony, but it was nothing compared to what I felt inside, knowing that if I didn't survive, it would be the end of both of us.

Suddenly, the ground began to shake and for a moment, Sofia stood in panic looking around the room as she tried to steady herself. She ducked her head and coughed as dust and small rocks began to fall from the ceiling. However, a few moments later, the earthquake stopped and the dust settled.

She looked up at me. "Derek, please..." She shoved her wrist right against my lips. "We don't have any time...we both know you have to..."

"If I drink your blood, Sofia, I'd have to turn you into one of us for me to stop craving you..."

She paused, but within a split-second, she immediately nodded. "Do what you have to...Derek, I can't lose you..."

When I turned my head away from her wrist, she quickly pulled my head back and kissed me, crushing her lips against mine. I could only groan at the gesture, because even the gentlest of kisses was painful. I was honestly relieved when she pulled her lips away from mine, but I found myself gulping when she bit into her lower lip, easily drawing blood.

My blood boiled at the thought of why she was so easily able to cut her lip. I noticed that they were slightly swollen. *He must've already drawn blood from her lips.* The thought of what Borys had been putting her through over the past twenty-four hours made me sick. Not once did Sofia leave my mind through all the torture Lucas and Borys put me through.

So pre-occupied was I over the anger I felt at how Borys treated Sofia that I didn't realize why Sofia was drawing her own blood until she once again kissed me, giving me the slightest taste of her blood through the cut on her lips.

"Sofia..." I gasped, pulling my lips away from her.

"I won't lose you," she said determinedly. She rose to her feet and took a dagger from the guard's corpse. She then cut her wrist open and steadied my head with one hand before letting her own blood drip over my mouth. I tried to turn away, but found myself unable to.

Having already tasted her blood, I lost the battle I was trying to fight. I bit into her already open wrist and began to drink deep. The moment her blood entered my system, it was pure ecstasy. I could immediately feel my entire body coming back to life, the agony easing into a dull ache and finally into what felt like complete restoration. It was unlike anything I'd ever experienced before. Her blood wasn't only the sweetest I'd ever tasted…it also seemed to have healing qualities the likes of which I'd never thought possible. I could feel my strength returning and the wounds on my body healing, but I knew that I had to keep my senses intact. I couldn't lose myself in the bliss the taste of her blood was giving me. I knew I had to be aware of when I had to stop. Her body could only give me a certain amount of blood after all. I had to be careful not to drain her.

When I pulled my mouth away from her, she looked deathly pale. I swallowed hard, panic overtaking me. "Sofia, are you alright? Did I…"

She nodded weakly. "I'm alright. Don't worry about me." She looked far from alright, however, and I knew it.

Adrenaline rushed through my entire body, giving me the strength I needed to pull away from my restraints. Sofia looked with shock as the chains broke. She knew I was strong, but she'd never actually seen me in full combat. She'd never seen me do anything beyond ripping out a heart or two. I looked beyond her surprise, however, and proceeded to check on her. *Have I gone too far?*

She gripped my arm, which was healing pretty quickly, and looked me in the eye. "I told you, I'm okay, Derek. Get me out of here."

I knew that we had to take advantage of Borys' absent-minded stupidity. I rose to my feet and checked the guard for anything I could use. He didn't have much on him, except the clothes on his back. Considering how I was stripped down to my underwear before Borys and Lucas had their way with me, I needed the clothes. I pulled his trousers off and to my relief, they were roughly my size. I put them on and looked at his shirt. I wrinkled my nose at the blood that stained it and decided that it was better off left on the guard. At this point, Sofia was sitting on the ground, her back leaned against the wall, still looking pale and slightly nauseous.

I frowned at the outfit she was wearing.

When Borys brought her in and I first laid eyes on her, the first thing I noticed was how beautiful her face looked. After that, I noticed the pendant on her neck and remembered my nightmare. I quickly tore my eyes away from the necklace, refusing to accept that she could be gone forever. That's when I noticed the dress. It had Borys written all over it. It was very similar to the outfit I found Vivienne in when I took her away from Borys. I hated the humiliation both Sofia and my sister had gone through in Borys' hands.

Sofia noticed that I was staring at her dress in disdain and wrapped her arms around herself to cover her cleavage. "I had no choice." I hated that he put her in a position like this—where she felt she had to explain to me why she was wearing a dress so revealing. I found myself wishing that I had a shirt to pull off my body and hand over to her.

She shifted her focus to my bare torso. "How could you have healed so fast? When you were whipped at The Shade, it took you..."

"It's a mystery to me. Maybe there really is something about your blood." The fact that I'd just tasted her blood hit me once again and I had to change the subject before I could mull over the consequences that came with that.

"Can you stand?" I asked her.

She answered my question with a nod before reaching a hand out toward me so that I could help. I pulled her to a standing position, checking if she really was strong enough to support herself. When I was sure that she was steady, I gently pecked her on the lips before assuring her, "We'll get you something to cover up with as soon as we can. Right now, we have to get out of here."

"Do I look *that* awful?" she asked.

"No, Sofia. It's the exact opposite. You look absolutely enticing. Any vampire who lays eyes on you in that outfit is bound to want you." I then heaved a sigh in an attempt to divert my thoughts. "How on earth do we get past all seven levels?"

"Maybe Ben got us some help..." she said hopefully, looking at the dust on the floor caused by the small quake we had just experienced.

I swallowed hard. *If he did, he most likely called the hunters. That won't go well for me.* I shifted my focus to the door. I walked toward it and used my whole weight to push it open. I broke through it more easily than I expected. I then walked out to check the hall for any guards. I frowned when I realized that it was empty. *Something's not right.*

We went through the corridors without encountering a single guard. We finally reached the center of level seven where a control room was located. Surveillance monitors showed what was going on in other levels. Ben had indeed called the hunters. The monitors showed that The Oasis—specifically levels one to four were under full-blown attack. The sun was shining right through level one, vampires burning at the glare. It was clear what the hunters did in order to get in. They simply blew the top level of The Oasis away. I wondered if it was safer for us to just stay at level seven and wait for all the killing to be over, but Sofia stepped up and brushed her fingers over one of the monitors, her eyes wide with surprise.

"What is it?" I asked.

She just stared at the monitor for a couple of seconds before responding. "It's my father." Her eyes moistened. She looked at me even as I looked at the image she was referring to. She then stated her next words more to herself than to me. “My father’s a hunter.”

# Chapter 53: Sofia

The moment the circular glass elevator stopped at level four, I saw my father rising up to his feet as he pulled a wooden stake from a vampire's chest. At the sight of me, his eyes widened.

More questions than I could make sense of flashed through my mind at the sight of him. My mother was a vampire and my father was a hunter. It felt like my entire life had been a lie. However, I knew that I wasn't about to get any answers, because this was no time for teary-eyed reunions. War was breaking out all around us.

As I stepped out of the elevator, I realized that my father had just begun to take note of the dress I was wearing and the blood on my wrists. He then saw Derek stepping out of the elevator right behind me. My heart stopped when I realized what it looked like.

"Dad, no!" I screamed, but he was already pulling out a gun and aiming it at Derek. I immediately acted out of instinct and used myself to cover Derek. I was about to tell Aiden—who was running toward me—that if he ever hurt Derek, I'd never be able to forgive him, but before I could make sense of what was going on, Derek was speeding forward.

I was sure that he was about to attack my father, but then he ripped the heart of a vampire about to pounce on Aiden instead.

My father twisted around in surprise. I moved forward and held hands with Derek as I looked my father in the eye. "Let the hunters know that no one is to lay a hand on Derek Novak."

A muscle in my father's jaw twitched as he gave me a disapproving look. "Why are you dressed that way and who drank your blood?"

"Borys Maslen had me dressed this way, because he intends to marry me. He's also had a drink of my blood. Derek came here to rescue me," I explained, conveniently leaving out the part when I let Derek drink my blood.

My father glared at Derek. "Get my daughter out of here."

I sighed with relief as I heard him spout out orders on the hunters' communications system that Derek was not to be harmed.

Secure that the hunters wouldn't hurt Derek and that our only problem would be encounters with the Maslens, Derek's grip on my hand tightened. "Where's your room?"

The goal was to reach my chambers and hopefully hide out there until everything had blown over. I was relieved that Derek suggested we go there, because I wanted to retrieve the diamond necklace he gave me. I knew how important it was to him and it had also become extremely valuable to me because of what it symbolized. We weaved past the halls, Derek having to take down a couple of vampires before we reached my quarters. I entered the room and rummaged through the drawers for the necklace. The moment I found it, I pulled off the necklace given to me by Borys and threw it on the ground. I then turned to face Derek and found myself surprised when I saw the alarm on his handsome face.

"We're not safe here. I didn't realize how close your room was to the Maslen family's chambers. Come! Hurry!"

He gave me no time to voice out my confusion; he just grabbed me by the waist and sped out of the room. He stopped when we were already at the main hall, right by the circular elevator, where the heat of the battle was going on. At this point, a hunter—one who either didn't hear, or chose to ignore, my father's instructions not to harm Derek—lunged toward him with a stake. Derek pushed me to one corner away from the chaos going on around us and I heard the hunter's neck snap.

I managed to tear my eyes away from the sight of Derek killing another person and that's when I got a full picture of what was going on around me.

My blood was pounding within me. A surge of horror rushed through my body as I scoped my surroundings. Gunshots were being fired all over the place. A fiery bullet hit a vampire about seven feet away from me, who screamed in agony as he burst into flames. He was only one among the many vampires present in those tombs—one among many dying excruciating deaths by those fatal gunshots. A few lucky ones were killed with stakes being driven through their hearts, but most were shot with the hunters' bullets, uniquely engineered to mete out death on the vampires.

The sight was sickening, but despite my horror over the sheer magnitude of death surrounding me, my prime concern was Derek Novak.

*I can't lose you.*

The mere thought of losing him made breathing a struggle. I looked around and gasped at the sight of him ripping the heart out of a vampire from the Maslen clan before moving on to breaking the neck of another hunter poised to attack him. He was headed straight for Borys Maslen. Fearing for Derek's life, I stumbled forward. As I weaved through the chaos surrounding me toward my beloved, someone grabbed my arm and pulled me back.

"Get her out of here!" My father, Aiden Claremont, was pointing toward the exit. He was speaking to the stranger gripping my arm. The sight of my father still confused me. *What is he doing here?* After all the years he abandoned me and left me under the care of his best friend, Lyle Hudson, he seemed out of place in this world—*my* world. His attempts to protect me were irritating. He had no business interfering with my life, not after all those years of ignoring me. Still, his presence moved me beyond words. He was still my father and I wanted to run to him and embrace him, feel his strength surround me, hear whispers of assurances in my ear—assurances that would answer my questions about why he had abandoned me.

But war was being waged all around us and the only thing that mattered at that moment—reaching Derek—was being kept from me. I struggled against the hunter's grasp as he dragged me in the opposite direction. He was far stronger than me and I couldn't break away from his grasp until he was tackled to the ground by a familiar vampire. *Claudia.*

Her mass of blonde curls covered her face as she let out a scream before ripping the man's heart out. Her big brown eyes then turned toward me, a manic smile forming on her face.

"Hello, Sofia."

I shivered as I looked into her eyes. A broken creature, she embraced darkness like no other and had become one of the most wicked beings I'd ever come across. She surged forward and pinned me against a wall with her bloody hands.

"This is my gift to you," she hissed before sinking her teeth into my neck. I'd been bitten by vampires before, but I felt right away that what she was doing was different. She wasn't simply feeding on me. She was trying to *turn* me.

"No!" I gasped, trying to push her away. "Claudia, don't...please..."

Before I could fully wrap my mind around what was about to happen to me, I saw my best friend, Benjamin Hudson, hurtling toward us. His blue eyes screamed bloody murder at the sight of what Claudia, the vampire who broke him in many ways, was doing to me. He aimed his gun at her, but she must've sensed him, because she whipped around and tackled him to the ground.

"Did you really think I wouldn't sense you coming to her rescue? Your blood still pumps through my veins, Ben..."

Claudia's hands rose in the air and claws came out of her fingers, poised to wound Ben. I threw my entire weight against her, hoping to push her away from my best friend, but she easily threw me back and I crashed to the ground. I cast my eyes away in desperation and scanned the hall, only to be met with another bone-chilling sight.

Across the vast hall, Derek stood bleeding and weakened as he faced off with Borys Maslen and three other vampires. And, in another corner of the room, a vampire was poised to attack my father who was fumbling to reload his gun.

Watching with horror as the lives of three of the most important men in my life hung in the balance, I felt an overwhelming sense of loss. Somehow, I already knew that this was going to happen, that the loss of life was inevitable, but finding myself right in the middle of it was something I wasn't prepared for.

A voice echoed in my mind—the voice of a friend who sacrificed her own life to bring me back into Derek's arms. I could almost hear her—Vivienne Novak, Seer of The Shade—speaking to me. Her words not only confirmed my worst fears but painted a future I wasn't sure I wanted to be part of.

The memory of her spoke to me and said, *"Blood will be shed."*

And just as the memory flashed through my mind, a vampire had me pinned to a wall. Lucas. "Hello, Sofia. I've been looking for you."

# Chapter 54: Ben

Amidst all the bedlam surrounding me, I was certain of one thing and one thing alone. Claudia had reverted to her old mad and twisted self. I knew it the moment she attacked Sofia and sank her fangs into her neck.

"What is wrong with you?!" I hissed at her after seeing her claws come out, ready to put me through another painful ordeal.

"She's safer as a vampire than she is as the pathetic little twig that she is," she told me. "I was doing her a favor."

*She wasn't feeding on Sofia. She was turning her.* I couldn't even begin to imagine what was going through her mind. "This place is filled with hunters. *Nobody* is safe, you crazy bitch."

Her claws retracted and she pressed her palm over my chest to keep me down. "You were going to shoot me," she accused.

"You were sinking your bloody teeth into Sofia's neck. Of course I was going to shoot you." I pushed her away from me and was slightly surprised when she actually backed off. I searched for Sofia in time to see her pinned to a wall, Lucas licking the blood off her neck. I scoped the room for help. Derek and Borys were still at each other's throats. Reuben, on the other hand, was already poised to shoot at Borys, but Ingrid was on her way to keep her former husband from doing it.

*They're pre-occupied.* I looked around for my gun. I couldn't find it. Claudia had knocked it off me when she tackled me to the ground. A Maslen vampire began to approach me. Claudia found herself distracted, battling one of her own kind.

Thus, I was left with a wooden stake and one chance to take Lucas Novak down. I ran toward him. I reached him in time to hear him whisper to Sofia, "If I can't have you, no one will." His intent was clear. He wanted to kill her.

*Over my dead body.* I lifted my stake, ready to drive it right through his back and into heart, but I quickly realized that I should've learned my lesson. *Never underestimate a Novak.* I was just about to make contact with him, when he unexpectedly turned around and drove his claws right through my gut. I could feel the blood trickling from the open wound and I knew then that nothing could save me. I felt little pain and for that, I found myself thanking Claudia for the first time in my life. She had numbed me toward physical pain, but not to the pain of seeing Sofia's face when she realized what Lucas had just done to me.

Lucas pulled his hand away from me and watched as I stumbled backward. My back hadn't yet hit the ground when a UV bullet hit Lucas right in the forehead. I strained my neck to see who had shot him and saw Reuben standing with his gun. I turned my eyes from the grotesque sight of Lucas Novak bursting into flames and focused on Sofia who was now kneeling by my side.

"Ben…" she gasped, tears flowing down her cheeks. She stared at my wound in horror. "No…no…no…" she sobbed.

I was fading in and out of consciousness. At one point, I saw Reuben rushing to me, Zinnia trailing behind him.

"We've got Ingrid!" she announced. "Now what?"

Reuben's eyes darkened. "Take her to headquarters," he instructed after giving Sofia a quick glance. I knew even then that had Sofia not been there, he wouldn't have hesitated to have Ingrid killed instead.

Everything once again blurred and when I came to, Derek was kneeling over me, blood dripping from his palm. Sofia had a hand under my head and was lifting it up. "Ben, you have to drink."

I shook my head and panted. "Never. After what Claudia put me through…I vowed to never drink a vampire's blood again."

"You have to, Ben…" Sofia cried. "It's your only chance. Ben, please…"

I looked up at her and reached out to wipe the tears from her face. "Derek will take care of you, Sofia. Tell my family I love them, okay? And know that I loved you from the moment I first met you. Vivienne was right. I see the world through your eyes now." I smiled, resigning myself to my fate. "And it's beautiful. Just like you."

# Chapter 55: Sofia

Ben's eyes slowly closed and I knew without a doubt that it was the last I would ever see those beautiful blue eyes of his. It was the last I would see him smile, the last I would hear him speak. I'd lost people who were dear to me before, but the immensity of the anguish that I felt upon losing Ben was more than I could handle.

I stared blankly at his still form for what seemed like an eternity, knowing that everyone around me—heads bowed in deference—could sense the pain that losing Ben caused me.

Tears flowed down my cheeks. I began to shake his motionless body, fooling myself that he might actually wake up. "Ben…no…" My sobs filled the air and suddenly, everyone else was deathly still.

I could sense Derek's eyes on me, his gaze a soft, concerned caress. Even his presence couldn't provide me with a shred of comfort. He motioned to touch me, but I shied away from him. I clung to Ben's lifeless form, wishing that I could somehow bring him back to life.

He was too young, too full of potential…he didn't have the *right* to just give up like that.

No one dared touch me. No one dared speak. Until my father decided that I had been given enough time to grieve my best friend's passing.

"Take the boy's body," he ordered one of the hunters. "We have to go before more vampires arrive. The sun is setting."

"No…" I sobbed, still holding on to Ben's still form, his blood soiling the white dress I was wearing.

"Sofia, we don't have time," my father insisted.

"We can spare her a few more minutes. She just lost her best friend." *Derek.* I adored him for that.

The hunters who were ordered to take Ben's body hesitated from prying me away from him.

"I should kill you," my father told Derek.

"And give your daughter another loved one to grieve over."

A collective gasp filled the room. I wasn't sure if it was because of Derek's bluntness or if it was because not everybody knew that Aiden Claremont was my father. Either way, tension sparked between the two men.

The urgency of the situation forced my attention away from Ben as it began to sink in to me that the love of my life was very much in danger of getting killed by my father.

Aiden quickly changed the topic. He gave Derek a momentary, questioning glare. "Borys Maslen?"

"He got away," Derek responded. "Ingrid?"

"We're holding her captive."

An awkward silence followed until Derek broke it. "I won't leave Sofia."

"Then you'll have to come with us. You sure a vampire like you would be willing to walk right into the hunters' headquarters?"

"Why not?" Derek shrugged. "I was once a hunter."

"Reuben…" a young woman with blue-streaked hair interrupted. "We have to go." She couldn't seem to bear looking at Ben. My father nodded. He gave Derek a cold and suspicious glance before shaking his head and saying, "Get Ben's body. Let's go." He reached his hand toward me at the exact same time Derek did.

I tore my eyes away from Ben's body—now being taken away by the hunters—and looked at the two men, holding their hands out to me. I didn't hesitate. I took Derek's hand, not missing the flash of hatred in my father's eyes at the sight of The Shade's monarch.

Derek pulled me against him and gently caressed my forehead with his lips. I turned to face my father to find him removing his jacket. He handed it to me. "Cover up."

Relieved, I took the jacket and put it on, zipping it up to my neck. I then clung on to Derek's hand as we headed for the elevator. As it rose up through the levels of The Oasis, I got a glimpse of all the bloodshed that had just occurred. I realized that it certainly wasn't just the vampires of The Oasis that had been slaughtered.

"They killed all the human slaves too," I whispered into Derek's ear when I saw the elderly maid who had dressed me lying motionless on the ground.

He nodded. "In the eyes of a hunter, Naturals and any human loyally serving a vampire are just as bad as the creature itself."

"Then they could just as easily kill me for my loyalty to you."

"Not as long as your father holds any authority with the hunters…"

Suddenly, I understood why Ben had turned his back on the hunters. My best friend was out for revenge, but he never would've willingly taken the life of an innocent.

We finally reached level one and just as we surmised from what we saw through level seven's surveillance monitors, the hunters had blown off the entire top level of The Oasis. I was relieved to find that the sun had already set by the time we reached the top level, because I dared not imagine what would happen to Derek should the sun's rays shine on him.

The bloodbath we had passed through before reaching the hunters' helicopters was sickening. At one point, I looked at Derek, silently admiring him for stopping something like this from happening at The Shade. I squeezed his hand and he looked my way. He smiled and that gesture alone made me feel a lot better.

"I didn't think we were going to make it out of here," he admitted.

"Neither did I, but we still have a prophecy to fulfil together, Derek."

"I don't know how I'll be able to keep myself from craving you, Sofia…"

"I trust you," was all I could think to say before I caught sight of my father who was waving for us to hurry up. We rushed forward until we reached one of the choppers. That was when I saw Claudia climbing into one of them. I pointed at her to get Derek's attention.

He frowned. "That vampire!" he screamed at my father through the noise of the chopper's propellers. "Why is she being brought with you?"

"Ben demanded it!" was Aiden's response.

Derek and I exchanged confused glances. *Why on earth would Ben ask the hunters to spare Claudia's life?*

"Let's go!" Aiden sounded impatient and borderline angry.

Thus, Derek and I quickly climbed into the chopper. I cuddled up against him as we got seated, my father sitting across from us. As the chopper rose in the air, I once again remembered Ben and grabbed Derek's hand as I sobbed into his shoulder.

He knew me enough to know why I was in tears, so all he did was hum our song and hold me tight. "There'll be better days, Sofia."

I hoped he was right. At that moment, everything was just too overwhelming, too dark, and through it all, Derek seemed to be my only ray of light.

# Chapter 56: Derek

It felt like I was riding to my death. I was surrounded by hunters and I was willingly heading toward the last place any vampire should be. The hunters' headquarters.

I could feel Aiden's glare burning through me. I knew that in his eyes, I was the enemy. In his eyes, I had brainwashed Sofia into loving me. I knew that he would do everything to take Sofia away from me. It's the way I would've thought had I still been a hunter.

I clung to Sofia, driven mad by how much I was craving her blood. I swallowed hard as I pressed my lips against her cheek. I couldn't remember ever wanting anyone as much as I wanted her. The fact that I was in love with her only added to the heavy ache that seemed to permanently settle on my chest.

*No wonder Lucas couldn't keep himself away from her...*

*Lucas.* My jaw tightened at the recollection of seeing my brother burst into flames. I'd never liked him, but he was still my brother.

Seeing him meet his end brought no satisfaction whatsoever.

I found myself wondering where my father was. *Does he know that Lucas is gone? That we're the only two Novaks left?* I held back the tears. I wasn't about to break down. Not in front of all these hunters.

Death and darkness surrounded us and it felt like there was more of it to come.

My arm tightened around Sofia, who gently whimpered at the motion as she snuggled closer to me, trying to sleep her heartbreak away. I knew she was hurting. I knew how important Ben was to her.

"So you're Derek Novak." The girl with blue-streaked hair, sitting next to Aiden, had been glaring daggers at me ever since she had laid eyes on me. "Ben's dead because of you?"

I narrowed my eyes at her, trying to make sense of her twisted logic. "How is his death my fault?"

She shrugged one shoulder. "Your brother killed him."

"I'm not my brother. Just in case you didn't notice, he's dead right along with every other person you murdered back there." The discourse we were having made it brilliantly clear that I wasn't going to get along with this particular hunter. From the way she was shooting glares from me to Sofia, it seemed she wasn't much of a fan of the girl I loved either.

"What did you do to her?" It was Aiden who spoke up this time. "Does she really believe that she's in love with you?"

"Why don't you ask her that question yourself when she wakes up? If you think I've somehow brainwashed her, you're wrong. I truly love your daughter."

The face darkened. It looked as if he was debating within himself whether or not he should kill me while Sofia was asleep. I wouldn't have been surprised if he did exactly that.

"I don't trust you," he eventually spoke up.

"The feeling is mutual, sir."

"My daughter is the only reason you're still alive, Derek. I can't promise that I'll be able to protect you from the other hunters once we arrive at our destination."

I stared right at him, making it a point to look straight into his eyes. No matter how much mistrust there was between us, he was still Sofia's father and for that reason alone, he deserved my respect. "I realize that."

"And yet you still came with us?"

I nodded. "I can't leave Sofia. Not after everything that happened at The Oasis. I was walking right to my death when I went there to get her. What difference does it make now?"

He eyed me warily, hatred one of the many emotions being channelled by his cold glare, but there was also one other emotion that wasn't there before. Respect. The rest of the ride was spent in silence, with me getting rather accustomed to the nasty stares I was still receiving.

Finally, Aiden and the blue-haired huntress started fidgeting in their seats and stretching their necks. I peeked outside the window and saw a long runway strip.

"Derek?" Sofia blinked her eyes several times, before full wakefulness came upon her. "Ben?"

I shook my head sadly. Tears once again moistened her eyes, but this time, none of them spilled over. She held back the tears and nodded in acceptance even as she gulped down the pain. This was her life now. A life surrounded by warring factions of vampire covens and hunters. Ben wasn't the first person she'd lost since getting caught up in this world I lived in, and he definitely wasn't going to be the last.

I could see her disheartenment, and I found myself fighting

against the idea that I would lose her to her own jadedness. I wanted to preserve her, keep her innocent.

"What's on your mind, Sofia?" I found myself asking.

Her hand caught mine, gripping tightly, before looking me straight in the eye. "I wouldn't know what to do if I ever lost you."

# Chapter 57: Sofia

After the chopper landed on the runway, both Derek and I were given a set of clothes we could change into before we were ushered into the private jet, a clear indication of the kind of affluence, power and wealth the hunters had. We made ourselves comfortable inside.

I could tell that something was bothering Derek as he sat on the seat next to mine. It was easy to see from the listlessness of his blue eyes and the many times I noticed him swallow hard.

I grabbed hold of his wrist and looked questioningly. He gave me a quick glance and I could swear I saw his lips quiver. He wiggled my hand away and shook his head. "I'm fine."

*You're headed for hunter headquarters. How could you be fine?* I knew better than to force information out of him when he was acting all broody and intense so I just nodded and kissed his cheek. The moment I did, I could sense him tense and I realized exactly what was bothering him. He was craving my blood. *Of course. He hadn't had any blood since I had fed him back at level seven.*

I wondered if there was anything I could do to divert his attention toward something else and I remembered by encounter with Claudia back at The Oasis. The fact that she was seated somewhere inside the jet was unsettling.

"Back at The Oasis," I spoke up, careful not to touch Derek in any way, wondering how we were ever going to last as a couple if we couldn't even make physical contact without him wanting to sink his teeth into me whenever he felt hungry. "I think Claudia tried to turn me."

His eyes widened. "She did what?"

"She told me that it was her gift for me. She bit into my neck, but Ben came to shoot her and she attacked him…"

"Sofia, if the serum's injected into your system…" Derek gulped. I knew there was fear and apprehension in his eyes, but there was something else… hope.

My heart fell at the thought that he wanted me to become a vampire. I understood why he would, but still, the thought of becoming one sent shivers down my spine. "Am I going to turn?"

He stared at me with a mixture of confusion and awe. "You're not exhibiting the symptoms. You saw how it was with Ashley…the moment the serum was in her system, the effect was instant."

"Strange…" I remembered what Borys kept calling me. *The immune.* I still wasn't sure what he meant by it, but I knew that somehow, it tied in to why I wasn't now convulsing. I didn't want to discuss that with Derek just yet, so instead, I diverted the topic back to Ben and Claudia. "It's hard for me to believe that Ben would ever vouch for Claudia, Derek. The fact that she's alive…I don't know…something's not right."

"We won't know for sure until we get to talk to her."

"That's assuming we even get the chance. How is this supposed to work, Derek? What's to say that they're not going to kill you the moment we step out of this plane?" I was voicing out fears that I knew he didn't have the solutions to. "By the time we get there..."

"Sofia..." he cut me off. "Let's just get through this journey and worry about all that when we arrive."

"Maybe we should escape now...while we still can..."

Derek eyed my father warily. Aiden had just walked in after having visited the cockpit. He gave me a quick glance and took his seat, talking to the girl with blue-streaked hair.

"I don't think your father will just let us go off after having found you. I'm sure he'll chase us down."

"At least we have a chance..."

Derek shook his head. "No. If I'm going to marry you, Sofia, then your father's approval is important to me."

I couldn't believe my ears. *What is wrong with you? Have you gone mad?* "His *approval*?!" I practically spat the words out. "Derek, my father is one of the leaders of an order sworn to wipe out every vampire on this planet. There is absolutely no way he'd ever agree to me marrying you."

"Maybe so, but you know that I value you enough to try."

I stared at him with pure admiration, humbled by the value he was placing on me. After all we'd been through, I found myself still wondering how a man like Derek Novak could possibly love me in that way.

I shifted my gaze from Derek to my father, knowing without a doubt who mattered more to me. While I ached with the longing to get to know Aiden Claremont, to find answers to questions I'd been asking my whole life, my loyalty remained with Derek Novak.

*Blood doesn't always run thicker than water. Or perhaps it does...because Derek's blood runs in me just as much as mine now runs in his.*

I knew then that should Derek ever ask, I would willingly let him have my blood. The thought scared me, because it was a stunning realization of how much I was willing to give up for him.

I drifted off to sleep for the rest of the flight, leaning my head on Derek's shoulder, hoping to escape everything through peaceful slumber. It was the sudden jolt caused by the wheels of the plane hitting the tarmac that woke me. My immediate instinct was to check out the window for the sun and I was relieved to find that it was dark. I knew we were in the US—that much I'd gathered from overhearing several conversations between the hunters, but where exactly in the States we were, I had no clue.

I checked on Derek and found him unbuckling his seatbelt. "Hey, beautiful," he said before quickly looking away.

Something about him felt distant and cold. I looked toward my father and wondered what he would have to say if I went to him to ask for blood to feed Derek. The prospect seemed insane.

I grabbed Derek's arm and was surprised when he flinched.

He gave me an apologetic look. "Sofia..." His lower lip twitched and it was enough for me to understand what he was struggling with, "If I black out..."

I nodded. "I understand." I knew I'd be able to calm him and keep him from sucking me dry, but if the hunters ever saw him attack me, it would be the end of him, the end of us.

He didn't respond but the look in his blue eyes was enough to let me know the anguish he felt over the idea of not being able to even touch me. I tried to push back the overwhelming sense of dread that I felt.

Aiden was the first to rise from his seat when the plane finally stopped. He gave me a quick look as he spoke through the intercom system. "We have two vampires from the Novak coven and one vampire from the Maslen coven. None of them are to be harmed. I want this made clear throughout headquarters—especially to those trigger-happy new recruits. The vampires are not to be harmed."

My mind couldn't help but add a "*for now*" to my father's statement. I would be a fool to think that a vampire as notorious as Derek Novak would be in any way secure at Hawk Headquarters.

"You have to wait here for a while." The girl with blue-streaked hair approached, sounding perky, but still not withholding any of her death glares from Derek. "I'm Zinnia Wolfe by the way. I was a good friend of Ben's. We were partners." She shook my hand but didn't even bother to look at Derek.

"Sofia Claremont," I introduced myself. "This is Derek Novak."

"Yeah." She gave me a curt nod. "I know. We're still trying to figure out what to do with you all. If it were up to me, I'd just have you vamps killed, but the boss seems to have other things in mind..."

Derek glared back at her. I noticed his fist clench and I knew that he was trying to keep his temper in check.

"It's the first time vampires have ever been treated as guests at Hawk Headquarters," Zinnia continued. She then cocked her head to one side as if she were listening in on something through her earpiece. She nodded. "Unbelievable." She drew a deep breath before giving both Derek and me pointed looks. "Follow me."

Derek and I rose from our seats and trudged behind the petite young woman. It gave me some sense of comfort when Derek took hold of my hand as we walked forward. I needed his touch.

We remained silent as we got off the plane and walked across the runway. We were not oblivious to the curious stares being thrown my way and the disdainful glares being shot at Derek. I swallowed hard at the tension, wanting to get away from everyone else and get to somewhere where Derek and I could spend time by ourselves.

In the back of my mind, I knew that there were a lot of arrangements that needed to be done over Ben's passing away, but I was too overwhelmed to dwell on it. I knew I needed to first catch my breath and gather my wits about me.

Once we reached the main building, glass doors swung open to allow us entrance. Zinnia, still leading the way, headed right in. We passed through several corridors and then an atrium filled with several men in black jumpsuits training in martial arts. We then reached an elevator with large glass windows—reminding me a lot of the central elevator at The Oasis. The mere remembrance of the Maslen coven sent chills down my spine. On the third floor, we stopped and went through another maze of walkways and corridors, before Zinnia finally stopped in front of a door with a brass number eight.

"This used to be Ben's suite," was all Zinnia said as she handed us a card key. "In my opinion, neither of you deserve to be in it."

*I doubt that either of us want to be. I think both Derek and I would rather be back at The Shade right now.* I hated that she was talking to me like Ben didn't matter to me. He was my best friend and I was his. *Who was she to him?*

"Reuben will be coming to have a talk, either later tonight or early tomorrow. We'll need to figure out what's to be done with the prince of The Shade here."

After Zinnia left us, we stepped into the room and closed the door behind us. I switched the lights on and watched as Derek walked right toward the full length windows that covered one side of the room. It was the first time in a long time that I could remember ever feeling awkward around him.

"Nothing's changed, has it, Derek?" I asked tentatively, afraid to hear his answer.

"Everything's changed, Sofia. I've tasted your blood. I can't even look at you without wanting to..." he paused and I could sense the inward battle he was fighting. "I'm so hungry."

I approached him, wrapping my arms around his waist from behind and resting my head on his back, breathing in his scent. "We belong together. We're going to get married. I am yours just as you are mine. My blood is yours to take whenever you want it."

"For crying out loud, Sofia..." He spun around so quickly, I found myself stepping back in surprise. "Do you even understand what you're saying? How can we go on this way? I..."

"Perhaps you *should* turn me..."

"If I do that here and now, they'll kill us both, Sofia. Hunters are merciless against vampires. The only reason I'm alive is because of you."

"And Claudia and Ingrid? Why are they alive?"

He began to swear under his breath. "I don't know...the world has turned upside down. Nothing makes sense anymore."

"Derek...I need you to be here with me. I need to know that we're in this together. If we keep on being distant and awkward because you've had my blood, then I don't know if I can handle it. I'm going to crumble."

"What do you want to happen, Sofia?" he asked, his eyes betraying the confusion he was experiencing inside.

"They're not going to feed you any blood while you're here and it's going to drive you crazy, so just satisfy your thirst, Derek." I tilted my neck to the side, baring my neck to him. "Drink."

I could sense his hesitation, his eyes hungrily staring at my neck.

His hands crept over my waist and he drew me close. I reminded myself that this was Derek, the man that I loved, the man who would do everything to protect me. The reminders, I thought, would help keep me from trembling, but still I found myself shivering when I felt the pointed end of Derek's fangs on my neck. I bit my lip to stifle a groan when his fangs dug in and he began drinking deep.

As it happened, I couldn't shake the feeling that I was about to lose more than what I'd already lost that night.

# Chapter 58: Derek

*What have I done?*

I stared at Sofia's sleeping form lying on the living room couch. Motionless. Serene. Beautiful. I hated myself for what I had just done. My eyes kept returning to the bite marks on her neck—ones I myself had punctured.

*I love her. I can't keep doing this to her.*

I ran both hands through my hair, not knowing what to do. I'd reached the point where I couldn't live without her, but neither could I live with her without destroying her. It felt like I'd been sitting there for an eternity, just gazing at her and chastising myself for taking advantage of her by drinking her blood once again. Still, the taste of her lingered on my mouth—sweet and enticing… So enraptured was I by what just happened, by my own confusion and my own guilt that I practically jumped from my seat when someone began knocking on the door.

I grimaced at the idea of it being Zinnia. I then realized that while I was indulging myself making dinner out of Sofia, she hadn't had a bite to eat since we arrived. I quickly opened the door, certain that it was somebody bringing her something to eat only to find myself disappointed to find Aiden Claremont standing on our doorstep.

"My daughter?" he asked. Straightforward and curt.

"Asleep."

"Good. We need to have a talk, you and me."

I nodded. He stepped in and I closed the door behind him. He spun around to face me. "Every single human in this building—me included—perhaps my daughter being the only exception—wants you dead."

At that, I couldn't help but chuckle wryly. "So I've gathered."

"The great Derek Novak. One of the best hunters the order has ever known…now prince of the vampires."

*King actually…*I looked up at him…*but then you don't really need to know that.*

"This *thing* you have with my daughter stops now. You can't keep using her for whatever reason you have for wanting her."

"I'm in love with her," I said through gritted teeth. "I fully intend to marry her."

"Marry her? She's mortal! If you loved her, you wouldn't deprive her of the future she deserves. You wouldn't deprive her of an education, a family, children of her own…"

At that, I couldn't find a proper response. I'd been plagued by that thought ever since Sofia returned to The Shade. I knew I was being selfish with her.

"Be straight with me, Novak. Man to man. Have you had a drink of my daughter's blood?"

I looked Aiden in the eye and nodded, guilt once again washing over me. His fists clenched and he stepped forward and I wouldn't have blamed him if he socked me right in the jaw, but he held back.

"You are only safe from us until after Ben Hudson's burial. It's you she's running to for comfort. It's you she needs. After the burial is over, you will return to your cursed island—wherever it is—and you are never to see my daughter again. And you will leave without telling her."

*He knows about The Shade. He just doesn't know where it is.* I knew the risk involved if I should ever travel back to The Shade directly from the hunters' headquarters. A plan of action formed in my mind, and I realized that in my head, I'd already agreed to his terms. I simply couldn't be around Sofia. *If I stay with her, I will ruin her. I can't do that. Not to her.*

I nodded at Aiden. "All right. But know, sir, that I love your daughter like I've never loved anyone before."

"Empty words coming from a vampire." He scoffed. "I'm not sure your kind is capable of love."

I once again looked at the bite marks on Sofia's neck and found myself thinking, *I'm not sure either.*

# Epilogue: Sofia

Truth be told, I found it terrifying how much I'd allowed myself to need Derek. While going through the motions of Ben's burial, having to look Lyle, Amelia and Abby in the eye and tell them what had happened, Derek was there for me, holding my hand, being strong when I was not.

Since the first night of our arrival at Hawk Headquarters, he'd not dared take a drink of my blood again. It was clear to see how guilt-ridden he was over the whole encounter. Aiden had been providing him with packets of animal blood to keep him from starving. Still, it didn't escape my notice how he often swallowed hard whenever we touched.

I knew he was tormented about something, but he was in a world all on his own, and nothing I did seemed to be able to penetrate through his walls—not the same way I was able to before.

It felt like he was slipping away from me…a sandcastle being washed away by cruel, violent waves.

But Derek wasn't the only reason for the chaos in my heart and mind. The mysteries of my past were about to unravel full force and I was completely unprepared for it. Tossing and turning in my bed, dreams reminded me of memories I'd tucked away, deep in my subconscious.

*I was listening to the pitter-patter of the rain over our roof, watching droplets form on my bedroom window. I was delighted to hear the familiar growl of a vehicle pulling up in our gravel driveway. I knew what that sound meant.* Mommy's home.

*I loved my babysitter, but there was nothing like cuddling against the familiar contours of my mother's body. I always thought of her as the most beautiful woman I'd ever seen.*

*But when I saw her face that night, I could immediately tell that something was different about her. She wasn't looking at me with delight. She was looking at me the same way I did the cookies stashed in one of the kitchen jars.*

*"Hello, baby," she greeted me before pushing my bedroom door wide open. "I want you to meet someone."*

*A man stepped in. I didn't know who he was, but I was immediately terrified at the sight of him. He stared at me and I wanted to shrink away from his gaze. "What's her name? How old is she?"*

*"Sofia. She's nine years old."*

*"She's young, but she'll do."*

*I couldn't make much sense of what had happened next. All I knew was that he took me in his arms and bit my neck. I lost consciousness from the pain. When I woke up, my mother and the man were gone. Only my father was there and I felt sicker than I'd ever been in my life.*

*"Shh, Sofia..." My father tried to calm me, terrified by my burning fever—a fever that should've already killed me. "You're going to be alright. Daddy's here for you. Daddy will always be here for you."*

I woke from my dream and sat up, utterly confused…but then the pieces of the puzzle suddenly came together all at once, and the realization hit me full force: *I should be a vampire. Borys Maslen tried to turn me and it didn't work. That's why I was so sick. That's why Borys kept calling me 'the immune.'* I checked the space on the bed beside me and found it empty. I ached for Derek's touch, his strong arms around me, his soothing voice calming my nerves. He wasn't there.

I then recalled what Vivienne's memories had revealed to me: *they are strongest together. They are weakest apart.*

"Derek?!" I cried out.

Panic was beginning to take over, so I sighed with relief when he stepped into the bedroom from the balcony.

"Sofia?" he asked, concern traced in his choked voice.

I said the words before I could think them through. "Turn me into a vampire."

"What? No! Sofia…we can't…"

"Do it, Derek. Do it now!"

"Why?"

"Because *I can't be turned.* I can never become a vampire. I will never be immortal."

His blue eyes darkened as he furrowed his brows. "Sofia…why would you…"

"I'm the immune."

Want to read the next part of Derek and Sofia's story?
*A Shade Of Vampire 4: A Shadow Of Light* is available now!

Visit www.bellaforrest.net for more information.

# NOTE FROM THE AUTHOR

Dear Shaddict,

If you want to stay informed about my latest book releases, visit this website to subscribe to my new releases email list: www.forrestbooks.com

Also, if you subscribe, you'll be automatically entered to win a signed copy of A Shade Of Vampire.

You can also check out my other novels by visiting my website: www.bellaforrest.net

And don't forget to come say hello on Facebook.
I'd love to meet you personally, and sometimes Derek Novak takes over as manager of the page:

www.facebook.com/AShadeOfVampire

Thank you for reading!

Love,
Bella

CPSIA information can be obtained at www.ICGtesting.com
Printed in the USA
LVOW04s2319121114

413440LV00015B/300/P

9 781490 505770